Ashwalk Pilgrim

UNBREAKABLE IRON
A.B. BRADLEY

Skull & Crosspens Press

www.abbradley.com

Cover design by: Lin Ling Hsian.
Back cover design by: AB Bradley.
Interior design template by: David Haden.
Author photography by: Dustin Vyers.

ISBN-13 paperback: 978-0692423509

AB Bradley
www.abbradley.com
Email: authorabbradley@gmail.com

ACKNOWLEDGEMENTS

Writing a book is only one part of creating the novel. It takes a team of people to build something worth your time and money, and without their expertise I'm certain this dream of mine could have never become reality. So, thank you to everyone who walked this journey with me and who will walk it with me in the future.

THANK YOU

This book goes out to all the mothers out there, because every hero had a mother once, and every mother is a hero.

TABLE OF CONTENTS

1

THE HOUSE OF SIN AND SILK

Never had she known another world outside the House of Sin and Silk, and never did she care to find another. Mara stretched and grinned at the horizon. Her back ached, her muscles throbbed, yet no smile on the pleasure barge could ever match her own.

A thousand ships floated on the gentle waves lapping at Sollan's rocky shore. Thick ropes dripping seawater and old chains kissed by stubborn barnacles moored the bobbing labyrinth of barges to one another. They rocked on rippling waves that glittered like oiled glass beneath a moon crowned by purest silver.

Mara ran her hand through her hair, savoring the silky strands tickling her fingertips. Her unborn child kicked against her swollen belly. She grimaced, slowly bending to her knees until they pressed against the barge's smooth deck.

"Not long now," she whispered. "But stay just a little while longer. I do not want the beating your birth would bring me, my love."

Grime and muck coated her arms to her elbows, the last remnants of yet another night of feast and pleasure for the patrons of the House of Sin and Silk. She dipped her arms into the cool waters of the Sapphire Sea. The smell of fish filled her nostrils. The breeze kissed her lips with a hint of salt. With a heavy sigh, she rubbed from her skin the oils of the feast she prepared but never enjoyed.

As the last of the spiced slime washed into the ocean, she flicked the droplets dangling from her nails and watched her reflection tremble. She ran her fingers across her cheeks. The child within her gifted her skin with a healthy glow not even endless days of sun and sea winds could ever bring.

"You are good for me," she said with a smile.

Mara straightened. She pressed her hand against her back to support her belly and looked toward the great Sapphire Sea. An ancient titan's bones divided the line of the horizon. The skeleton towered over the waves, its hollow eyes facing the unknown and daring all Good King Sol's enemies to strike at the heart of his mighty empire.

"I said enough!"

Gia's harried voice jolted Mara, her friend's words drifting from within the barge's long hull. Mara's heartbeat quickened. Her child twisted in the womb, its blood rising with hers.

Mara turned to the open door. "Gia?"

She faced the House of Sin and Silk, her home, her kingdom, her silken prison. It dwarfed all others in the Floatwaif in size and reputation. Polished brass braziers cast their flickering firelight against the barge's mahogany walls. Scarlet ribbons hanging from its roof rippled like serpents' tongues in the wind.

"Get off, you pig!"

Gia's words sent Mara's blood to a boil. She clenched her jaw and headed for the pleasure rooms in the barge's belly. With the aid of her heavy push, the door widened enough for her stomach to pass. She waddled inside. Scarlet doors set in neat, even spaces lined the hallway. Beyond each door, there was a room containing throws of fine silks, pillows soft as satin clouds, and a woman or man serving an eager patron.

Mara hurried past the first few doors as best she could and planted her feet before Gia's room. A dark and hungry laugh filtered from behind the door's wooden face.

"Gia, is everything okay?" Mara rapped on the door. "Gia!"

Moon maidens occupied the rooms beside Gia's. Of course the other girls would never help. Kindness was rare as diamonds in the Floatwaif, and in the House of Sin and Silk, it was a thing of myth and legend.

Mara took a deep breath and slapped her palm against the wood. "I'm calling the strong boys! You're out, Kard. I knew you had a sour look in your eye when you came aboard."

She heard a grunt, followed by a deep laugh.

"*Madame Olessa!* Strong boys!" Mara gripped the handle in one hand and her belly with the other. She shoved her shoulder against the door and pushed, flinging it aside. Gia squatted like a caged lioness in the corner, her arms trembling and ready to strike.

The woman glared at her patron with poisoned-tip daggers in her eyes. She held her silk dress over her breasts, her polished nails shining in the lamplight. Her patron swayed barely more than an arm's length from Mara's friend. He was a sailor from Skaard and painted in the flowery tattoos of strange lands. He wore a black loop pierced through his nose like one might see on a bull and snorted as he took heavy, hungry breaths.

Mara smelled the reek of wine and saltwater gin coming from the man. Red rimmed his dark, bleary eyes, and sweat shimmered on his bourbon skin. He glanced at Mara from the corner of his eye. A long, pale scar cut his face from his hair to his grizzled chin, and he wore the old wound as proudly as a king would wear his crown.

Kard's gaze drifted to Mara's belly. He licked his lips and faced her. "Someone looks ready'ta pop. I'd no idea that oiled slug of a woman let her maidens have whelps. Might be some good fun, eh, Gia?"

Mara stepped back. Her shoulders pressed into the doorway.

Gia snarled and stood to her full height. Like most people born in the eastern kingdoms, she wore her hair in long, oiled braids. Like all moon maidens on Madame Olessa's barge, she wore a brass collar tight around her neck, the cheap, plated metal staining her luminous skin a sickly olive wherever it rested.

Mara's friend stood as tall as her drunken patron, and even though she was both a slave and moon maiden, she carried herself with all the royal pride of a mighty queen.

"You will not touch Mara," Gia spat. "Kard, leave the barge. Leave it now or I swear I'll cut your manhood and feed it to the coral sharks."

Kard howled with laughter, his cheeks blushing as he bent backward. "You will? Bless me, I've got myself a fiery maiden tonight! I paid good money for a girl from the East, so you'll lay on your back and be a good maiden or I'll slit your throat and get my coin back from that hag madame of yours."

"You think I'm lying? I'll cut it off, you pig." She marched forward, pausing before him with a smirk spreading on her lips. "Once I find it, that is."

Kard tensed. "Why, you'sa little…"

The sailor pulled his fist back. Gia lifted her chin.

Mara lunged. She grabbed Kard's wrist before his fist could slam into Gia's jaw with all the fuel and force of a fearless drunk. Mara twisted his arm behind him and shoved it against the small of his back. "You think Madame Olessa leaves us defenseless? You aren't the first drunken idiot to wobble on deck thinking he owns all he sees."

Kard cried out. She pushed harder.

Gia twirled. Her silk dress fluttered to her ankles like an undulating wave and exposed her bare body in the dim gold light. She balled her fist and slammed her knuckles against Kard's jaw. The man's head spun to the side, a shower of rosy droplets bursting from his lips and splattering on the floor.

"Pig!" Gia shouted. "Drunk, stupid glimmer fiend!"

He fell upon the room's fine rugs, landing on his knees and palms. Groaning, he shook his head, an oozing line of blood dripping from his lips and staining the room's carpet.

Mara sidestepped the dazed drunk. She embraced Gia, the woman's chest heaving with her heavy breaths, her shoulders slick with oils ripe with jasmine.

"Are you hurt?" Mara asked. "What did he do?"

"He said pain was pleasure. He tried…he tried wrapping a silk scarf around my neck. He said I would enjoy it. I knew he would kill me, Mara. I saw it in his wine-stained eyes. He didn't care. The bastard took a full vial of glimmer. It's made him wild. He'll start seeing ghosts soon enough he took so much."

Mara pulled Gia closer and stared directly in her eyes. "Everything will be okay. I came as soon as I heard. I always will."

"You are the only one who would." Her eyes locked on something behind Mara and widened. "Watch out!"

Gia pushed Mara back as Kard sprang from the floor. He struck Gia in the arm, and the woman stumbled back. Mara's heavy belly nearly toppled her, but she caught her balance at the last moment. She pressed a hand against her chest and exhaled, hoping her heart wouldn't burst from her ribs.

Mara spun to face their attacker, fists balled and shaking. The sailor kicked at Gia. She caught his ankle and threw his leg aside. He brought his fist back in a hit Mara knew would break Gia's jaw. Mara lurched forward, veins burning with her adrenaline, and caught the man's wrist.

A jagged, silvery point glinted between his fingers. Terror flooded Mara, and she released the man.

Gia scrambled toward them. "Mara, watch the razor!"

Mara shielded her face, her only thought the beating she would get from Olessa if the fool scarred her cheek. A hot slash raked her forearm. She cried out, collapsing to the floor. Her hand wrapped around her arm and gripped the burning wound. Tears came to her eyes, but they were of anger, not of fear.

Kard stood over Mara, a tiny, dripping razor wedged between his fingers just beneath the knuckle. "You's gonna dare get in my way, you whore? You're nothin' to me. You's the filth I scrape from my boots after a stroll through a pigpen and a hike through shit. Just 'cause you got some bastard in that belly, you think that keeps you safe? Your lovely madame's gonna tie a rock to the whelp's legs and toss it to the sharks soon as it slides out o' that swollen belly. Don't think your fate's any better. Who'll want to bed a maiden stretched and broken by pushin' out a melon?"

Mara clutched the cut on her arm and breathed through the wall of her teeth. Blood wet her fingers, her pulse throbbing beneath the wound.

Gia lunged at Kard, but he kicked her in the stomach and sent the woman flying. "Not yet, m'dear Gia, let me finish this business first."

The man sneered, wiping his bloody jaw. He clenched the tiny blade in his fist and licked his lips. "Let's give that pretty face of yours a few cuts. Maybe a scar like mine? Olessa'd sell you to me then, and then I could sell that rat in your stomach for a polished coin, maybe might make up for the trouble you caused tonight."

Mara dragged herself away. Her hand left her wound and went to her belly. She saw the glee swirling in Kard's eyes. His pupils were black, new moons, and they twitched from the heavy dose of glimmer in his blood.

"That's right, fear me," he whispered. "It's so much sweeter that way."

Her child kicked and twisted. She swallowed, lifting her chin. "I will be a bitter poison for you."

Kard flashed his eyes and wagged his tongue. "I'll tell you how you taste once you're on my lips."

He stalked forward. Mara glanced at Gia. The woman rolled over, arm clasped over her stomach and eyes dully dazed. She would never reach Mara in time. Mara closed her eyes and grit her teeth.

"*Enough!*" Olessa's blessedly familiar, deep voice bellowed into the room.

Kard halted. Relief washed over Mara like a tide held back for generations and loosed that night.

Madame Olessa had no last name. She needed none. She was the empress of Sollan's most prestigious pleasure barge, the House of Sin and Silk, and every moon maiden and strong boy living on the ship bent a knee or trembled on the floor for her passing.

Once she must have been a beauty to behold. Mara could see the remnants of her youthful life hidden beneath the mask of sagging cracks curtained over her high cheeks. She wore a wig colored burgundy as rich, red wine and kept the locks at bay with a net of golden chains.

On her left hand, gold and silver bands coated her fingers while rubies, her favorite gems, glittered on her knuckles. On her right hand, she wore not a single jewel. It was the right hand Mara feared the most, because that was the hand of discipline.

Olessa's dark eyes narrowed at Kard. "You glimmer fiend of a fool. You dare hurt my maidens? Boys, get him away from my girls."

She motioned to the strong boys rushing in behind her. The two tall, muscular men lunged at the sailor. Kard tried scrambling out of reach, but one of the strong boys fell on him before he could make another move. The bodyguard planted his heel against Kard's already swollen jaw and grabbed the sailor's wrist, yanking it to the side.

"Get your freak dogs off me!" Kard rasped.

"Watch your tongue in my house, Kard." Olessa crossed her arms and smirked. "My strong boys may lack that oily worm wagging between your legs, but there's no guard more loyal than they, and believe me when I say they'll have no problem forcing you into their ranks…if you get my meaning."

Kard's face paled. Olessa's eunuchs grinned.

Gia groaned and sat up, grabbing her loose chiffon dress to cover her nakedness. "Thank you, Madame Olessa. It was the glimmer. I think it's turned the idiot's brain to mush."

"Eh." Olessa waved her off. "Boys, throw this puke overboard. Kard is not to return to the House of Sin and Silk unless it's as a spirit to haunt my dreams."

Kard's eyes widened. He reached for Olessa, but the strong boys forced him back. "Banned? Please, Madame Olessa, I—I promise I'll quit the glimmer. It won't happen again."

"You're right. It won't. No one strikes my moon maidens except their madame, and not only did you strike two tonight, you cut skin! That is my asset, Kard. *Mine.*" Olessa turned from the sailor as the strong boys dragged him kicking and wailing from the room.

He managed to hook his foot on the doorway and delay his exit a moment longer. He snarled, spitting at Olessa. "You and your cows' days are numbered, madame of the Floatwaif. Mark my words, you're a dyin' breed. Change is coming, and there's no room for sin and silk beneath the Serpent Sun."

She rolled her dark eyes as the strong boys yanked Kard away. "Yes, yes, the serpents are coming, magic is dying, the Fourth Sun rises. We've all heard what those snakes say. Why am I so thoroughly unsurprised you bend a knee to them? I swear, fools will follow any hollow promise if it means avoiding a long, hard look at their own life."

Her gaze settled on Mara. Her lips puckered like she smelled soured milk, her eyes glaring disapprovingly on Mara's swollen belly. The woman's steely glare shifted to the slash along Mara's forearm. Her frown warped into an angry scowl.

Mara never should have been with child. Olessa demanded all moon maidens take an ebon orchid draught after they saw a patron. Mara did so, and she did it faithfully, just as she did everything Olessa commanded as if a god had carved it into stone for her to read. Even after Mara discovered the child in her belly, she still took the draughts. Yet for her, they did not work.

The woman's jaw clenched, her chin inching up. "Mara, he cut you? Not deeply, I hope."

Gia swallowed, glancing nervously at her friend. "It's my fault. She did it to save me."

"Did I ask you a question? Don't speak unless I speak to you, Gia." Olessa strolled forward. She grabbed Mara's arm and inspected the wound. "If the Six look favorably on you, this won't leave a mark. Bad enough you've got that worm squirming in your womb and ruining my good property. Now I see you might have a scar to further lower your stock in my house? Tell me, Mara, what patron will pay me coin for a whore with a flapping womb, sagging sacs of milk, and a scarred body?"

Mara winced at her madame's words. "I'm so sorry, Madame Olessa. Please forgive me. I'll—I'll take care of the wound. It won't scar if I use honey paste. It will be gone soon after the birth."

Olessa's bare backhand caught Mara square in her jaw. Hot pain flared against her cheeks, and her ear rang as her world spun.

"Come with me, Mara," Olessa commanded.

No one disobeyed Madame Olessa, even if their world spun and the child in their belly protested angrily from the chaos. Mara sucked in her breath, and she wobbled to her knees. Gia threaded her arm beneath hers and helped Mara to her feet.

Gia kissed her lightly on the cheek. The faintest scent of sweat and jasmine drifted from the woman and tickled Mara's nose.

"Thank you," Gia whispered. "Be strong. I will light a candle to the Six for you. You know how Olessa worships them. Use that to your advantage and avoid the bruises."

Mara squeezed her friend's arm and forced a smile. She pressed her palm against the small of her back to support the weight of her unborn child. Her jaw throbbed. Blood oozed from the cut on her forearm. Each step pained her sore and swollen ankles. She would not speak of the pain. She would not show it.

She trailed Olessa out of Gia's room. She would welcome sleep when it came. But first, Olessa would beat her until the woman was satisfied by Mara's tears.

Mara sighed through her nose. She shook her head. Just another night in the House of Sin and Silk.

2

OLESSA'S RIGHT HAND

Teardrops splattered over Mara's trembling knuckles. She stared at the the fine rugs masking the floor, their intricate weaves a swirling labyrinth of gold and crimson before her bleary eyes. "I beg forgiveness, Madame Olessa, I did not mean to let him cut me."

Mara sucked the snot dribbling toward her lip and lifted her chin. Olessa glared at her property down the bridge of her long nose. Like always, gold and silver and glittering rubies covered her left hand. On her right, she wore a snowy glove over otherwise bare knuckles. Jewels and precious metals cut the skin. Silk and knuckles would not draw blood, but they would leave a bruise that taught a hard lesson.

Olessa shook her head. She turned her back to Mara and headed for a plush bench. She kept her personal room sparse save the rugs, a bench, a pedestal for wine, and a shrine to each of the Six so she could pray to whichever one the occasion demanded.

The woman admired her silk glove and wagged her fingers in the light of the oil lamps dotting the walls. "The Harvest Festival is upon us. Visitors from every city in the kingdom of Eloia will flood the Floatwaif, looking for wine and glimmer and a taste of sinful flesh. Ships will sail from all corners of Urum, from the icy land of Skaard to the eastern kingdoms Blail and Hine, each tired sailor on their decks looking for a soft pillow and a moon maiden's gentle stroke. Yet my most beautiful maiden will remain untapped, her bulging belly ruining the years of etiquette, lessons, and fine food I've invested in her. You have ruined my profit in this endeavor, simply ruined it."

Mara dipped her chin. Harvest Festival would be Olessa's most profitable night. The Floatwaif would teem with countless revelers. Normally chaste men and women would take a second look at the enchanting House of Sin and Silk with its great braziers and billowing ribbons and wonder if they should visit a moon maiden if only for a night.

"You were my best maiden by far, Mara." Olessa closed her eyes and pinched her nose. "What happened to you? Why would you claim you took the ebon orchid draught when you clearly did not? Why would you launch yourself at a fool drowning in wine and glimmer and let that beautiful body of yours be further marred? Do you hate me so much? Do you wish to singlehandedly sink this home and serve the coral sharks a feast for the night?"

Mara dug her nails into the rug. She squeezed her eyes shut, feeling the rhythm of her heartbeat. "Madame Olessa," she said, daring to lift her gaze to her madame. "I swear upon the Six I never once missed an ebon orchid draught. I even took it after I knew I was with child. You made the draughts yourself and watched me. I do not know why the child survives, but it does. Please, my madame, I only live to please you. I know no other world than yours, and I fear you will cast me from it once my child is born. I was not sure, but now that I am cut—"

"Mara, Mara." The woman plucked a wineglass from the nearby pedestal and savored a sip. "Do you remember how you came to me?"

Mara leaned onto her knees and followed the woman's gaze to the shrine of the Slippery Sinner. The statuette within the shrine watched Mara with wide eyes and a sly smile, dried rose petals and old incense littering his feet.

"I only remember small things. I remember a big man's hand. I remember people in streets. I remember a boat, and the big man's quiet smile. Then, we were here, and you were all I knew because you were all I needed to know."

"His name was Laedon." Olessa smiled, her fingers tapping her collar. "And he was from a time long ago, when things in Eloia were simpler and the old king ruled with a righteous hand. Before his son took the throne and renamed our fair city of Thean to Sollan in homage to his own stupid name. Who renames a city? Really, it's quite foolish. I'm sure the mapmakers collectively fainted when they heard his proclamation."

Mara tensed. Her eyes searched the shadows. Even she knew none spoke ill of Good King Sol. Those who did often disappeared, leaving whispers that they had become food for some great serpent lurking in the king's palace.

"Was Laedon your patron?" Mara asked, trying to focus on something other than the king.

Olessa laughed and gazed upon Mara like she was a foolish puppy. "No, of course not. He was my brother and an acolyte of the Burning Mother. You can thank him for saving your life. You can thank him for your survival in the House of Sin and Silk. You can thank him that I don't sell you for a tarnished silver when one of your many disappointments burdens my ledgers and lightens my purse."

"I will light a candle to the Burning Mother for him tonight."

"Do what you will." Olessa took a sip of her wine, her eyes fixed on Mara. "He's dead anyway, so perhaps he might hear your prayers himself and pinch your nipple if your words have a honeyed taste."

Mara dare not laugh even though Olessa chuckled at her own words.

Instead, she swallowed and nodded.

Olessa swished her wine and leaned forward. "So you speak true when you say you remember nothing of your childhood? Not a single memory of your mother or father? Siblings, perhaps? *Think*. Reach into that shallow sea of a brain and find some hint of who you were."

Countless nights Mara spent on her knees before Madame Olessa. Each time, Olessa asked the same questions, demanded answers Mara knew would never come. As far as she knew, Olessa's brother had plucked her from the ground like a flower from a garden on his way to the pleasure barge.

"Please forgive me, Madame Olessa. I have no memory before your brother."

"Bah!" Olessa launched her glass. It careened over Mara's shoulder and smashed against the wall. Drops of wine slid down Mara's cheek and stained her chiffon dress. Mara hunched on her knees, still as one of the statues in the shrines.

Her madame floated from her seat like a wraith cloaked in flowing red and gold. The woman cupped Mara's chin in a hand slathered with citrus lotion and weighed by jewelry. "Strange times are these, and stranger still the girl named Mara. Laedon wouldn't say a word to me, either. We never really had much in common, you know. He loved the Burning Mother while I've always favored the Coin Counter. He used that to my advantage and told me you'd turn a profit fast. I should have known better. Gods, I should have known."

Mara's child kicked. She winced, her hand clutching her belly. "I only ever wished to please you and your patrons."

"Yes, my patrons." Olessa chuckled and released Mara's chin. "The House of Sin and Silk has treated king and queen, sailor and scoundrel. We are as much a part of this city as the palace and the temples. Tell me, Mara, what do you know of the wider world? What do you know of the Six?"

Her madame's questions confused her. They were different questions than other nights, and Mara feared where the conversation might lead. "I…I do not know much other than that you worship them and so do most throughout Sollan and the other cities of Eloia. My patrons, their tongues wag for flesh, not faith, and I would not trust the other maidens even if they would answer my questions. The Six are a thing outside the House of Sin and Silk. Patrons do not speak of their lives outside our gentle walls. I suspect they do not speak much of us once they leave, either."

Olessa retook her seat and smirked. "It's good to know I only purchase smart girls. I have always believed we are the unspoken priestesses of the Six. Most clergy choose a single god to serve. Their god is their patron. Not us. No, a moon maiden serves all gods."

"How do we serve all gods?"

"We are a place of sin where for a night a patron may indulge in the fantasies that the world will only let them dream of. For a night, we give them a sinful kiss, and in the morning, they may run to their gods and pray for forgiveness. We are the fuel for the holy fire and the food for the heavenly feast."

"I do not understand how that serves the gods, Madame Olessa."

"Of course you don't. Mara, here's a hard truth: There are no gods without sin to bring the faithful to them."

"Oh." Mara clenched her knees. She still didn't quite understand, but she feared looking foolish before the woman.

"Indeed." Olessa's dark eyes drifted to Mara's stomach. She clucked and straightened, her shadow swallowing Mara. "As I said, my word to Laedon is all that's kept you around. You're lucky he took pity on you, because my pity spout ran dry long before your birth. That said, my word was to keep you safe. That bastard you bear is a different story."

"What?" Mara's hands tightened over her belly, and she recoiled, fearful Olessa would somehow rip her child from her then and there. "Madame Olessa, but I—"

"Want to raise it here? Or maybe you'd like to leave?" She raised a brow and motioned for the door. "You are not a prisoner here, although I wonder how long you would last with an infant in your arms in a city like Sollan these days."

Mara's jaw quivered. Olessa was right. Mara's first memory was leaving the city. Since then, she had never returned. Sollan would eat her like an ancient titan come back to life, and then it would take her child.

"That's right," Olessa cooed, guessing her thoughts. "You have nowhere to go. You know nothing of Eloia or the many strange lands of Urum. This barge is your world, and I am its goddess. This goddess does not care for another mouth to feed, especially one that won't turn a profit for years to come."

"Is there no way? Is there nothing I could say or do to keep my child with me?"

Olessa's features hardened. "Unless your infant pisses gold and shits diamonds, it's off this barge as soon as it draws its first breath. You understand me? That is my word, and as you know by now I never break my word. You'll watch iron rust and turn to dust before I reconsider."

Mara grabbed her dress and wrung it in her fists. The babe within her kicked, its hand moving like a wave across her belly. "What will you do?"

"As if I have to tell you." Olessa snorted and looked to the side. She rubbed her wrinkled hands on an armrest and puckered her lips. "But…I am not a cruel madame. The lesser pleasure barges on the Floatwaif, they would have tied stones to your ankles and tossed you to the coral sharks long ago. I am not them, and this is the House of Sin and Silk."

"Praise to the Six," Mara whispered, her knuckles whitening.

"Indeed. As to your whelp, I have decided to show it a kindness undeserving of its station. Once you give birth, I'll have it sent to the noble palaces in Sollan. Nobles pay good coin for well-fed infants. Raising them as servants from birth allows them to properly train them in the fine art of knee-bending and chin-dipping."

"A servant? I—I never thought…" Mara's gaze drifted to her belly.

Olessa cackled, her chortle twisting into Mara's heart like witch's nails. "What did you think this world would hold for your child, Mara? Did you think it would be some kind of mighty warrior, leading battalions to slay titans? Maybe a famed acolyte of the Six, performing their wonders throughout Urum to adoring crowds even as magic fades from our world with each passing generation? Or maybe you just want it to be happy, to live on a little farm outside Sollan and watch its kids grow old and have children of their own?"

Mara bit her lip. A tear slid down her cheek and splashed onto her knuckles. "I did not think, Madame Olessa."

"Of course you didn't. None of those things can ever be for that child, Mara. You are young and still bathe in your hopes and dreams, but one day, you will see that nothing can wash away the reek of our lot in life. Your child will be born a bastard to a faceless father and a moon maiden mother.

"Like you, it will not have a last name because it does not deserve one. Sending it to a noble to serve is a kindness children of the docks would gladly slit a throat for given half a chance. Pray you never see what that life is truly like."

"Thank you, Madame Olessa, for showing me and my child such a blessing."

Mara fought down the urge to leap into the sea and drown in salty sorrows. Friends were rare in the pleasure barge, and at times, she even hesitated before telling Gia something close to her heart. Having a child with her would have been different. She would love her son or daughter, and they would love her.

She could whisper secrets to them until the rising sun cast pale gold over the horizon and snuffed out all but the brightest stars. They would laugh at jokes no one knew but them, not caring how the other girls would roll their eyes and turn their backs. They would have each other, and nothing could ever break that bond between them. Nothing except the razor tongue and hard truths of Madame Olessa.

"Tell me then," Olessa said in a flat, cold voice, "that when the time comes, you will willingly give me the child."

Mara lifted her chin. Olessa considered her with hard eyes.

"You want me to promise this now?"

Olessa nodded. She tucked a curl behind an ear weighed by gold and smiled cooly. "I'd rather not be forced to have this conversation again. If we come to an understanding now, that will make what happens after the birth so much easier on us both, don't you think?"

"I...I don't know..."

Olessa sucked in a breath, her anger lifting her brow. "Mara. Promise me now you'll give the child to me. Do not fight me on this. You are no prisoner here, but if you do not agree to this, I will not let you stay. I'll have a strong boy drop you at the docks before sunrise, and then you'll see what happens to a moon maiden when she's plucked from the sky and buried in the sewage of that city."

"No, no," Mara pleaded, "I can't survive there."

The very thought of being marooned in the vast, teeming maze of streets and towers sent her heart clawing up her throat. Sollan was danger. Sollan was darkness. Olessa kept her safe on the barge. Mara knew that world, and if she stayed in it, Olessa would keep her from the wicked children of the docks and their long knives.

"Well?" Her madame arched a brow. "You know what you must do if you wish to stay."

Mara placed her hands gently on her belly. She felt the life inside her, the ball of warmth and hopes and dreams, a child who would grow that she would never know.

You have my heart, she told her child. *I will love you until the end of my days. When you cry, think of me to dry your tears. When you smile, know that I will smile with you. When you dream, know that I will dream of you. I love you, I love you, I love you.*

Mara lifted her chin. A strange calmness washed over her body. Her tears disappeared. Her aches and pains and bruises faded. "I promise, Madame Olessa, that you may take my child once it's born. I will not fight you because I know I cannot give it the life it needs."

Olessa clapped her hands and smiled. "See? That wasn't so hard. Now get out. Oh, be a dear and send a strong boy in to clean that broken wine glass."

Mara nodded. She tottered from Olessa's room, her aches and pains slowly creeping back into her bones.

3

FLIGHT OF THE LANTERNS

The first paper lanterns of Harvest Festival drifted from the docks as the sun slowly sank beneath the horizon. The rectangular lanterns would drift on the glassy waters of the city's bay until they reached the Floatwaif where the heat of their flames and the ocean breeze combined to pluck them from the waves and pull them toward their starry brethren.

Mara never lit a lantern of her own. Olessa never allowed it, even though her madame always lit one herself. One day, Mara wanted to light a lantern. Maybe she would for her child once it was born. Once Olessa took it from her to a life that would never intersect with hers.

"Each one is a prayer for the Burning Mother," Gia said, tucking her legs to her chest.

"May she bring another plentiful harvest this coming year," Mara murmured.

"And a year of healthy..." Gia's voice faded. She looked to her knees, her cheeks flushing red. It was an innocent mistake, the phrase she nearly muttered. All muttered it on Harvest Festival. All prayed for it on that night.

"...Babes," Mara finished. "It's okay, Gia. I know you didn't mean anything by it."

Ever since her talk with Madame Olessa, Mara had meticulously avoided the subject of her child. Gia eventually gave up her friendly prodding and hid her worries behind a warm smile. Mara wasn't sure if she would ever tell her friend the truth until the deed was done and her child gone. By then, every moon maiden and strong boy would know the truth and it wouldn't matter anyway.

The first paper lanterns reached the bobbing mess of the Floatwaif barges. The lanterns lifted from the calm waters, floating in an ever-rising wave toward the titan skeleton proudly facing the horizon.

Cheers erupted from the shore and quickly spread to Floatwaif. Drums beat a merry rhythm. Sea and shore came alive with leaping, dancing peoples of all shapes and sizes. Ferry boats unmoored from Sollan's docks and disturbed the glassy waters, their pointed prows aimed like arrows for the heart of the House of Sin and Silk.

Gia stood and smoothed her shimmering sheer dress. "And Harvest Festival begins. Is my collar polished?"

Mara stood with a little help from her friend. So long had she worn her own brass-plated collar that she often forgot it hung around her neck.

She licked her thumb and rubbed a speck of grease from Gia's collar. "There. It looks like it's never been worn before."

"You know I envy you, Mara."

Mara furrowed her brow and paused her polishing. "Envy me? Did you take a dose of glimmer?"

"No," Gia said with a laugh. "But you'll be cooking in the kitchen while I'll be serving the whims of drunk fools. Sometimes I just wish I…I just wish I had my body back."

"I can't remember a time when it was mine." Mara looked to her belly. "I've been Olessa's slave since my youngest days. As soon as I was old enough, she had me taking patrons so she could turn a profit. Now, I share my body with my child and wonder if tomorrow Olessa will grow tired of the expense and throw me to the sharks."

Gia laughed and leaned back. She tossed a dark braid behind her shoulder and glanced toward the horizon. "I think you would like freedom if you ever got the taste of it. It's sweet like honey but strong like saltwater gin. You'd be worse than a glimmer fiend on it because you'd never want to let it go, and if you did, there would always be a cold pit of longing for it in your heart."

"Why do you think that?"

Gia smiled and pinched Mara's chin. "Because I see a fire in your eyes that I don't often see in others. Even the girls who knew freedom for years before debts, desperation, or a slaver's whip brought them to the House of Sin and Silk often lack the spark of freedom. But it's there inside you. It's why your body fought the ebon orchid, and it's why you are the only one to show kindness even in a place like this where every girl plots her sister's downfall. Never let that fire burn out. I feel like one day, it will free you."

"What was it like?" Mara asked. "The world beyond the barge, what do you remember of it?"

Her friend's eyes lit up, her inky orbs glittering with the light of the lanterns slowly drifting overhead. "Oh, Mara, the world beyond the barge is like nothing you've ever seen and even greater than anything you could imagine! One day, we'll both leave this rotting ship, and I'll take you to the eastern kingdoms. Blail and Hine are beautiful beyond words. They put even the king's palace to shame."

"Do they worship the Six in Blail and Hine?"

"Of course." Gia turned to the ocean and held her arms tight against her chest. The barest breeze kissed her gauzy dress, its shimmering folds fluttering in the wind. "In the wider world, every city of worth has a titan standing guard. Some even more than one. I remember a time when I was across the sea in a city called Silph with my father. It was the summer before the slavers killed him…"

Gia relaxed her arms and opened her palms toward the sea. "We came upon a priestess of the Burning Mother performing magics no words can truly describe. Her eyes were like two suns, her hands weaving patterns of flames that could burn through solid stone."

"It sounds beautiful. And frightening."

"Things are only truly beautiful if they frighten you a little. As I watched that priestess, I knew then that my life's dream was to be a someone like her, to serve the Burning Mother and spread her wisdom throughout Urum."

Silence settled over them. Lanterns filled the air from the shoreline to the titan. They drifted over the skeleton's broad shoulders and through its massive ribs, painting the bones with the warmest gold.

Even in the beauty of the moment, Mara couldn't help but pity Gia. Instead of a maiden of the Burning Mother, she had become a maiden of the moon, chained to the earth by a cheap brass collar.

"Gia, I—"

"*Shh…*" Gia spun around and pressed a finger to Mara's lips. "We cannot regret where we are. We can only look to where we want to be. I want to be on the steps of the Mother's temple. I know in my heart that one day I will be there, and when I finally make it to the steps, everything I do will be for her, and I will finally have my body back."

"And I'll do what I can to help you."

Her friend smiled and clasped Mara's wrists. "Will you help me with something now?"

"You know I will. What do you need?"

"Turn to the Sapphire Sea. Close your eyes."

"Gia…"

Gia faced the ocean and closed her eyes. "Please, Mara, just do this with me."

Slowly, Mara turned to the horizon and took a deep, calming breath. Salt spray wet her lips. The breeze caressed her neck like a patron who truly loved her. The low din of revelry gave her a sense of being a blissfully small part of something much greater.

"We are prisoners here despite what our madame says," Gia said, "but not even Madame Olessa and her brass collars can chain your spirit. I find when I am calm and close my eyes, my spirit takes flight, and I am beggar and noble, moon maiden and patron, coral shark and bay gull. Then, in the small quiet before my next patron arrives, I am truly unchained."

A smile inched up Mara's cheeks. Already she smelled the cooking fires of the Floatwaif. They carried the rich scents of fried shrimp, coral shark stew, and soft fin bass that was the staple of their diet.

Yet Mara sensed more than just food and cooking fires. In her mind, she saw the people of the Floatwaif, their smiles and laughs, their stories, their hopes, and even their fears.

"She made me promise to give the child to her," Mara finally said. She opened her eyes and looked at Gia. "And I did."

The muscles in Gia's throat tensed. Her friend opened her eyes and glared at Mara. "Your child? Why does she want it? For another servant?"

"Not a servant for her but one to sell to a noble house. Was I right to agree? I carry this guilt, and it makes me feel like my heart has swallowed rocks."

"There are worse ways to live than as a servant of a highborn fool. You may only know the barge, but the pleasures of nobility are far beyond anything you've ever seen and probably even imagined."

"Then it is the only way." Mara cupped her round belly. "My child will never have a life with me."

"Remember what I told you? Don't regret. Look to your dreams, and you will achieve them. Once this child of yours is born and Olessa takes it from your arms, if you wish to see it again, then dream it. Breathe it. Live it, and it will come true for you."

"I don't know if I could ever leave the barge," she said, grimacing as the child kicked her stomach. "It's frightening beyond our house. Olessa says the children carry knives at the docks. They will slit your throat for a promise of a better life."

A grin notched up Gia's cheek. "I think Madame Olessa doesn't want to lose one of her most profitable assets. The world is dangerous; she is right about that. Look at the titan that guards Sollan's bay, Mara. When the First Sun shone, they walked this world. They owned it. They punished the creatures on it. Yet the Six saw their corruption and took pity on the lesser beings. The Six struck the titans down and raised the Second Sun..."

Gia hesitated. No one spoke of those that walked beneath the Second Sun. To speak their name invited ill fortune. To think of them welcomed a curse with open arms.

"The alp," Mara whispered. She glanced around like a girl discovering how to steal. "The demons of the Second Sun. Pale patrons of death. Tamers of the glittering dragons."

Gia's gaze darted around them, searching for a specter that might leap from the water and latch around their throats. "The alp," she echoed. "And when they waged their war against the Six and sought to raise the titans, even they were toppled and the Third Sun raised for the thrones of men. Who says something won't come and topple us next? There are dark things out there and there always will be, but there are also things of such wonder they will steal the breath from your lips in the best of ways."

"I wish you were cooking with me tonight."

"Me too. I'd rather steal fried shrimp from platters than handle raw ones in my room until the sun rises."

Mara laughed, and the motion caused the child to press against her bladder. "I have to relieve myself. Again. Sometimes I wonder if I'm growing a mermaid in my belly."

"Or merman," Gia quipped. "It could be a boy."

"You're right. I hope for both, truth be told. Twins would make my night."

"And you really don't know who the father is?"

Mara shook her head. "The way Olessa works us, it could be any number of men. You and I both know that many of our patrons don't reveal their true identities to our madame. I've heard rumors from my patrons that Good King Sol does not look kindly on the pleasure barges, so to avoid his disfavor they use false names and dress in rags when they may have riches."

"Good King Sol?" Gia spat into the sea. "He can run into a cooking fire after an oil bath for all I care. He's some spoiled brat who took his father's throne and now looks to take the thrones of the Six for himself. He thinks he's holier than all of us, but mark my words, Mara, I bet that man's stepped foot in the House of Sin and Silk looking for a maiden's touch."

"But you can't deny the rumors. Even Olessa talks about the king's cult of the Serpent Sun and its spread not just in Sollan, but throughout all Eloia's great cities. If Olessa's talking about them, then I know she fears them. You think he'll come for us, come for the barge? Are we even safe here anymore?"

Gia swept her arm toward the last of the paper lanterns floating toward the titan. Beyond the towering skeleton, the night sky was a dome of twinkling silver jewels and bobbing gold points of light.

"Those lanterns are not for the Serpent Sun," Gia said. "They are for the Burning Mother. Each one of those lights is a prayer for *her*, not that snake born of fire the king and his cult worships. Sol can't crush the Six. He's a young, foolish king of one country amongst many others. He cannot hope to conquer an entire world and its faithful, no matter how hard he tries."

"I hope you're right, Gia." Mara stared at the floating lanterns. Her gaze drifted to the titan, its body illuminated by the flickering orbs.

The Six destroyed the titans under the First Sun when the world was young and burning with greed and magic. Any gods powerful enough to slay such creatures would surely squash a king if he became a threat. They even buried the demons of the Second Sun, the alp who tamed the forces of magic and the dragons of old.

Yet, Mara heard the rumors about the Six just like everyone else. Whispers of the priests and their dying magic filtered through the Floatwaif. Without power in their blood, no number of prayers would keep men faithful to the Six when the blades of King Sol's armies demanded otherwise.

A strong boy rushed around the corner. Mara didn't pay much attention to Madame Olessa's eunuchs, but she recalled that one. His short hair glittered like gold, and his round, blue eyes gazed at the world like he was still a child despite his imposing height and brick body of rippling muscles.

"Tolstes," Mara said. "Do you need something?"

"Gia, Mara, I thought I might find you here. Madame Olessa is searching for you. The first boats are arriving."

Gia held out an arm for Mara. "Then I guess we should be off. I'm sure she has a line of patrons already forming for me."

Tolstes nodded, hurriedly motioning around the corner. "You will have a long night swimming in silk while Mara swims in shrimp grease and picks bits of shark stew from her pretty hair. The Mother has brought us a plentiful harvest and patrons wish to kiss the moon."

Mara took Gia's arm and nodded at Tolstes. "May she bring a year of healthy babes to add to the bounty."

Gia and Mara shared a smile. They followed Tolstes around the barge, the sound of laughter, drums, and clinking wine growing louder with each step.

4

THE HARVEST

Mara tightened the bun of her hair. All around her, smoke from cooking grease filled the clattering, chaotic kitchen in the pleasure barge's belly. Oyster shells lay in broken mounds at Mara's feet. Strong boys entered the kitchen in pairs, bringing baskets of squirming shrimp caught fresh from the Sapphire Sea. Moon maidens past their prime hacked away at coral shark fins and cut thin slices of soft fin bass for heavy silver trays.

She took a deep breath, savoring the garlic and dill dulling the reek of grilled onions. Mara wiped her arm over her sweaty brow and sunk a wooden spoon into a thick brew of shark fin soup. She grunted as she slowly stirred the thick, gurgling broth, careful not to let the hot stew bubble and pop grease onto her cheeks.

Faratta eyed Mara from across the kitchen. The old woman was one of Olessa's first moon maidens, but age had pulled her out of active service and buried her in the bowels of the pleasure barge where she cooked for patron, maiden, and strong boy alike. Time had stolen her once smooth, porcelain features and replaced them with deep wrinkles and weary rings beneath her eyes. Constant exposure to grease and oil gave the woman's puckering lips and wide cheeks a bright sheen. Some of the meaner maidens called Faratta the Buttered Puffer. No matter how brave they were, none would ever dare say it to her face.

The cook strode across the kitchen, muscling past strong boys and kitchen aides. She came to Mara's pot and leaned over the column of twisting steam rising from the stew. Her nostrils expanded, the trails of grey rushing into her nose.

"More garlic," she said in a low and crackling voice, "and a pinch of thyme. Don't let the bottom burn or it'll ruin the whole batch, you hear me?"

Mara nodded eagerly. "Yes, ma'am."

"Good." She glanced at the piles of shells around Mara's feet and puckered her lips in a gesture Mara thought might be approval. "You work well. Most of the younger girls who come to me fuck up the food so badly I wouldn't feed it to a pig."

"Thank you, Faratta." Mara gripped the spoon tighter and stirred. "You wouldn't need more help in the kitchen after this, would you?"

"What's that? What do you mean?"

"If you needed it…after the, ah, after Harvest Festival…"

Faratta's cheeks swelled with the snort she tried desperately to hold back. The woman waved dismissively and turned from Mara, heading back to the table of half-sliced soft fin bass. "Someone sounds like they've gotten tired of taking patrons' orders and wants to hear this old hag bark at them instead."

The other kitchen girls giggled. A few of the nearby strong boys grinned.

Faratta glanced over her shoulder and winked. "We'll see. Night's still young, Mara, and there's plenty of time yet to fuck up a batch of soup or two. You keep working as you are, and maybe I pull a few strings with Olessa and get you down in this dump with me."

"Yes, ma'am!" Mara stirred more eagerly than ever, her smile shining on her face.

Her babe kicked. Mara grimaced, leaning over the hot pot. Despite the child's constant twisting and turning, despite the pressure on her bladder that made her body cry for relief after what seemed like every breath, despite her swollen, aching ankles and sore back, Mara was happier than she had been since she could remember.

Maybe Faratta could also convince Olessa to let Mara keep her child. Faratta could find some use for the boy or girl in the bowels of the barge, and then Mara would have everything she ever wanted. She could live out her days in Olessa's world while the wider one with its evil, selfish people, petty kings, and false religions passed her by.

* * *

Mara cooked and cooked. As soon as she finished one plate, a strong boy would heap the fresh ingredients of the next before her. On her fourth round of stew, Faratta returned. The woman dabbed the sweat on Mara's brow and brushed a moist lock of Mara's hair behind her ear.

"You've been doing well, Mara. If you don't get some fresh air, this grease smoke will have you croaking like a frog just like me."

Mara grinned, politely swallowing her chuckle. "I can go on. I'm not tired."

"Hah!" Faratta swept her hand toward the pile of oyster shells beside Mara. "How about this: Bundle up those shells and dump them in the rear. Coral sharks love greasy oyster bits. They'll go wild, you'll get some fresh air, and my kitchen'll be a little cleaner. We all win, and that's the best kind of winning."

Mara lifted the spoon from the stew and tapped it against the pot's rim, shaking clumps of cream and shark from the utensil. The air in the kitchen thickened as her gaze swept over the room. The pungent aromas filled her lungs with grease and oil. A quick trip for a few breaths of sea air sounded intoxicating by comparison.

"If you wish it, I will do it," Mara said.

"That's the spirit." Faratta took the spoon and began stirring the pot. "Now get before I change my mind."

Mara scurried over to the shells. She used a broom and pan to sweep them into a reed basket. Wiping bits of shell from her palms against her apron, she grabbed the rough container and slipped through the kitchen door. It swung closed behind her, and the din and smoke of the kitchen vanished. With the basket resting on her belly, she waddled up the short flight of stairs to the barge's aft deck.

The festivities at the House of Sin and Silk took place on the long, wide decks at the prow or in the luxurious pleasure rooms within. Not a single patron, maiden, or strong boy lingered on the quiet aft deck, its simple wooden floorboards sheltered by a flapping canvas canopy.

A few potted aloe plants and other succulents dotted the deck. They loved the sun and sea and required little care, so of course Olessa thought them perfect for the barge. In the offhand chance someone burned themselves on a brazier, or more commonly, burned their skin from candle wax dripped onto their back, Olessa would cut the leaf and use its juices to soothe the burn.

Mara dropped her basket by one of the plants at the edge of the deck. She looked into the Sapphire Sea's waters and stared at her reflection staring back with its wide, youthful eyes and shiny cheeks rounded with a mother's glow.

The image brought a smile to her face, but she did not forget her chore. If she wanted Faratta to convince Olessa of her worth in the kitchen, she couldn't idle like a foolish girl in the aft while the rest of the barge was hard at work.

She knelt to the basket and gripped the rim. The rough and awkward container wobbled in her hand. Her bloated belly made tipping the shells toward the water even more difficult, so she planted her feet to give her extra leverage. She placed her other hand beneath the basket and angled it over the edge.

The oyster shells shifted, clattering toward the basket's lip in a shifting pile of bone grey and tarnished brown. The shells gathered near the edge. A little more, and they would tumble into the waves.

With a grunt, she tipped the basket. The shells piled higher, but they refused to fall. It was as if they knew their doom waited patiently beneath the waves.

Mara frowned and dug her nails into the bottom of the basket. She shuffled her feet closer to the ledge.

"Get in there, you stupid shells!" Mara lifted the basket—just a little higher.

Both shells and reed container splashed into the sea. Mara's burdened belly tipped her forward. Her heart fluttered. Her arms swung in wild circles. She toppled over, and the dark, glassy Sapphire Sea swallowed her whole.

She spun and splashed through a torrent of foam and rubbery bubbles sliding up her arms and cheeks. The sea's sour brine stung her lips and burned her throat. She reached for the deck, but in her panic she hit her knuckles against the wood, and a jolt of pain lanced through her hand.

A soft form slid across her knee, gentle as a first-time patron's playful caress. Another form glided across her back. In her periphery she caught a fin slicing the sea like a black knife tearing through a thin curtain.

Mara knew coral sharks well. They swarmed the shallows just off Sollan's shores. Most people in the Floatwaif ate them daily so plentiful were their numbers. Normally, the sharks feared men. That fear vanished in a frenzy brought on by things they ate like greasy shells and bits of soft oyster inside them.

She swallowed another bitter gulp of seawater and coughed, flailing madly for the deck. Once calm waters bubbled. Fins cut the waves. Mara finally grasped the deck with her red, bleeding knuckles. She heaved and pulled. Her arms trembled. Her body shook. She lifted her chin just over the deck, but the child in her belly weighed more than her arms could bear, and Mara slipped.

Mara cried out. Weighed by her child and exhausted from stirring thick stew, not even the terror electrifying her blood gave her the strength to save herself.

"Help..." she rasped through her sobs. "Please...I can't..."

A coral shark's tail slapped her face and stung her cheek. Her babe twisted and kicked. Through some miracle, she grabbed the barge's lip once again.

She heaved, but she also tired. No matter how hard she tried, her arm would not bring her above the waves. A finger slipped. Her adrenaline faded, and the sea gently coaxed her beneath its surface.

A strong, steady grip clamped around her wrist. She stuck her other hand above the waves, and her savior took it, yanking Mara from the water in a shower of sea and foam and bits of sharp shells.

The saltwater stung her eyes and blurred her vision. She pressed her palms against the deck and coughed until her lungs burned. Blinking, her world slowly came into focus. So did her rescuer.

"Tolstes!" Mara laughed, grasping the man's hand. "Thank you, thank you, thank you."

The strong boy knelt beside her. He lifted her knuckles to his eyes, his blond brows knitting together as he inspected the bloody scrapes. "There are much easier and faster ways to take your life than putting coral sharks into a frenzy and throwing yourself to them."

"I—I fell. The basket..." Mara coughed. She turned and vomited seawater on the wood. "I couldn't pull myself up, Tolstes. You saved me. Why are you even here? Did I take too long? Did Faratta ask for me?"

"It's not that at all. It's crowded up there. This is the busiest Harvest Festival I have seen in all my years. You'd think they knew we'd never celebrate the day again by the drinking and mounds of glimmer they're shoveling down their throats. I came out to check the aft for thieves and heard the splash. To be honest, I almost hacked your hand off when I saw you."

"I'm glad you didn't." Mara smiled, but a sharp pain in her groin wiped it from her face. The pain twisted up her body and coiled around her belly where it clenched like a snapping eel around her womb. And then, it vanished as quickly as it came.

"What's wrong?" Tolstes asked. "You have an odd look about you."

"Because I felt something odd about me. It's gone now. We should go inside before Faratta thinks I've run off."

Tolstes nodded and gently clasped her hand. He helped Mara to her feet and rung the seawater from her dress. "The Buttered Puffer might not even notice," he said.

"Let's hope. I've been gone long enough."

The strong boy stood and guided Mara toward the doorway leading inside. They slipped beneath the canopy's shadow. A familiar burning hardness clamped her groin and shot to her womb.

Mara doubled over. Her knees hit the deck. Tolstes kneeled and clasped her shoulders in his strong grip. Concern contorted the boyish innocence of his features. "Mara, something really is wrong."

"No, not now…Not tonight."

"What is it? You know what ails you?"

Mara twisted around. She scooted to the wall and panted, her arm resting over her belly. "I think I'm having this child, Tolstes."

"You mean now? On Harvest Festival?" He shuffled to her, eyeing her belly like it was a kraken that just crawled on deck. "What—what—what—what do I do?"

"I'm not ready. I'm not ready." She grabbed Tolstes' hand and leaned forward. "Olessa will take my child. I do not want to say goodbye. I promised, but I can't. I can't."

"Six save me. Don't worry about that right now, Mara," he said, twisting his hand out of her grasp. "Worry about a safe childbirth. I'll go get help. Maybe Madame Olessa has delivered a child before…"

"No!" Mara grabbed the man's loose shirt and yanked him to her. His eyes widened into full moons before her. She pulled him so close his breath washed over her face.

"Do not fetch Madame Olessa," she hissed through the wall of her teeth. "Find Gia. You must find Gia and bring her. She will help. I know she will."

Tolstes looked unconvinced. He bit his lip and glanced toward the doorway. "We could get in trouble. I really should get Olessa."

"Tolstes, since you have no manhood, I can't cut it off. But I promise you that I will haunt your dreams through this life and all others if you bring our madame to me before my child takes its first breath. I promise upon the Six and all other gods from all other ages that were and have yet to be. Bring my madame here, and I. Will. Haunt. You."

The strong boy recoiled. He blinked, his jaw loose while his mind processed her words. "I'll, uh, I'll go get Gia, then."

"Thank you."

Tolstes stood. He darted into the doorway but paused before he disappeared down the hall. "You're frightening when you've got a fire in you."

"*Go!*"

He bolted into the shadows. Another snaking pain gripped her womb. Mara dug her nails into the wood. Her body pushed even though her mind protested.

5

ASHWALK PILGRIM

"Push, Mara, push!" Gia's dark eyes loomed large in Mara's vision. Her fingers wrapped around Mara's wrist and squeezed reassuringly.

The pain. Mara had never felt a pain like that before. She'd suffered Olessa's beatings many times, but the child forcing its way from her womb into the world was an ever-heaving torment unlike any silken fist her madame ever slammed against her jaw.

Labor was an agony that blossomed within the deepest parts of her. Nothing dulled it. Nothing lessened it. Her groin was fire, her legs slick with filth, her brow soaked in sweat that stung like jellyfish poison in her eyes.

Her deep muscles flexed and twisted. Mara cringed and grabbed Tolstes' hand in an iron grasp.

The poor strong boy looked frightened as a fish on a sand dune. His eyes darted to Mara's stomach and back to the door leading inside the barge. If she released him, he'd either jump into the sea to face the sharks or run screaming to Olessa, begging for forgiveness.

Mara clenched her jaw and tightened her grip. "It hurts, Tolstes. It hurts so much."

Gia grabbed Mara's sweaty chin and jerked it toward her. "You just push and that's all you do, do you hear me, Mara? Push and do not stop. You're strong. You can do this!"

She heaved a sob as the pain erupted in her belly. "I don't know—"

"Push or I'll slap you so hard this child flies out your belly!"

"Slap me then. Slap me so hard I spit out my teeth. Just get this child out of me!"

Gia smiled but quickly forced her lips down. Tolstes snickered and dipped his chin. Mara whipped toward him and glared daggers in his eyes. "What's so funny, strong boy?"

His face paled. He looked to Gia for support. "But it was—I thought—a joke?"

Gia rolled her eyes. "Just hush and sit there for her to hold."

"I'm scared." Mara squeezed her eyes shut. Hot tears streamed from the corners of her lids. "Tell me everything will be fine."

"Everything will be fine," Gia cooed. She stroked Mara's temple. "It will be just fine."

"You'll make it through this," Tolstes added. "The Six will bless this child. I'm sure of it."

Another burning, twisting pain coiled around her womb. Mara sobbed, pushing with all her might.

Gia looked between Mara's legs. The woman's dark eyes swelled, and she shuffled to a better position. "I see the head! Once more, Mara. Once more!"

Mara gathered all the energy left within her and opened her eyes to the world. In the distance, on the horizon, the bright moon glittered on the calm sea. The silver disc crowned the titan's bones like the halo of a mighty god.

"I can't do it," she told the titan.

"You can," Gia answered instead. "Push, damn you. I said *PUSH!*"

Mara screamed and poured all her strength, all her hope, and all her fear into a final, terrifying push. She clamped her teeth into a tight, trembling wall. Her vision faded into a tunnel. Only Gia remained, framed by the dark sky and the black silhouette of the titan's bones.

Ever so slowly, Gia smiled. A satisfying weight slipped from Mara's groin, and her body relaxed. Her tunnel vision expanded. Her strength flowed away on her sigh. The inferno in her body faded into an aching burn. She released Tolstes from her grip and shuddered.

The strong boy slipped a small knife from his pocket he'd swiped from the kitchen and handed it to Gia. "Cut the chord from the child. I would do it, but, ah, you're already down there and all…"

Mara's friend nodded and plucked the knife from Tolstes. Licking her lips, she cut the chord.

Mara smiled. She ran her hand through her sweat and saltwater soaked hair and waited for her child's first wailing breath. "Boy or girl, Gia?"

Gia's brows knitted in a wrinkled wedge above her smooth nose. Her dark eyes glanced worriedly at the strong boy. "Boy…"

"Wonderful," Mara said. "A boy. Let me see my son, Gia."

Tolstes caught Gia's worried look, and his own brows knotted together. His bright eyes flicked from Gia to Mara and back again.

A new kind of fear worked its way up Mara's spine unlike any terror she ever imagined. "Gia, what's wrong? Let me see him, Gia. Give him to me. Oh Six, please give me my son."

Tolstes edged over to Gia. His lips pressed into a flat line. His eyes caught sight of the child. He swallowed and shuffled back. His chin trembled, and he looked away.

"What's wrong, Tolstes?" Mara asked.

She couldn't see her son, and neither could she hear his screams. The terror racing through her veins clamped a cold hand around her heart. "Why isn't my son crying? Shouldn't he cry? Shouldn't he scream?"

Gia choked down a sob. A tear slipped down her cheek, but she quickly wiped it away. "He should, Mara. I'm so sorry, but he should."

"No. N—no!" Mara twisted forward. Pain racked her body. Filth and blood stained her legs. The reek of her urine accosted her nose as it soaked into the shadowy deck.

Mara focused on the infant lying on the wood. Gia had cut his chord to Mara. Blood and bits of womb covered his tiny, plump body and stained his pink skin scarlet.

His closed eyes were soft and puffy above cheeks no larger than spring plums, and his lips were two silken caterpillars softly embracing. He looked hale. He appeared healthy. But the boy who only a few hours ago kicked and squirmed within her belly lay still as stone and lively as brick.

In that instant, Mara knew two indisputable truths about her son. Mara knew he was more precious than all others who had ever existed in the history of all the Suns of Urum. She also knew he drew not a single breath.

She grasped her child, prodding his tiny chest for a heartbeat that never came. "Why isn't he breathing, Gia?"

Gia did not answer. The woman sat hunched, hands buried in her lap, sorrowful gaze trying to hide in her thighs along with her hands.

"Tolstes!" Mara looked frantically to the eunuch. "Help me make him breathe. Help me give him life! Please."

The strong boy stared at the babe with a face as grey as old ash. "Stillborn. On Harvest Festival…" he wobbled to his feet and stepped back. "An ill omen, Mara."

Fluttering red and gold silks from a fine dress drifted into Mara's periphery. Mara choked on a sob, a cold, numb dread sinking deep into her stomach as her fingers continued searching her son's body for a spark of life.

"So Mara had the child," Olessa said, her voice flat as a frozen lake. "And it is stillborn?"

Mara wept. Her fingertip caressed her son's lips, feeling their silky flesh tickle her skin. Teardrops splattered against his dirty cheeks—salty, glimmering tears that should have come from his eyes as he opened them to his first night on Urum.

"Gia, is the child stillborn?" Olessa asked again.

"Yes, Madame Olessa," Tolstes answered for her, "the child did not draw a breath."

"That is…unfortunate. And on Harvest Festival, a day for celebrating life. This is not a good sign for any of us."

"Ma—Ma—Madame Olessa?" Tolstes' voice trembled like he'd just lost his manhood a second time. "What do we do?"

"We wrap him in cloth. Send him to the Sapphire Sea in a box and light it on fire or tie a rock to his feet and let him sink beneath the waves. Stillborns are never a good sign. Stillborns on Harvest Festival will ruin me."

"What?" Mara looked up, blinking the angry tears from her eyes. The thought of her infant as a meal for coral sharks twisted her stomach into a burning coil not even the threat of Olessa's silken glove could cool. "Beneath the *ship*? You would have me work and serve patrons above the floating corpse of my *son*?"

"What would you have me do, Mara?" Olessa snarled. "We can't leave him here. There's no place in Lower Sollan to bury him on the busiest night of the year, and every drunkard in the streets is going to be howling curses for trudging that ashore tonight. Might as well tell the world the House of Sin and Silk only serves lepers because that's all who'd come knocking at my doors!"

"There has to be a way. There has to be something we can do—"

"Ashwalk!" Gia's eyes finally darted from her lap. They focused on Olessa with a desperate, hopeful glimmer shining deep within them. "Let Mara take the ashwalk. It is a right of every mother whose newborn draws no breath on the holiest day of the year."

Madame Olessa stared blankly at Gia. She blinked and burst into laughter, waving at the maiden like the woman was a silly child. "Ashwalk? Mara? The girl hasn't been to Sollan in ages. She's probably never even seen Upper Sollan, let alone Hightable or the temples. Some beggar would slit her throat and take her maiden collar as soon as she stepped on shore."

Mara's gaze bounced back and forth between the two women. "What is this ashwalk? Gia, if this will help my child, I will do it. I will do it a hundred thousand times over until the last stars die."

"See?" Gia flashed her brows. "Please, for Mara, let her make the ashwalk. She is of no use to you tonight anyway. She is…she is a burden on your books tonight. Let her do what the Burning Mother requires of those who birth stillborn children on this night."

"What is an ashwalk?" Mara asked.

Olessa sighed and pinched the bridge of her nose. She turned her back to Mara and faced the glittering sea. "It is a very old tradition of the Burning Mother's and one that I am loathe to let you honor because you will never succeed."

The woman shook her head. Her wig's curls bounced over her shoulders. "But I do fear what might happen should you not at least try to save his soul."

"Save his soul?"

Madame Olessa turned to Mara and nodded. "All stillborn children have a soul, but since they never took their first breath, their body is a prison for their spirit. That cursed fool of a brother of mine. Damn him for making me love the Six so much."

Gia turned to Mara and placed a hand lightly on her knee. "She speaks true, Mara. His soul is trapped. It is so rare for stillborns on harvest I had forgotten the ritual, but I remember my father telling me of it."

"Is it—is it true? Is his soul really trapped? I must take this walk to save it?"

Olessa's features hardened. "I wouldn't stick my finger in the Mother's eye if I were you, and I'll be damned to dine on ash for eternity before that child's curse turns my profits into penance for my property's heresy."

You are trapped, Mara thought. She cradled her son's soft, minuscule body and looked into his closed eyes. *I will not let you suffer, my love.*

Madame Olessa swatted Tolstes' arm. "Go inside. Find some burlap for a cloak—use an old potato bag for all I care. Then find ashes from a cold brazier. Make sure you also find burlap for the child, and do not go sparingly with the ashes. I wouldn't want any demons sniffing him out before he leaves my house."

Tolstes nodded and bolted from the deck as if scorching flames had been nipping at his heels. Mara's frightened gaze fixed on her madame. "Ash and burlap? Demons?"

"Mara." Madame Olessa went to her knees. For the first time in the many years Mara had known her madame, she saw genuine warmth in the woman's eyes and the slightest sag of pity in their lids. Her gaze drifted to Mara's son, and the soft look quickly hardened.

"You have had a stillborn son on Harvest Festival," Olessa continued. "Any child born without breath tonight night is cursed by the gods. His soul is trapped within his body, and there it will fester while dark spirits from the Second Sun gather. They will seek those who witnessed the birth. They will bring plague and rot and horror. This place of pleasure will become one of pain and death."

"No, you're wrong," Mara said. She clutched the child firm against her breast. "My son would never do such a thing."

"Stupid girl. Your child is the bait for a demon feast like oysters amongst a swarm of coral sharks. With his birth, it has begun. It will not end until we are dead or you complete the ashwalk. If you do not do this, the first victim they take will be the infant's soul. Yours will be next. And damn my fate, damn my brother, and damn my years of coin spent on your upbringing, because those demons will come for me next."

"I won't let them have his soul. I'll rip every demon apart who tries to take it."

"Calm down." Madame Olessa snorted. "You are not all that you think you are. The demons of our Sun were the ancient races of the Second. No moon maiden could stand against those horrifying things."

Olessa's shoulder slumped. She reached for Mara. Mara flinched out of habit.

Her madame's hand held nothing but a soft caress. Olessa pulled Mara's chin to her, her eyes hard with the determination within them. "You can save his soul, Mara. You can save yours and ours, too. You must make the ashwalk. Cloaked in burlap and ash, you must journey to the Burning Mother's temple. There, in witness of the High Priestess, you must set the child before the Mother's Ever-Burning Flame. Only within the Mother's arms will you save him. Only then will you save us."

Mara shuddered. The well of her emotions bubbled up her aching throat. They spilled out, carried on her heavy sobs. She'd cried more in those past few hours than every day before combined. She kissed her son's soft brow and nodded, her tired eyes drifting closed. "Then take me there, and I will do the right thing."

"Take you? We cannot take you."

Mara's eyes shot open. Visions of young children with hollow eyes and long knives lining the shore peppered her thoughts. Behind them, a writhing monster of a city waited, full of dark people and dark tidings, and there she was, lost deep in its heart with nothing but burlap as her armor and ash as her shield.

"But you must take me! I've never been to the city. I—I don't know Lower Sollan or High Sollan or Hightable! I would be lost. I—I would be alone. I've never been alone. Never."

"Mara, I cannot take you. Gia cannot take you. No one can take you but yourself. The ashwalk is a journey for one and one alone. That is the price of holy pilgrimage. That is the lonely cost of saving souls."

"Please, Madame Olessa!" Mara reached for her madame, but the woman recoiled.

Olessa straightened, smoothing her silk dress and standing stiff as the titan skeleton rising from the sea. "Enough. I'm giving a worthless whore like you the chance to save your child's soul and for once do something in return for your gentle master. You will leave this place at once. Tolstes will take you to the docks on a skiff, far away from any of my patrons or maidens.

"Under cover of night, you will go to the docks and make your way through Sollan to the temples in the shadows of the king's palace. There, you will complete your ashwalk by giving the child to the Burning Mother. If you don't, I'll send the child to the bottom of the sea for coral sharks and sell you and your black womb to the highest bidder. Do not test my patience with this. Do not second guess my kindness in the matter."

Mara's arms shook. She clutched her son like a frightened toddler might clutch a soft pillow. "I'm afraid. I do not know the city. What if I fail? What if I'm not strong enough?"

"Then you will die there, your child's soul will never reach the Six, and if the stories are true I will spend the rest of my very short days fearing demons leaping from my chamber pot."

Mara stared blankly at Olessa, the only mother she had ever known and loved despite her many cruelties and hard lessons. Mara's gaze drifted to Gia, the one and only friend she ever had in the tiny kingdom called the House of Sin and Silk.

Her friend still tightly clasped her hands and buried them in her lap. She stared at Mara with eyes that glittered with her tears.

"It is your choice, Mara," Gia said. "I know you're afraid of the city, but I know you would want to give your son the respect he deserves—the respect the Six demand. Remember what I told you? The world beyond the barge is big and full of wonders. There is plenty darkness, but there is also light. Put your faith in the Six, and they will guide you. You may find you have yet to discover the real strength within you."

"Do you—do you think I can do this?"

Gia smiled and leaned forward. "I do. You are stronger than you know. Maybe this ashwalk will teach you that."

Tolstes burst out of the doorway carrying a messy bundle of burlap stained by soot and ash from one of the ship's brass braziers. He threw the fabric before Mara and stepped back. "There is a makeshift robe for you and a strip of burlap swaddling for the child. The ash will protect you both from the demons searching for your son, and in the city, no thief will bother an ashwalk pilgrim for fear of catching the curse. You should be, ah, safe. I think."

Mara reached for the smaller strip of burlap. Her fingers clasped the fabric. Slowly, carefully, she wrapped her son in the material until it cocooned him in its ashen folds. She took her burlap cloak and placed it over her shoulders, fastening the rough threads with frayed twine around her collar. Its fibers fell down her back. Soot stained her arms and added to the filth on her dress.

Tolstes had fashioned a rough hood from the cloak. She pulled the hood over her head, and the scent of burnt wood clogged her nose.

Mara struggled to her knees. She looked to the strong boy for a hand, but his eyes told her he would never extend it. Her gaze passed quickly over Olessa, who stood farther back than her bodyguard with arms locked over her sagging chest. Lastly Mara looked to Gia. Even sweet, strong Gia, so unafraid of anything, slowly drew her hands behind her back and looked to her feet.

"We are alone then," Mara whispered, kissing her son's brow.

She took a deep breath, and after some struggle, came fully to her feet. Her knees wobbled under her weight and the utter exhaustion thinning her resolve and tamping her will. Blood drained from her head, and the deck spun. She placed a hand upon the barge's wall and waited for the world to still.

Once it did, she pushed away. Olessa nodded. The woman turned to Tolstes. "Take us to the skiff at once. Make sure not a single patron, maiden, or strong boy sees us."

Tolstes spun on his heel, and they headed for the small rowboat moored beside the barge. Mara trailed after, taking the first steps of her ashwalk pilgrimage.

A SKIFF AND SILENT SON

The small skiff bobbed like an arrow pointed toward the shore. Tolstes secured the ropes tying the boat to the House of Sin and Silk. The eunuch leapt into the vessel surprisingly lightly, his feet accustomed to balancing on a wavering surface.

Mara blinked. It took longer than usual to open her eyes again. Her knees knocked. Her body ached. She shook her head and forced her eyes wide. Holding her son close to her chest, she stepped from the deck and tumbled into the skiff.

The boat rocked violently. Her knee buckled and hit a rough wooden seat. She winced as a flash of pain coursed through her leg. Mara grabbed the skiff's lip and bit her own, swallowing the burning slosh of bile lurching into her throat.

She turned to the House of Sin and Silk, the safe haven she'd known all her life, the one place she knew that would soon fade away beneath the stars of Harvest Festival.

Olessa grabbed the thick rope mooring the boat to the barge and tossed it to Mara's feet. "Goodbye, Mara, and good luck. You will have until sunrise to bring him to the fire. A moment after, and it will be too late for him. Remember that. Do not let the sun rise before you finish the ashwalk."

Mara's free hand went to the heavy jewelry clasped around her neck, her fingertips gracing the brass-plated collar staining her skin sickly green. "I'm afraid, Madame Olessa."

"We all are, but I'll be less afraid when I can no longer see this skiff darkening the Floatwaif." Olessa placed her heel upon the rowboat's stern. "May the Six guide your steps to safety. Fail, and the alp will devour his soul. Then, their eyes turn to *us*."

"Wait!" Gia grabbed Olessa's arm.

Their madame's lips pursed into a single venomous point. "Explain yourself. The girl needs to go."

Gia realized what she'd done. She released Olessa, recoiling like she'd accidentally thrust her hand into a baker's oven. Gia quickly fell to a knee. The oily braids cascading down her back glimmered in the starlight. "She's exhausted. She's just given birth, and now we send her on this…on this journey. She will never make it in her current state."

Mara's heart skipped a beat. Perhaps Gia had seen the insanity of the ashwalk. Perhaps her friend would demand Olessa give her leave to accompany Mara with two armed strong boys.

Olessa cleared her throat, her wrinkled lips melting into a disapproving frown. "And what do you suggest we do? She will not stay. I will not have her tainted womb and cursed child on my most profitable night."

Gia's gaze drifted to the deck where it paused for a long moment. Then, it darted up to meet Olessa's. "Give her something that will at least give her a chance. Give her a dose of glimmer. It will dull the pain and sharpen the senses if it's only just a little. She'll run through Sollan in no time with that coursing through her blood."

The visions of Mara walking through the streets with Gia by her side and two strong boys cracking knuckles hard as granite vanished. Instead, Kard's wild eyes appeared, hungry for violence and crazed for flesh.

Would that be me? Mara wondered.

"Glimmer?" Olessa laughed and turned away. "Mara's never taken glimmer. It would make her wild and loosen her tongue. I can't have her flapping that pink slug all over Sollan that Olessa gives her maidens glimmer. I'd have the the king's soldiers or worse swarming like hornets by morning."

"Just a small dose, please," Gia begged. "I know you bow to the Six. I know you want Mara to finish her ashwalk and return home to set things right. Without the glimmer, she will collapse on the shore, and then it won't be the soldiers swarming, it will be the spirits of the alp circling the House of Sin and Silk. Do you wish that on any of us?"

Mara knew not much of the histories of Urum, but she had learned enough to know the alp were the lords under the Second Sun after the titans fell beneath the First. The alp were a race of power and beauty, able to weave great works of magic and perform feats that rivaled even the titans. They rode the skies on glittering dragons and tamed all the wild beasts.

But under the Second Sun, they grew arrogant and turned from the Six. They sought to raise Urum's fallen monsters and harness their power like a rider breaks a wild horse. It was said even the Six feared them, and so the Six utterly destroyed them.

No one knew much of their fall. From their ruins dotting Urum's lands nothing had been discovered, and so they became the stuff of myth and legend, tales told to keep children behaved.

Olessa crossed her arms and thought. "Gia, Gia, always so brave when bravery would make you look like a saint, yet here you are standing before me and not on that skiff with your friend."

The woman wheeled around and backhanded Gia with her bare hand. "Do not presume to tell me what I believe and what I must do. Be careful to remember your place in the world."

Mara winced as Gia winced. The girl turned to the side, meeting Mara's eyes. *I tried*, they said.

Madame Olessa reached into her dress pocket with a sigh. She produced a corked vial filled with glittering gold. Uncorking the container, she dipped her pinky in the powder and shoved her powdery nail toward Mara. "Put this under your tongue. Try to remember your wits when the glimmer takes hold. If you tell anyone you took this and they find their way to my house, I will deny I ever knew a moon maiden named Mara. Understood?"

Slowly, Mara nodded. She opened her mouth and leaned toward Olessa. The woman dropped the powder beneath Mara's raised tongue.

The glimmer tingled against the soft flesh beneath her tongue. It sent dazzling sparks racing down her spine. Colors gained crisp clarity. Her aches and pains ebbed.

Mara straightened. Olessa kicked the skiff with her heel, and the boat slipped away from the House of Sin and Silk.

"The glimmer won't last all night," Olessa said. "Best hurry, or you'll collapse somewhere in an alley and be the plaything of every drunk and scoundrel in the city."

Mara nodded politely, even as Olessa's warnings fed another log to the fire of her fear. She turned to her friend and waved. "Goodbye, Gia!"

"You will do this, I know you will!"

"Goodbye, Madame Olessa!"

Her madame turned and strolled casually toward the front of the barge as if nothing had occurred. The woman paused at the bend. She lingered there as if she wished to speak, to call reassuring words to Mara as the distance grew between them.

Olessa stiffened. She darted around the deck and disappeared. Mara sighed and turned away, her eyes set toward the long, crowded docks of Sollan.

* * *

The House of Sin and Silk retreated behind the bobbing labyrinth of the Floatwaif. They passed between a line of carved statues of Sollan's past kings, a barrier that separated the Floatwaif from the docks so larger ships sailing into the city wouldn't shatter the tangled barges.

Tolstes rowed into the open water. Not a word slipped from his lips, and his eyes kept well away from Mara. She didn't know if it was his fear or pity that kept him silent. She suspected it might be both.

His oars dipped into the glassy waters. They came out, tossing droplets that rippled the smooth waves the skiff made on its journey to the shore.

"I'm sorry, Tolstes," she finally said.

His bright, blue eyes flashed toward her. "It's fine. It really isn't your fault. Sometimes the gods just spite us. It is the price we pay as their creation."

"I didn't mean to bring any of this on you. I just—what's that?"

Mara's eyes caught something ahead bobbing on the dark waters. Because Tolstes rowed at the prow, he faced the stern and couldn't see the silhouette approaching.

Frowning, the strong boy turned and peered over his wide shoulder. "Looks like another skiff. Probably heading to a party on the Floatwaif, maybe even going to Olessa's. Keep your head down and don't say a word."

Mara did as she was told. She cradled her child and took deep, calming breaths as she cowered in the shadow of her burlap hood.

"*Ho!*" Tolstes called. He rested the oars on his knees. "On your way to celebrate another plentiful harvest?"

She heard no reply. Mara held her son tighter against her chest. "Six, keep us safe," she whispered.

Tolstes cleared his throat. "You're coming awful close, friend. Mind giving us some room? I've got a sick one here and I'd hate to ruin your festival with a fever."

Still, not a single voice answered the strong boy's call. The skiff rocked as Tolstes came to his feet. No strong boy carried a sword because Olessa feared they may accidentally scar her maidens in a tiff. A strong boy's skill at brawling, however, held no equal in Floatwaif.

Mara risked a glance up. The strange skiff floated close enough to paint its passengers in starlight. Terror jolted Mara's glimmer-fueled veins. "Tolstes, watch out!"

The eunuch tensed. Silver flashed from the strange skiff. Tolstes' hands went to his throat. He gagged and coughed and fell into the sea in a splash of fear and foam, leaving Mara and her stillborn child alone in a rocking boat facing the sailor Kard.

The man's dark eyes focused on Mara. He grinned, bending his serpent of a scar along his cheek. He stepped on the prow of his boat and leaned forward. "Well, well, if it isn't the moon maiden from the House of Sin and Silk. How fortunate to find a whore so far from her hag's protection."

Two other sailors manned the oars of his skiff. Mara saw the starlight glitter on their toothy smiles.

Her gaze darted to the water. Tolstes' floated to the surface, eyes wide and dulled. His boyish cheeks paled from the blood draining from his throat, a gift of the dagger sticking from it.

"What do you want, Kard?" Mara asked in a voice much more confident than she thought possible. "I have nothing to give you. I'm on an ashwalk, and…"

She lifted her chin and glared at the man down her nose. "…Unless you'd like to dream with the alp tonight, you'll let me go."

His companions laughed. Kard snorted and crossed his arms over his burly chest. "I don't fear tales told to little shits before their bedtime. I've seen the alp's sunken cities. I know their ruin. Your superstitious madame might get her wig knotted thinkin' about them, but I've sailed the seas and faced what really lives in Urum's shadows. There're greater things to fear than ghosts, and those things fear me."

"What do you want?" she asked again, her voice harder.

Kard picked dirt from his nail and flicked it in the water. "I knew you were special when I saw you. We all know you girls slurp that ebon orchid. It's a nasty draught, ya' know. Works like a charm every time. In fact, I've never heard of the stuff failing. Not once, and I've been to many a pleasure house in my day. So when I saw you, I knew something must be odd with the pregnant maiden at the House of Sin and Silk."

Mara glanced at their surroundings. Not a single other boat disturbed the waters between the Floatwaif and the docks. For all the people flooding Sollan's streets and barges, she was more alone than ever.

"Rare things happen, Kard."

"They do. When they do, people take notice. Important people, if you get my drift."

"No, I don't."

"Why Mara, how unfortunate of you to live in Olessa's silky prison out of earshot of the happenings in the world. You're a wanted woman. A very wanted woman."

"What?" Mara recoiled and nearly fell into the sea. "Why? I've done nothing!"

"You've done something, that's for sure. I heard whispers out in the street the king's eye has turned to the Floatwaif, looking for a mother and child. He sent his serpent priests from that cult of his looking for her. Those same whispers say any who bring the woman's child to them will be rewarded with the mother's weight in gold."

"But why would the king's guard want me? I haven't done—"

"You?" Kard laughed and slapped his knee, and the other men joined him. "They don't want you. They want the child. You can die for all they care. You're a moon maiden. That's less than nothin' in their eyes. And really, who'll miss you? Gia? She's probably already forgotten all about you. She's likely tickling some bloated whale of a highborn or three, glad to see you and that cursed corpse out the way."

"No, no." Mara clutched her son tight against her neck and squeezed her eyes shut.

"Give it up. Maybe if you hand him over real nice, I'll give you a little tickle of my own."

Mara heard the hunger in his voice. She knew he would never be gentle, and once he finished, she would float alongside Tolstes until the sharks stripped her to the bone. But worse than all of that, the despicable sailor would have her son.

"I won't let him have you," she whispered. "Please, Six, Burning Mother, any of you, help me. I will finish the ashwalk. I swear I will. Just please, give me the chance. I'm at your mercy."

She waited for Kard's rough, calloused grip. She waited to fall into the cold, unforgiving waters. She waited for the coral sharks to nibble at her feet.

But Kard's grip never came. No waters embraced her, and no sharks tasted her flesh.

Mara opened an eye. Kard still stood at the prow of his skiff, his two companions holding the oars behind him with trembling grips. No longer did the sailor have the confident, hungry glimmer in his eyes. No longer did his chest swell with arrogant pride.

The color drained from his skin. "S—Silent son..." he stammered, falling back into the rowboat.

A shadow slipped over Mara like the boughs of a tree sheltering a weary nomad. Mara's heartbeat thundered in her ears. She cupped her son's head and slowly looked behind her.

A towering figure stood upon the calm waters. A black drape covered the silent son from the crown of his head to the water's surface, making him appear to grow from the Sapphire Sea as a tree grows from soil. Like all priests of the Loyal Father, he wore a pale mask where his face should be.

He lifted an arm. A porcelain hand extended from the black. Its palm flattened before Kard's skiff, and the boat gently careened away, picking up speed as it headed for the distant, open sea.

The sailors paddled frantically. Kard yelled curses at them, his voice growing more panicked as the boat glided in circles toward the horizon.

Mara sat as a statue. She had never seen a silent son and only knew they served the Loyal Father. Neither had she ever seen an act of magic.

Gathering her courage, she turned as calmly as she could toward the cloaked figure. "Did you hear my prayer?"

The silent son said nothing. She knew he wouldn't. Those of their order bound their voices to silence until death claimed them. Still, she had to try.

Like a ghost, the silent son wafted toward her. He reached the edge of the boat.

Mara cowered in his shadow. "Please, don't hurt me."

He extended a hand sculpted from starlight and reached for her. She winced and closed her eyes, pressing her son against her bosom.

"Please," she whispered.

A touch soft as silk and light as a feather caressed her jaw. She opened her eyes, and they met the expressionless stare of the silent son's mask. The man's long fingers traced the curve of her jaw and stopped at her chin.

He cupped her cheek and squeezed so gently she almost didn't notice. Straightening, the silent son grasped the lip of her skiff. He pushed the boat, and it glided toward the shore as if the vessel skated over ice.

The silent son shrank against the dark table of the Sapphire Sea. A few moments later, he disappeared, and the skiff came to rest upon Sollan's rocky shore.

7

SOLLAN

Alone on the edge of a raucous tempest of revelry, Mara stepped from Olessa's small rowboat and onto Sollan's rough and unforgiving shore. So many crowded the docks the land seemed to sway with the drunken dancing of men and women working their way through foaming mugs of ale or tin cups sloshing with saltwater gin. Multicolored ribbons and banners of Harvest Festival fluttered above the packed and winding roads leading deeper into the city.

Mara trembled and wrapped her arms around her son. The city had always been so close. She had often dreamed of visiting. Yet standing on the dark shore, staring at the streams of bodies laughing and rocking to the rhythm of drums and mandolins, she wanted nothing more than to crawl into the sky and paddle back to the House of Sin and Silk.

Despite her fervent searching, she spotted no children with knives or villainous scoundrels licking their teeth within Lower Sollan's shadows. "Sollan's not evil at all."

She smiled, the spark of her courage gathering strength. "They're celebrating. It is a happy time. It is celebration. I will save my son's soul and be back home long before dawn."

Her sandals crunched over the shore's smooth rocks as she stepped away from the waves lapping at her ankles. She glanced over her shoulder, peering through the great ships moored to the docks. Beyond their bobbing hulls, the empty sea stretched to the titan at the bay's mouth. To the side, the Floatwaif glittered with the lights fastened around the small boats.

She imagined Gia gazing at the shoreline, praying to the Six that Mara landed upon the rocks unharmed.

"It was close, Gia," Mara said, "that bastard Kard killed Tolstes. He would have killed me, too, but a silent son saved me. He used magic, Gia. Maybe it isn't really leaving the world. Maybe if you really do believe in the Six, they can still grant you the power."

Her gaze lingered on the stretch of water where the strong boy's body fell. Whispering a quick prayer for the eunuch, Mara turned from the world she knew and faced the strange one before her. She darted from the docks, carefully avoiding clusters of sailors downing shots or crying out toasts that boasted of their exploits.

Mara stepped out of the shadows and onto the first stony avenue of Lower Sollan. Scents of fried shrimp seasoned with paprika tickled her nose, the inviting aroma drifting from a noisy tavern a few steps from where she stood. Her belly rumbled and gurgled like an old bog, and for the first time that night, she felt the empty, ravenous pit within her stomach.

Swallowing, she peered into the city rising before her, graceful towers thrusting against the sparkling sky, ropes intertwined between them hanging glowing lanterns from their lines. The ground sloped upward, revealing Upper Sollan in the distance, and beyond it on a raised plateau, the tall wall of Hightable where the Mother's temple waited.

A fish merchant leaned against his stall and stared into a cup of wine. A wooden pipe hung from his swollen lip as he mumbled quietly to himself.

"Sir?" Mara took a shaky step toward the man. "Can you tell me the quickest way to Hightable? I'm heading for the Mother's temple, but I'm afraid I don't know the way."

"Hm?" The man's lips tightened around his pipe. His eyes drifted from his wine and focused on Mara. "Brave girl to head so high when Good King Sol's got his blades out for—"

His bleary gaze looked Mara up and down. He stiffened with a sneer. "Ashwalk pilgrim, are you? Out of my face with that dead thing in your arms. I'll not have any demon alp or king's blades in my room tonight."

"Just point, and I'll leave. I just—"

"Out!" He threw his cup at Mara, and a burgundy trail of wine lashed out like a striking serpent. The wine splashed against her filthy cloak as the cup careened over her shoulder and smashed against a wall.

The man thrust his shoulders back and hooked his thumbs into his belt. She caught the glint of steel tucked behind the strap of leather.

Her eyes widened, and she spun from the merchant.

The long knives of the docks. They really do exist.

She bolted headlong into the city and nearly crashed into a roving band of sailors. They recoiled when they saw her. One spit and another cursed. The third sneered and licked his lips in a way that said, *you might be fun.*

Mara twisted from them, her fingers tightening on her babe. Their gazes latched onto her back like insects hungry for her blood.

"You see that?" one hissed. "That was a moon maiden's collar on her neck."

"Aye, and one whose womb's been poisoned. The serpents are right. The pleasure houses are a curse for any who have a taste for their sweet sin. You won't be seeing me out on the Floatwaif any time soon, no sir."

Mara frowned. She did not look back or stop and tell them how harmless the pleasure barge really was. No one spoke much of the Serpent Sun cult in the House of Sin and Silk, but she did not like hearing how the its priests spoke of her home in the wider world.

Ahead, a juggler tossed flaming swords high above his head, the flickering weapons a hypnotic pattern that brought claps and silver coins tossed into the hat at his feet. When she drew near, his merry face melted into fright. He backed against the wall and lifted his hands, his flaming weapons clattering to the ground.

"Get away, woman!" He slapped his hands against the wall and searched the bricks like he hoped his fingers might find a door. "I'll be a poor man tonight if I've got an ashwalk pilgrim stained with piss and wine skulking in my shadow with a dead rat in her arms."

"Could you please just—"

He swiped a sword from the ground and pointed its burning tip at her chest. "I said get!"

Mara twisted away. She ran through the crowds, doing her best to ignore the gasps and curses and old fruit and fish heads hurled at her back. She ran into an alley. Its calm shadows embraced her as beads of sweat traced cool lines down her back.

She wove between piles of rotting garbage and ignored the hissing cats with eyes glittering like jewels dipped in hateful poison. Huddling in the corner, she sobbed, a pool of spoiled water soaking her burlap. "Olessa was right, Gia. The world is full of hate. I can't make this walk. I am alone."

Mara adjusted her son's swaddling and gently stroked his soft temple. "We are alone."

A small figure traipsed into the alley. Mara caught her breath and stared at the silhouette drawing closer with each silent step.

Her imagination painted features on the child, giving it pale skin and eyes hollowed like a skull. It grinned with pointed teeth, and behind its back it held a long, sharp blade with her name etched on the steel.

The child edged closer. It stopped barely an arm's length from Mara. She could see its chest rise and fall with its breaths even though shadows hid its features.

"Have you come to kill me?" she asked. "I have nothing. I am an ashwalk pilgrim. I am a curse to you if you stay nearby. The alp will come for us both."

The child cocked its head. "I seen you come into the alley," he said in a light and scratchy voice. "I haven't come to kill you. No, not that at all."

"Then you have no long knife?"

The boy giggled and bent to Mara. "I wish. I've got a dagger, but it's a little dull and could use a bit o' cleaning. I like to keep it rusty, though. Folks don't want to lose a leg to rot from a beggar boy's bad blade. My name's Tag."

He had a little arrow of a nose stained by dirt that also stained his dimpled cheeks. He flashed a wide smile, slipping the pink curtain of his lips from his broken front tooth.

Tag extended a hand. "Who might you be? I mean, I know you're an ashwalk pilgrim and all, but you've got a real name, right? One you go by on the regular."

"Mara…" Slowly, she took his hand.

He squeezed, and she gasped, yanking her hand from his grip. "Your finger!"

"It's missing. The price of bread's pretty high if you're caught without the coin for it." He slid next to her and lifted his hand. A stump wiggled where his index finger should have wagged.

"They say in the early days of the Third Sun," he continued, "that the priests of the Gentle Lover could regrow fingers and sometimes even arms or legs. These days with magic as it is, I doubt they could grow a nail. It's too bad, too. I'd have gone to the temple and said all my prayers and then some if they could bring my finger back."

"I've never seen magic," she said. "Not until tonight. I think—I think a silent son used some to help me get to shore."

He shrugged and lowered his hand onto his lap. "It's nothing special if you ask me. They say it's dying. It's why the priests of the Six keep to their temples. They're afraid if people know the truth, they'll turn their backs to the Six. Can't say I blame folk when there're other faiths out there with gods who listen."

"I've only ever prayed to the Six. Madame Olessa wouldn't allow for any other gods."

"Madame? You're a moon maiden, then. I thought I caught a glimpse of brass around your neck when I saw you on the road." His lips split in a cock-eyed grin. "Yeah, there're many other gods out there, and with the Six's power what the way it is, I hear about more every day. Even the king's got himself a cult. They call themselves the Serpent Sun. Fitting I guess. There's supposed to be some kind of crazy monster lizard holed up in his castle with him."

"I've…I've heard of the serpents. I don't like snakes very much."

"They don't like moon maidens much either I bet. I hear they've got wicked powers, and the snakes they wear around their necks have a bite that'll drop even the toughest sailor in a breath."

A shiver raced down Mara's spine cold as ice melting down her back. She licked her cracked and peeling lips and glanced at the boy from within the safety of her hood. "What do you want, Tag?"

The boy blinked. His chin dipped to his chest. "I don't want a thing."

Her mother's instincts wanted so badly to embrace him, but her fear held her back. "I'm sorry. It's just you're the first kind person I've met in Sollan. I've never been to the city before, and it's odd for one so young to know so much of the Six and the ashwalk."

He sucked in his breath, lifting his chin. "It probably does seem odd. You hear about ashwalks, but it's not often you see the pilgrims in the flesh. When I saw you, it reminded me of…it, ah, it reminded me of someone I knew."

The boy's fingers fidgeted in his lap. She sensed the knotted ball of emotions twisting in his heart.

"Who did I remind you of?"

Tag turned to her and flashed his broken smile. "My momma was an ashwalk pilgrim. She had my sister, but my sister never took a breath. I helped cloak her in burlap and ash, and together we walked to the Mother's temple. Well, almost to it."

Dread sunk into her stomach like a weighted fishing line. "And where is your mother now?"

His smile faded. "She never made it. We were robbed on the way. They had a blade, and we tried to run, but the blade was faster than Mom's feet."

Tears glimmered in his little almond eyes. "I was fast enough to outrun them, though. I made it. I'm very quick. I'm very smart. My momma always told me so. She told me to run and never stop. I never have, except maybe when I see another pilgrim like her on the road."

"I bet you're very fast." Mara smiled, and it was the first real smile she had in a city of unfriendly roads and dark alleys.

A thought sprung like a weed in her mind. "Tag, do you know how to reach the Mother's temple?"

The boy nodded enthusiastically. "Of course I do! It's in Hightable, and it's the grandest thing you'll ever see! Marble pillars carved like women, ceilings so high you could never reach them, the Mother's statue, and at her feet the Ever-Burning Flame."

"Could you—could you take me there?"

He bit his lip, his brows pinching together in a boyish frown. "I don't know…we've got to go through Upper Sollan first. The nice roads aren't paved for poor folk like us. The serpents don't want us there and neither do the nobles." His gaze drifted to his missing finger. "If they catch us, I could be down to three fingers. Probably worse."

"Oh." Mara stared blankly at the alley wall, and a silence settled over them even as the city thrummed with the flutes and drums of the festival.

If a child who knew the streets feared the journey to the temple, she could only imagine what might be waiting for a stranger to Sollan like her. She imagined her own hand missing its finger. Olessa would never take her back then, even if she somehow finished the ashwalk.

Tag sighed. He jumped to his feet, brushing the grime from his hands onto pants that Mara suspected held much more filth. "My momma never reached the fire. Maybe it's a sign from her that I take you now. Maybe that's what I need to do to put their souls to rest."

"But it's dangerous, Tag. I could never ask you—"

He waved her off, spinning toward the alley exit. "We can do it, Mara. Trust me. I'll get us both there and back with no fingers missing. No more than when we have left, that is."

Her heartbeat quickened. She grinned despite the pain in her throbbing ankles and the looseness in her tired knees. "You are a good boy. Thank you for showing me kindness."

Tag paused just where the shadow's alley met the bright lane, his back still facing Mara. "Everyone could use a little kindness." He glanced over his shoulder and flashed his brows. "You hungry?"

Mara's stomach rumbled. She tightened her rough cloak, and with her child cradled in her arm, she followed Tag into the bright roads of Sollan.

8

THE BRASS COLLAR

Tag led Mara through the winding roads of Lower Sollan. Crowds packed the avenues and spilled from Sollan's many taverns with wine-stained lips and laughter bubbling from their slurring tongues. Joy hung in the air, carried by the song of countless drums, flutes, and mandolins casting their notes toward the heavens.

Only magic could keep her invisible among the multitudes, but only priests new such spells, and so far, Mara hadn't seen a single one. In fact, the only clergy of the Six she'd encountered was her quiet savior on the calm waters beyond the docks.

She and Tag paused behind a dive of a bar, its only sign the scratched painting of a grapevine on its wall. Men and women drifted in and out its doors, eyes glassy from wine, steps unsteady from their many drinks.

Mara noticed Tag staring from their hiding spot at the train of visitors filtering inside. His little fingers danced over a crate of rotten food. She saw the longing in his eyes. She could practically hear him praying to the Six to gift him a life like the ones he watched.

He licked his lips, and his stomach grumbled. Mara frowned and gently clasped the back of his neck. "You really are hungry, aren't you?"

"A little." His chin dipped to his belly. "I haven't eaten in a few days, and the, ah, the food smells really good."

"You don't eat every day?"

The boy smirked and shook his head. "I wish! They hate us beggars more than strays, even in Lower Sollan where the richest are still a little poor. I usually sneak through the trash for my meals after everyone's gone to bed and hope the cats and curs haven't got the good stuff first. I had...I 'd hoped tonight would be so busy, maybe I could snag something still a little fresh."

Mara's belly rumbled with his words. While Olessa's glimmer gave her energy and focus, her body still cried for sustenance.

The night was young. With Tag as her guide, they would reach the temple long before dawn. A scrap or two of food might even make the journey quicker.

Tag looked up at Mara, his small, almond eyes glittering with the all the innocence of a child. "Do you have coin? Maybe we could get a bowl of stew or a few fried shrimp?" His eyes widened as he hung his hope on his words. "Maybe even a glass of wine!"

Mara smiled sadly and caressed her fingers down his dirty jaw. "I'm sorry, but I have no coin. I don't have anything of value except…" her hand drifted from the boy to her brass collar. Her nails clinked on the metal. "…This is really the only valuable thing of mine, and I don't even own it. It's Olessa's. Everything is hers."

"What's it made of?" he asked.

"Plated brass. I don't think it's worth very much."

"It would be a meal at least. Maybe a few. Do you think…?"

"No." Mara clenched her collar. "I—I could *never*. My madame would have my head if I returned home without it."

"Oh." His chin dipped as his tattered shoe toyed with the dirty stones. "Then let's keep going to the temple. There's always tomorrow for food."

He darted from the alley. Mara propped her child against her chest and bolted after the boy. Her stomach gurgled as she wove in and out of crowds that gasped and cursed when they saw the pilgrim cloaked in ashen burlap.

She could never give up her collar. It had hung around her neck for years, a symbol of her station and life aboard the House of Sin and Silk. Yet, she could not shake the boy's disappointed look and the knowledge that he hadn't eaten in days. He risked his fingers to bring her to the Mother's temple, but she couldn't risk a simple collar?

His mother died a pilgrim, Mara thought, a*nd he risks gods know what to take you to the temple. Are you such a selfish woman you wouldn't help a child who's helping you and yours?*

They reached another alley and slipped into its shadows. A man sat against the wall, covered in tattered rags. His eyes were blue and clouded, and his matted, silver hair stained with dirt and refuse. Long, deep cracks carved channels in his spotted skin, and one of his legs rested at an awkward angle. He toyed with a tin cup but otherwise ignored the two newcomers to his space if he even realized they were there at all.

A long line of people passed like a slow centipede in the lane. Mara watched them from the darkness, her arms wrapped around her child.

"There are too many of them," Tag whispered. "We can wait here until they pass."

Tag eyed the man warily before turning to the trash piled deeper in the alley. He pressed his hand against his stomach and forced a smile. "I think I'll look through the trash a little. Maybe there's some meat that isn't rotten. If I find it, I'll bring some to you."

He took a step toward the alley's back wall. Mara cursed herself and clasped his bony shoulder, pulling him to a halt. "Wait."

The boy looked behind him. "What's wrong?"

Sighing, she closed her eyes and brought her hand to her collar. "We both need food or we'll never make it. If I give you my maiden's collar, will you get us something nice to eat?"

His eyes lit up with his toothy smile. "You would do that? You really would? Even if your madame will be really mad?"

"I…I will. Olessa's not so bad," she said. No need to worry the boy with the beating she would get for losing the collar.

Mara took a seat near the blind beggar. The old man wheezed softly, mumbling incomprehensibly to himself. Mara placed her son in her lap and searched for the collar's clasp. Her fingers found the chain.

She closed her eyes and took a breath. Tag showed her such kindness when no one else in Sollan would. He lived a hard life, having lost his mother so young and a finger soon after just to fill his belly. Despite his past, despite the danger Mara placed him in by taking the boy on her ashwalk, he still helped.

"Olessa, forgive me," she whispered. "I have nothing else to give, but I give it to one who needs it more than I."

Mara unclasped her collar and pulled it from her neck. She looked at her chest, at the olive stain above her breasts where the plating mixed with her sweat and colored her skin sickly green.

Unburdened by the metal, she rolled her neck. It surprised her how light and free her shoulders felt. The soft breeze rolling in from the sea cooled the sweat glistening where the collar once laid and sent a tingle down her spine.

Mara held the jewelry in her hand. She stared at the tarnished metal glinting in the dim light and at her warped reflection on its surface. "I've worn this for so many years. I did not remember what it felt like to have it off."

"How's it feel?" Tag asked.

"It feels…" Mara smiled and met the boy's gaze. "It feels nice."

She handed Tag the collar. He took it in his hands as if a queen had just given him her crown. He clutched it against his chest and bounced on his heels. "I can almost taste the food!"

"It will be a good meal we share. Now hurry and find us something tasty," she said, pinching his cheek.

He nodded enthusiastically as he shuffled toward the alley's exit. "You can just wait here for me. I'll be right back, okay?"

"How long do you think it will take? I have to finish the ashwalk before dawn, so we can't spend the whole festival nibbling on soft fin bass."

His gaze drifted to the ground. He paused at the alley's mouth. His knuckles whitened on the collar.

Mara frowned. She opened her mouth.

The boy's gaze shot up, and he beamed a happy smile. "Not long, Mara."

He turned his back to her and glanced over his shoulder. "Thank you."

The boy pierced the crowd like a dagger through flesh and disappeared behind a shifting wall of legs. She licked her lips and tried not to imagine buttered shrimp melting on her tongue, a little bite of pepper hitting her throat as she savored the taste.

Mara plucked her child from her lap. She kissed his soft, tiny brow and ran her fingers through hair soft as spun silk and so dark it might have been threaded from night itself.

* * *

The crowds passed the alley, coming and going in an endless train. Mara stared at the exit, searching, thinking every child she spotted might be Tag returning with an armful of steaming food.

"I was a soldier once," the old man croaked.

A bolt of fear jolted Mara from her thoughts. She turned to the geezer. He stared dully into his bent and rusted tin cup. His wrinkled, bony finger ran lightly over the rim.

Mara scooted out of arm's reach and shifted her son to another shoulder. "You…you were?"

He smacked his lips and squinted. Deep cracks spread from the corners of his eyelids. "That I was. I served the old king long before his son took the throne. Those were different times. Better times. The things I saw, the places I went, they would amaze you. Sollan is a wondrous city and the jewel Eloia, but let me tell you a secret: Urum holds many more jewels far more beautiful than Sollan. Some you can find sailing the seas. Some are buried and better left forgotten."

Mara swallowed the lump down her sandpaper throat. "I'm sure the world holds many secrets. The titan's bones are proof of that."

He cackled, picking up his tin and shaking it, but no coins rattled within the container. "Don't worry, girl. There's no need to fear a nearly blind beggar. Unless you fear my cup, the fine weapon that it is."

She relaxed a little, smiling sheepishly. "I'm sorry. I just haven't met many kind people. The boy Tag has been the only one, really. I should not have judged you harshly. It's just—I'm not what people want to see on Harvest Festival." Her eyes watered and her chin trembled. "I haven't had the best night."

"Ah, but I can hear you've got a decent head on your shoulders. Trust your first instinct, my friend. You *should* judge me harshly. You are a stranger to this city, correct? Mara they call you, if these hairy old ears of mine heard your name right? Do you have a family name?"

"Yes and no. They call me Mara, but I…my madame is my family, but her family's name isn't mine. Who might you be, brave soldier?"

The man grinned, flashing a broken wall of bent and yellowed teeth. "Galladus Fel. It is a pleasure to meet you," he said with a courteous nod.

"You as well, Galladus."

"As I was saying, I saw many wonders on my travels before my eyes betrayed me and left me to this life. I saw cities greater than Sollan even though their walls had long since crumbled. I saw creatures I thought nothing more than myth and legend. I witnessed the magic of the Six when it was at its zenith and priests were feared more than any good king."

"It sounds like you lived a wonderful life. I'm from the Floatwaif, but I've never been in Sollan. Well, I was in Sollan once I think. I don't remember much other than my madame's brother and maybe a street. His smile…I do remember that. But then I was at the House of Sin and Silk, and that was my life."

"Interesting." Galladus smacked his lips. "And here you are on Sollan's grandest night, a night of celebration. But it is no celebration for you, a woman wrapped in unforgiving burlap stained by unwanted ash. It is a long journey for an ashwalk pilgrim. Longer now these days with the eyes of a king on you who has no love of the Six."

Mara's grip tightened on her child. "I know the city is dangerous, but Tag will guide me. We will make it to Hightable and the temples, and I will give my son to the Mother's Ever-Burning Flame. Everything will be fine."

"Mara, how can it be that I have found the one woman in Sollan with sight who does not see? Can I have your eyes since you don't seem to want them?"

"I use my eyes. I do." Mara's heart picked up its pace. "Tag will take me. I will make it."

"You pretty little ashwalk pilgrim. The streets are more your enemy than you think. The Six are not looked kindly upon beyond Lower Sollan. The Serpent Sun will never let an ashwalk pilgrim to the steps of the temple."

"But…but it's Harvest Festival!"

Galladus spit. "It's a party. The king would be a fool if he banned the city from the one night all within it could get drunk and fill their bellies. Tell me, Mara, what priests of the Six have you seen? Have you caught the eye of an acolyte of the Burning Mother and received a blessing? It is her festival, yet strange how it seems she hasn't been invited to it."

Mara's stomach twisted. She glanced out the alley, desperately hoping Tag would come darting into its shadows any moment. But Tag did not appear. Only a sea of unfamiliar faces continued rolling by.

"I saw a silent son on the waters to the city," she said, "but no, I haven't seen a priest in Sollan."

"And you won't. The king will not let them out of their shining temples. The Serpent Sun has spread poisonous rumors like a plague from house to house. Mark my words, soon I will hear of the day when those temples are crushed to dust and burnt to cinders. It will come soon, very soon."

"I will make my ashwalk before then. Tag will take me."

Galladus dipped his chin and placed his tin on the stony ground. "I was a soldier once."

"You told me this already, Galladus Fellinus. You fought for the old king."

"I did," he said with a nod. "And I saw many wondrous places. But above all else, I learned one thing about the world."

"And what is that?" she asked despite the creeping dread sinking deep into her bones.

"Kings and beggars, priests and sinners, soldiers and thieves—Trust not one of them. In the end, they will leave you for dead in a dark alley if you have nothing left to give them."

Mara's gaze shot toward the alley exit. She hoped to see Tag's toothy smile, his bright, almond eyes, his arms burdened with meats and figs and a flagon of cool water.

Tears wet her eyes. Her chin trembled as her grip tightened on her son. "He will return. He showed me kindness. He was hungry, and I gave him the only thing I had. He will return and take me to the temple."

A rough and calloused hand gently lay over hers. She turned to Galladus. The man stared at her with blanched eyes that somehow saw so much. Liver spots dotted his sagging brow. His breath reeked of rot and decay. Yet, when he smiled, it wasn't one of hate or hunger, but one of pity. He wasted away in that alley, bent, broken, and forgotten, and still he pitied her.

"Mara," he whispered. "The boy called Tag will not return. He has taken from you what he wanted, and with that oily brass he'll fill his belly for a night or two. You must understand that he was not evil. He did not want to hurt you. But if a rotted old beggar in an alley knows the danger of the ashwalk, then a boy who knows the streets understands it much, much better."

"No…" Mara dipped her head, touching her brow to her son's. "He showed me kindness."

Galladus squeezed her hand. "And if there truly is any in him, he'll regret tonight for the rest of his days."

"What do I do now? I couldn't find my way back to the docks if I tried. I'm alone, Galladus." She looked to her child, wiping the snot from his nose. "We're alone."

"If I had useful eyes I would fight each of the king's heretic priests myself to take you to the Mother's fire. But I have no useful eyes, and my legs fail me. So instead I'll arm you with my words, my warning: Trust no one. Do not waver. Do not bend. March ever on, and the Six will guide you.

"You are in Lower Sollan now. There is a wall that keeps Upper Sollan protected from the riffraff like you and I. Beyond Upper Sollan's apartments, you will find a great round plateau dotted with stairwells to the Blooming Ring. The Blooming Ring encircles the mighty wall of Hightable. There is only one gate into Hightable, and it is always manned. I hear from thieves who've wandered in my alley that there are other, more secret ways to enter the high-born realm if you have a sharp eye, but those ways are old and full of danger."

"Thank you for your knowledge, my friend."

"Trust the Six, and they will see you to the Mother's steps. They will show you signs along the way. Follow them, and from the serpent's fangs they will deliver you."

Mara blinked away her tears. She stared at the green stain her collar left behind and the child who would never wake wrapped in burlap just beneath it. She shifted to her knees.

"I will trust the Six," she said.

The old man smiled, clasping his hands. "And no others."

"I will not falter."

"Bless the Six, then." The man's cracked grip tightened on his cup. "Now go, Mara, and hurry! The serpents slither in the night. Watch for them. Keep away. No priest of the Serpent Sun is your friend. If you see them, run and hide and do not whisper a single word. Now go!"

Mara took a deep breath and bolted from the alley.

9

SERPENTS IN SOLLAN

A rock whistled past Mara's ear. She ducked, and the stone clattered against the bricks of someone's home. She turned a corner, darting into a blessedly empty avenue walled by tall, ramshackle brick and adobe houses.

With her free hand she touched her bruised shoulder, wincing at the flash of pain that washed through her arm. Not every rock hurled at her met its mark. The ones that did bruised both flesh and soul.

Mara leaned against the wall and stared into the starry sky. Loose lines hung from one rooftop to another. A single paper lantern swayed from a drooping rope. The lantern's once bright light dimmed and painted the narrow lane in an eerie blue.

She took a deep breath and closed her eyes, letting her spirit flow into the world like Gia had taught her. For that moment of tranquility, the world slipped away, and her spirit danced among the stars.

"I'll get through this, Gia," she whispered. "I'll see you soon."

A smile grew on Mara's face. She knew the glimmer probably tugged it there because any normal fool who'd let their one valuable thing be stolen by a child with a sad story would have been furious with themselves.

"Tag, Tag. I hope you eat well." Mara smirked and pulled away from the wall. Securing her son's burlap around his tiny form, she inched down the lane.

A cool breeze whipped through the narrow avenue. It carried with it the faintest hint of sage and salt. Overhead, ropes crisscrossed from window to window, their lines weighed by linens drying in the fresh air.

The lane gently turned and sloped upward. She followed the curve of the wall and spotted an intersection with another avenue.

Mara hesitated in the safety of the blue lights. Unlike most other roads she traveled, not a single passerby drifted into view. Even the drums and flutes grew distant in her solitude.

After a few calming breaths, Mara straightened and padded toward the exit. The curved wall cast a shadow angled inward she did not want to leave. She reached the edge of darkness, the city beyond awash in the gold of burning braziers and the strange blue lanterns hung from high lines.

"Where did everyone go?" she wondered.

She stepped from the shadow and into the wider lane. Beyond the curve, a pale wall rose above the buildings built snug against its side. An arch set within it opened like a titan's mouth into Upper Sollan.

"Walls within walls," Mara said. "This city fears itself."

Through the archway, Mara caught a glimpse of the next district waiting patiently. Luxurious apartments connected by bridges crowded the street. Delicate fountains poured graceful arcs of crystalline water into glittering pools walled by blooming poppies and the delicate spears of lavender blossoms.

She bit her lip to keep her smile down, and for the briefest of moments, her fears and trepidations flowed away on her girlish giggle. Without another moment wasted in the darkness, she darted for the opening.

Each step she took brought the wide mouth closer. Iron braziers burned on either side of the archway, their flames beckoning her nearer like maidens teasing a patron. Not a single reveler or guard lingered at the entry. It was as if the Six had finally bestowed some small blessing upon her after a night tinged by glimmer and fear.

"Get back to your posts, you lazy fools!" a woman called, her voice a fiery lance tearing from beyond the arch.

All of Mara's hopes vanished in a puff. She skidded to a halt and spun between two homes, crouching at a corner so she could peek longingly at the destination that was so close and so far all at once.

Clattering metal echoed near the archway. Long shadows stretched down the lane. Two tall men clad in shiny breastplates and metal greaves scurried to either side of the arch. One of the soldiers kicked a flagon, and the container spilled ruby wine that filtered slowly down the sloping road.

The soldiers stiffened and lifted their chins. They stared down the lane where Mara had just been sprinting like a fool. They pressed their hands against their legs. Their arms shook. Their skin glinted with sweat in the firelight.

A long shadow split the archway in half. The darkness bled down the lane and swallowed the snaking line of wine making its way past Mara. The shadow grew in rhythm with the footsteps of the woman who made it, her footfalls hard and steady.

Mara squinted and leaned forward just enough to get a better look. The woman strolled through the archway until her back faced the men. She had the body of a dancer and the stature of a general. She wore a pale mask with a hungry scowl framed by elaborate gold and a shimmering robe of white that hid every inch of her features. Around her neck rested a loosely coiled serpent, its scales pale shades of desert sands. Strapped to her side hung two swords secured in scabbards painted with swirling gold curves and strange symbols.

The masked woman paused, hand resting on her hip. The breeze toyed with her robe and sent it whipping around her ankles. She stared down the lane, the frozen scowl of her mask surveying Lower Sollan.

"Filth," she said. "They are filth, these lower folk, getting drunk and tasting flesh for some dying goddess who couldn't care less for them. Yet still they sing. Still they dance. Still they drink until cheap wine soaks their beards and saltwater gin rots their teeth. Pathetic."

Mara did not know much of Sollan. Patrons did not speak of politics at the House of Sin and Silk, and Olessa's protective shadow kept much of the world at bay. Even then, she knew beyond a doubt the robed woman standing in the lane was a priest of the Serpent Sun.

Waves of power billowed from the woman as if her very soul rejected the air of Lower Sollan. Behind her, the two soldiers shifted uncomfortably. They shared a sweaty glance and wrapped their hands on the grips of their swords. The priestess stepped forward. Her foot planted on the trail of wine. She looked down at the burgundy staining her boot.

"Tell me," she said in a voice clear and sharp as a polished trumpet, "why you two thought it wise to get drunk on wine when you have a duty to perform?"

One of the soldiers cleared his throat. "My deepest apologies, Sister Ialane Donra, we merely had a glass to celebrate Harvest Festival. You have my word not another drop will touch our lips."

The woman called Ialane said nothing. Her serpent lazily lifted its head, flicking a pink, forked tongue toward the lower city. Ialane brushed her fingertip beneath its jaw as her robe rolled with a gust of wind.

After a pause just long enough to become uncomfortable, Ialane dropped her hand from the creature. "I'm curious why you celebrate Harvest Festival. Enlighten me."

Once again, the soldiers exchanged glances. The same soldier licked his lips. "Because we must give thanks for a year of plentiful food so the next will be just as plentiful."

"You must give thanks?" Ialane strummed her fingers on one of her sword's hilts. "Why must you celebrate it?"

"Because, ah, because the king has blessed the celebration, and we would not go against Good King Sol's wishes."

Mara frowned. Harvest had nothing to do with the king. It had everything to do with the Burning Mother. It was for her they lit the paper lanterns that carried their prayers to the stars.

"Good," Ialane said, her back still to the men. "Because our king would not be pleased to know his men thought that whore the Burning Mother would ever grant them kindness or care about their stupid paper lantern prayers. Has anyone passed into Upper Sollan? The low folk should know better, but they're drunk tonight, and tonight more than all others we need to keep the trash out of the true city."

"None have passed. We have kept careful watch like you commanded. The, ah, the trash know to keep far away from Upper Sollan tonight."

"Yet I feel as if that little fact is not known to all who prowl the streets this evening. Keep an eye out, and if I catch you leaving your post again, my serpent will be spitting out the remnants of your manhoods by morning. Then you can join the trash. I hear the Floatwaif has use for men like that."

Ialane whipped around, finally facing the soldiers. Somehow the men both managed to stand even more rigid than before. Mara watched the priestess march back into Upper Sollan. Her serpent's eyes gleamed like Olessa's polished rubies, their cold stare sweeping one last time across the lane.

The priestess disappeared beyond the archway. Mara squatted in her hiding spot. Her babe weighed on her already tired arms. She adjusted him against her shoulder and watched the men, hoping they might return to their wine now that Sister Ialane left them in peace.

Mara waited. A cricket picked up its chirping. The soldiers didn't move. They didn't speak. She might not have known they were more than statues had she not just witnessed the encounter with the priestess.

If she could just find a way to distract them, she might slip through unnoticed. Frustration tied a knot in her chest. She knew no other way through and feared wandering around to find another gate would lead her away from her goal.

I needed you, Tag, she thought bitterly. No longer did she smile thinking of him licking butter from his thumb. *I needed you and you left me to this.*

After a few moments thinking in the shadows, she noticed the cricket no longer chirped its song. A gaze weighed on Mara's back. Her heartbeat quickened. She tightened her grip on her son and slowly turned.

Instead of a small, empty alley, a silent son stood tall and imposing. His black robe blended perfectly with the darkness and framed his pale, expressionless mask.

Mara lurched to her feet. The ball of her foot planted on a jagged rock. She yelped, yanking her foot from the stone. It clattered into the lane. Mara's eyes widened. She twisted around and watched the stone come to rest on the wine-stained stones in the middle of the road.

She grimaced and leaned back, her hood slowly slipping to her shoulders. She peeked into the lane.

Both soldiers glared from their posts. Their knuckles whitened on the hilts of their swords.

"You there," one said, "why are you skulking in the shadows like some thief? Come out where we can see you."

"She wears a burlap hood," the other man said, his voice trembling. "You know what this means, sir? An ashwalk pilgrim! Just like they said would be crawling about tonight."

Mara twisted into her hiding place. The silent son's hand lanced from the black and wrapped around Mara's wrist. The guards' footsteps pounded on the stones, their scabbards clattering against their breastplates.

She hoisted her son against her neck and frantically searched the priest's eyes hiding behind his mask. "What do we do? There's nowhere to go!"

The silent son did not answer. His hand tightened on her wrist. He spun around, and the pale wedge of his other hand swept in a great arc before the wall. A hole opened in the stones, and the priest pulled them through it.

Mara stumbled after the man as the opening shrunk around her. She leapt through the hole and landed on the other side. Turning, she spotted the men barrel around the corner she had occupied seconds before.

"Halt!" one shouted, clumsily yanking the sword from his scabbard.

The second soldier bolted for the hole. Mara watched, frozen in horror, as the man's brawny frame swelled within the shrinking gap. He ripped his sword from the scabbard and screamed, thrusting the blade into the opening.

The gap sealed around the sword with a hiss. Its razor tip wriggled like an angry snake inches from Mara's face, the stone wall keeping the steel from burying between her eyes. From the other side of the wall, guards screamed for reinforcements.

Long, pale fingers rested gently over Mara's shoulder. She turned to the masked priest, and he motioned to follow.

"I've never seen magic before today," she said. "And that's twice now a silent son's used it to save me. I thought your power faded from Urum?"

He brushed his knuckles over her cheek and shook his head side to side. She started to speak again, but he turned his back and floated like a phantom over another wide lane.

Mara followed the silent son in and out of narrow alleys, across lanes, and between spaces so small she feared she might crush the child in her arms. Alarm bells rang out. The rhythmic march of guards on the move echoed all around her.

The silent son and Mara slipped into an alley that turned sharply toward a familiar wall encircling Upper Sollan. The barrier towered over her, its long, cool shadow snuffing out the light like wet fingers pinching the dying flame of a candle.

"There's nowhere to go," she hissed as the silent son picked up speed.

"Please," she begged, "slow down. You're too fast. I can't—I can't keep up!"

The silent son disappeared within the darkness. Mara slowed in the deepest depths of the shadows and searched the black with her free hand. The wall rose not inches from her face, and yet, she found no solid surface.

Mara leaned into the darkness. "Silent son? Are you there? Will you take my hand and lead me through?"

No one answered.

Mara licked her lips. She glanced behind her. Guards' harried voices grew ever louder. She faced the black and stepped into it.

10

A GOOD KING'S UNKIND WORDS

From the shadows Mara stumbled. She wheeled around and searched the darkness. Instead of an opening in the wall to Lower Sollan, now only thick, solid stone remained.

She spun back around, her rough burlap cloak itching her legs. If the silent son who opened the wall for her came through, he had either long since left or cloaked himself in invisibility. Mara had no idea if the man really could do that, but then again, before that night she'd never seen someone move a wall like a velvet curtain.

Tall apartments dotted with graceful balconies lined Upper Sollan's wide avenues. Thin curtains fluttered from wide windows thrown open in the cool night air. Murmuring fountains quietly poured pure water from the mouths of lesser gods and creatures of the First and Second Suns. Tall pillars supported angled roofs tiled richly red, a stark contrast to the smooth marble of the homes and luxurious shops of the neighborhood.

None of the intricate fountains, graceful pillars, or thin veils billowing from the windows captured Mara's heart more than the flowers. Lavender grew in great bushels on every corner. Poppies spread their brilliant petals beneath nearly every window. Wax flowers bobbed on their rigid stems, their tiny violet petals casting shadows over their spindly leaves.

"It is not a different neighborhood," she said, looking to her son. "This is a different world."

Mara closed her eyes and smiled as she lifted her chin. "And it smells wonderful!"

Tall poles set at even spaces lined the road. Bulbous lanterns grew from the poles like fungus. The lights cast a calm glow on the serene district and filled the air with a sense of tranquil security.

Mara stepped into the lane. Her smile quickly faded beneath the lanterns' light. Despite the beauty, despite the tranquility, she did not belong. She was a splinter in a foot. She was a beggar at a ball. She was an other, and the people in that place would quickly mark her for it.

With her free hand, she clasped the hood that had fallen to her shoulders. She drew it over her head until its shadows locked her in their safety.

A light breeze played with her burlap and toyed with the dark locks protruding from her hood. She hoisted her babe against her collar and stalked forward, eyes casting about for any sign of soldier, or Six forbid, the frightening priestess with the foreign-sounding name and scowling mask.

"Silent son?" she whispered. "Where did you go?"

She waited in the quiet. A moth fluttered by. It rose to one of the lampposts and flapped around a lantern, desperately trying to find a way to the light it could never reach.

Mara cradled her child's head. She pressed her lips together and took a deep breath through her nose. She darted into the lane, passing a tall fountain of a woman pouring water from a vase.

"Where is everyone?" she wondered. Not a soul milled in the avenues, and not a single resident lingered outside their home. The music of Lower Sollan drifted from beyond the wall, but the tall barrier muted the merry tunes as they passed through hewn rock.

The road wound like a serpent through the city. Tall apartments with their overhanging roofs blocked most of her view, but she could tell she headed in the right direction. The homes grew taller, their columns crowned by more intricate vines of ivory. The gardens grew richer. The fountains became monuments to an artisan's skill.

"Citizens," a voice called from beyond a bend in the road. "Calling all citizens of the upper lanes. Your Good King summons you. The Good King calls!"

"Well at least I know there are actually people in Upper Sollan," she said.

Mara slowed and twisted to the side of an apartment. She pressed her back against the wall and leaned toward the edge. Beyond, the lane spilled like the mouth of a river into a wide plaza. A crier stood upon a platform raised in its heart, a great lamppost dotted with lights towering over him.

The people missing from her walk through Upper Sollan had gathered there. They formed a crowd packed shoulder to shoulder, a multitude of heads and and faces robed in fine silks and gold-hemmed dresses.

A large apartment in the plaza's corner thrust a short flight of stairs not far from the crowd. Mara waited for the right moment and sprinted for it. She padded up the stairs and crouched behind a column, just close enough to hear the crier's voice ring out Good King Sol's proclamation.

"Dear citizens of Upper Sollan. Good King Sol regrets interrupting your revelry. He knows his compassionate hand and bountiful wisdom has blessed the people of the Kingdom Eloia with yet another harvest that will feed all bellies for another year."

"He calls himself Good King Sol?" Mara rolled her eyes. "You are no good king."

The crier looked up and waited. The crowd clapped. A few halfheartedly cheered. The crier forced a smile and locked his gaze on the parchment unfurled in his hands.

"The Serpent Sun has seen calamity on the horizon. This night of celebration hides a grave danger to our peaceful kingdom. There is a threat among us, an evil so dark it imperils the souls of every man, woman, and child of Sollan... of Eloia...of even Urum!"

His words finally animated the quiet crowd. Whispers erupted. Husbands and wives exchanged worried glances. A few slipped their hands into one another's grasps.

"The king has summoned the mightiest soldiers Eloia has to offer to protect the innocent in our city from this threat. He wishes nothing but safety and celebration for this night. So the normal guard shall be doubled until sunrise. No villainy shall disturb your merriment, of this Good King Sol swears upon the Serpent Sun!"

Many more than before clapped. Heads nodded in agreement. Mara seemed to be the only one wearing any kind of frown.

The crier cleared his throat and continued his message. "Thanks to the dedication of the one true religion and the ancient serpent who grants their wisdom, their power, and our bountiful harvest, the king has thrown away the shadows hiding this threat. He has uncovered the vile plot. He knows the faces of those who seek to bring you violence.

"They worship the Six. They are the Six. Their power wanes, and their bitterness has poisoned their hearts. They are angered that the Serpent Sun rises. They hate the king for recognizing this truth. Good King Sol does not know how many in their ranks plot this vile treachery, but he believes the corruption may reach even the highest of priests and priestesses."

The crowd gasped collectively. Priests of the Six were not necessarily pacifists. In fact, many old stories Gia whispered to Mara involved a warrior priest laying waste to armies or moving mountains to topple monsters or changing the flow of rivers to save towns. Gia never whispered of priestly plots to kill kings. Priests did not rule. They served. First they served the Six, and then they served their kingdom.

"Therefore," the crier shouted, "all priests and acolytes of the Six are confined within their temples. None shall walk the roads of Sollan tonight, pestering its good and faithful folk. Keep an eye open for them, especially the silent sons of the supposedly Loyal Father and the men of the Slippery Sinner. They toy with shadows and cloak themselves in darkness. Their hands make doors from solid stone that could lead straight into your child's chambers."

Mara glanced at her son and clenched her jaw. "How dare they. No silent son would hurt an innocent. I do not need to see the eyes behind their masks to know that truth."

She looked back to the crowd. Soldiers lingered at its edges like vultures might linger above a dying hare. They eyed the people within the mass, searching for someone. Most likely that someone just happened to wear burlap stained by ash and carried a dead child in her arms.

"But why?" she asked herself.

"If you should see a priest or priestess, raise the alarm at once," the crier commanded. "Your king will greatly reward all who are loyal in this request. To those who may harbor the Six's servants…" the man pursed his lips, his gaze sweeping over the crowd. "…You will see a good king sour."

The crowd took a step back from the crier's platform. He smirked and pushed his shoulders back, gleefully soaking in his own obnoxious self-worth. "Now to the threat itself. A woman walks among us…"

Mara wrinkled her nose, her lip protruding. "Now here's my grand entrance I suppose."

"…She is not like any woman you have ever known. She will be sweet. She will weep and pluck at your heartstrings. Do not listen! Do not allow her into your heart! For she is not a woman. She is a sorceress, raised from the dead by the Six, a creature of the Second Sun whose power will burn the souls of all who touch her."

Mara brought her fingers to her lips. She almost laughed at the thought of her being some ancient, resurrected sorceress of a forgotten age.

"Yes," the crier continued, "she seeks to take Good King Sol's life this night, and she will stop at nothing until she swallows his soul as a serpent might swallow a hen's egg. If you see her, scream. If you see her, run. If you see her, call out and do not stop calling until the king's men come. Do anything else, and she will pluck the soul from your body, and you will never have a room in the Serpent Sun's golden palace. Heaven will be forever out of reach, and you will scream through eternity in an endless void."

"But what does she look like?" someone asked. "How do we know this demon sorceress when we see her?"

"That is her true villainy," the crier said. "She has come to Sollan on this holiest of days dressed as the only one who could come within reach of Good King Sol without being troubled. Her face, it will be beautiful. Her skin, it will be soft and smooth as silk. Her eyes, they will be like polished jewels. Yet, you will not see her beauty. You will avoid her. You will turn from her as she moves from shadow to shadow…"

The crier paused for effect. His eyes darted over the crowd, and he leaned forward. "For she will be cloaked in burlap, covered in ash, a stillborn child cradled in her arms."

Mara's throat twisted. She gripped the pillar, her knuckles whitening. "Bastard. I am no sorceress! I am a moon maiden. A moon maiden!"

The people hated her. The serpents sought her. The king wished her dead. Yet Mara had no idea why. Worse yet, her only allies in the city were men who could not speak because their faith forbade them to utter anything but prayers of adoration to the Six.

"That's vicious!" a man shouted. "To use the ashwalk in such a way. It is a crime against divinity."

The crier nodded in agreement. "Indeed it is. It is why Good King Sol has proclaimed the ashwalk is forever forbidden. All newborns from this day forth shall be inducted into his glorious house, the temple of the Sun Serpent. Born wailing or still, all babes will be received into his open arms. They shall all taste of heaven with Good King Sol's guiding light!"

Cheers erupted from the crowd. Mara slumped, dipping her chin. She focused on her babe, the stillborn boy whose puffy, swollen lids hid above his round, pink cheeks.

She tapped him on the nose and smiled. "You had just been kicking, my son. What happened? Why did you not draw breath? I felt such a fire in your spirit, but when you came to the world, the spark would not light. Now the king wants us dead. For what? A newborn's soul?

"Yesterday, I was no one. Yesterday, I was property and a plaything for any patron who might have enough coin. Tonight, though…" she stared into the overhang. "…Tonight I am wanted by a king."

Mara had no idea if it was her fiery spirit flaring or Olessa's glimmer making her more a fool than anything else, but the shame and fear and self pity weighing on her shoulders lightened. A king wanted her. The jewel of the kingdom. The lord who wore the crown. He wanted her.

Never had she wanted to finish her ashwalk more than at that moment. An evil king desired her, and she held the secret to his defeat.

Rolling to her knees, she tightened the burlap wrapped around her child. She rocked to her feet and stood within the shadows, staring into the crowd already disbursing and retreating to their silk-draped apartments.

"Olessa said I would never be anything." Her jaw tightened, and her gaze locked onto her son. "She said I would never be anyone. She told me you would be the servant of a rich family, that you would never achieve anything else because this was our lot in life and we should accept it with the grace of an obedient slave."

Mara sped down the stairs. She slipped into the shadows, walking backward between the strip of grass separating two tall apartments. The darkness encased her like comforting veils.

The crowd ambled down the lane, couples whispering plans in their ears of what they might do should they see the great sorceress of the Second Sun. Husbands balled their fists and spoke of meeting the witch in battle. Wives promised to say extra prayers to the Serpent Sun to guard their children.

She watched them all, still as one of the marble statues crowning the fountains of Upper Sollan. The people walked not a stone's throw from her. Had the sun been shining, she would have been spotted, and the soldiers would have been thrusting swords into her chest in moments.

But no one saw her, and a mighty king feared a lowly whore. Mara closed her eyes and felt her spirit flow into the world. She lifted her chin and smiled at the stars. "I will overcome this. No king will stop my ashwalk. This I swear to the Six. I will find the Mother's temple before dawn, and damn the king to the hells where the other demons wail if he tries to stop me."

The last of the crowd drifted down the lane. Mara scanned her surroundings before slipping into the city streets, ever onward, ever closer to Sollan's heart.

11

THE WIDOW AND THE MAIDEN

Burlap and ash fluttered around Mara as she darted from building to building. Her child's weight began to wear on her arms, but the mix of her determination and Olessa's glimmer kept her moving at a steady pace toward Hightable where the Mother's temple waited.

A new determination also blossomed within her. Knowing that Good King Sol wanted her, a simple moon maiden and ashwalk pilgrim, it gave her something in life she never had before. She had meaning. She had *value*, and not just value to another, value to herself. For the first time in her life, something important hinged on her actions, and not even the king would stop her.

"I can do this," she muttered, twirling into a grassy strip between two tiered apartments. "I can really do this!"

Mara pressed her back against the cool marble of one of the buildings and listened to the rhythmic steps of soldiers as they marched through Upper Sollan's stony lanes. Evading them had almost become a game of cat and mouse, but while sidestepping the men and lurking in the shadows thrilled her, more rational thoughts eventually prevailed. Once when Olessa had caught Mara stealing buttered shrimp from her madame's table, the woman told her the cat always eats the cocky mouse first. The beating her madame gave afterwards etched the words onto her heart.

The soldiers' rhythmic marching died into a muted echo. She darted through the grass and spilled into another avenue. Ahead, a few small but ornate apartments appeared stacked one atop another like the tiered steps of a queen's wedding cake. Interlocking decks and balconies strung with loose lines weighed by lanterns gave the stonework an inviting glow.

Mara focused on a line of linens drying in a yard beside the homes. A taupe robe fluttered like a moth's wings in the breeze, beckoning her with the promise of soft threads free of ash. She looked at her arm, at the rough burlap threads fraying at the edges and the soot marring the brown fibers. "Maybe it's time for something that blends a little better…"

She licked her lips and scanned the lane between her and her goal. No guards lingered in the street. No watchful eyes peeped from within the curtained windows.

With a last, deep breath, she sprinted for the courtyard. The pitter-patter of her sandals on the stones echoed on the apartment walls rising around her.

Her feet landed on the yard's soft grass. Sweat rolled down her back in cold lines. She twisted into a dark nook and stared down the lane she had just crossed.

A door opened. A man stepped onto his patio. He held a sword that gleamed in the lantern light. His narrow gaze swept down the road. Mara inched deeper into the corner, lifting her heels and pressing her back as deep as she could into the darkness.

The man grumbled something. He disappeared within his home, and the door clicked shut behind him.

Mara exhaled, her shoulders slumping. She bit her smiling lip and spun from the nook. Before her, the linens billowed just above the grass, pinned to a line stretching from one apartment to another.

One robe looked about her size. She could easily toss the burlap and hide her son against her bosom. No one would be the wiser.

Mara approached the line. She grabbed the soft linen. Looking left and right, she yanked the robe from the rope. The clothing fluttered from the bobbing cord.

"Like my robe, do you?" a woman asked. "It is simple, but simple is the fashion this season, or so they tell me."

The fabric rolled in gentle waves toward the ground. Behind it, a woman appeared wearing a deep frown.

Mara's hand trembled. "I…"

The woman wore her hair tied in two buns just above her ears and oiled them to a glimmering polish. Grey and silver streaked the brown, but her smooth cheeks and bright eyes revealed an age much younger than her hair displayed.

They stared at one another for a long moment. The linen in Mara's hand tickled her knuckles and wrapped around her leg like the curling tongue of a lizard. She released the robe, and it collapsed in soft waves onto her feet.

"I—I—I wasn't…"

"You are an ashwalk pilgrim," the woman whispered. "Are you the one the crier spoke of? Are you the sorceress?"

"No!" Mara held her son tighter against her chest. "I swear I'm no sorceress. I never walked under the Second Sun. I never danced with the alp and cursed the Six. Not once."

"Good King Sol doesn't like you very much. There's a reward out on you. It's no small sum. It would buy me a thousand dresses and then some."

Mara stepped back. "I've avoided the soldiers long enough. I can run. By the time they get here, I'll be long gone. You'll get no reward. You'll get punished for wasting their time."

The woman considered Mara for a long moment. Mara lifted her chin in a childish attempt to appear formidable.

"And so I might," the woman said. Lightly she shook her and laughed. She turned on her heel and padded toward her apartment door. "You want a bite? Maybe some water to wet your tongue? Your lips look like they're about ready to crumble to dust."

Mara's stomach grumbled. She swallowed and watched as the woman paused before her doorway.

Mara took a step back. "I can't trust you."

"Spare me. I could have called the king's men when I first saw you when you ran down the road and hid while my neighbor searched for you. I could still call them if you like. They will be turning down the lane soon. Really, how long you've survived is beyond me. The Six must be escorting you to Hightable themselves."

"Then what do you want from me? Why should I trust you?"

Sighing, the woman rolled up her sleeve. Two circular scars marred her forearm.

"Scars," she said, quickly rolling down her sleeve. "A gift from Sister Ial-ane Donra and that devil serpent she wears around her neck. My husband worshipped the Coin Counter. He dared stand up to her, so she cut off his legs and watched his blood wet the ground until no life remained within him. Her snake would have stolen my life, too, had she not called it off as my world faded. She chopped my poor Decimus into bits and buried him in a box of copper coins. I hate that masked priestess with every drop of blood in my body."

"That's horrible," Mara said. "How could anyone do such a thing?"

She smirked and stepped inside, holding the door for Mara. "She is the law made flesh. The king's tongue commands, but she is his sword in the city. Now, will you come inside? Or would you rather run into the arms of a soldier?"

"I…" Mara wrapped both her arms around her son and tightened her jaw. She took a last, fleeting look at the outside world before slipping inside the apartment with the woman.

Inside, the woman walked to a hearth where she had water set to boil. Steam curled from the kettle and tickled Mara's nostrils with the faintest hint of hibiscus and lemon.

"Tea?" her host asked.

"It smells nice," Mara said.

The woman chuckled, plucking the kettle from the flames. "Your words are modest but your eyes are as ravenous as a feral dune dragon. I have some salted pork as well. I'll pour a cup and fill a plate if you'd like to have a seat and rest those weary feet of yours."

"You're very kind," Mara said as she sat on a stool before a long table. "I don't even know your name."

"Vibiana Kel, widow to the late Decimus Kel."

"I am Mara."

"No last name?"

Mara's gaze dropped to the floor. "No. I am a moon maiden from the House of Sin and Silk. My station did not earn one, and if I had one at birth, I do not remember it."

"I like to thank Decimus never visited the pleasure barges." Vibiana looked into the corner, lost in thought. She blinked and smiled. "I thought about it once or twice when I got wild and took too much wine on Harvest Festival, but it's just never struck me as worth my while."

Vibiana placed a teacup with a teal braid around the rim onto the table. Mara leaned over the tea and inhaled its sweet aroma. "My madame makes sure all her patrons leave with a smile."

"Sounds like a competent business woman." The woman slid a plate of salted pork next to the tea.

With her child in one arm, Mara plucked a strip of meat from the porcelain. Her throat watered, saliva rolling in lines down her scratchy throat. She ate the meat, smiling as the salt melted on her tongue.

"I've never tasted pork so good."

"Welcome to Upper Sollan," Vibiana said with a laugh."I doubt there's any pork half as good in Lower Sollan, and if they eat pork on the Floatwaif, it is a meal had once in a lifetime."

The woman eyed Mara's son while she ate. Vibiana interlaced her fingers on the table and smiled. "I'm sure your arms are tired. Why don't you give me the child? I'll wrap him in something proper so he looks less suspicious once you continue on your journey to the temple."

Mara nearly choked on the pork. She grabbed her teacup and swallowed a honeyed gulp of hibiscus tea. Her fingers instinctively tightened on her son's burlap. She looked into his sealed eyes. He looked so peaceful, so serene. A stranger might think him sleeping had he not been wrapped in the ashen fabric.

"He's been with me since the birth," Mara said. "I haven't let him go. Not once."

"Then your arms must be absolutely dying. Here, give him to me, and I will let you rest." Vibiana held out her arms and wagged her fingers. The urgency tinging her voice turned Mara's stomach, and the room warmed a few degrees.

Mara pulled her son closer to her chest. "You aren't scared of stillborn on Harvest Festival? They told me the dark spirits of the demon alp would swarm him and all those who came near us on the ashwalk. Ash and burlap keeps us hidden from them until sunrise."

"Old, silly stories." Vibiana laid both arms on the table, palms out. Her fingers waggled harder, beckoning Mara lay her son in the woman's arms. "Now give him here and let me take care of things."

Mara's heart fluttered. The look in Vibiana's eyes was one of hunger slipping into frustration. She wanted Mara's son. Mara could see it. As a moon maiden, she knew hunger and lust when she saw it better than most.

"No," Mara said, scooting from her seat. She licked the last of the salt from her lips and bowed respectfully. "Thank you Vibiana Kel for your hospitality, but I fear I've already lingered too long. I must be on my way."

Mara turned, heading toward the door she only just realized had its bolt thrown. The walls closed in around her. She hurried past the table, flashing a polite smile at the woman.

"Wait! Before you go…" Vibiana slid from her stool and turned her back. She hurried to a counter and opened a drawer, searching contents that clanked and clattered within.

"You've already given me far too much. Thank you, Vibiana."

Mara turned to the door. Her fingers fumbled with the lock, but it held fast. "I did not listen to the beggar's warning, Gia," she whispered, her fingers clawing at the lock. "I should not have trusted a soul in Sollan tonight."

Vibiana shut the drawer with a bang. Mara wheeled around, pressing her back against the sealed door. The woman smiled with one hand behind her back. With the other, she hooked her finger on a necklace and pulled it from her bosom. A brass key swung on the chain, glimmering in the hearth's firelight.

"It requires a key to open. Sollan is so dangerous these days, even here. As a widow, I have to ensure my own safety, lost as I am to my own devices."

"I have nothing to give you," Mara said. "A boy took my brass collar in Lower Sollan. I have nothing else but burlap."

Vibiana laughed, dropping the necklace from her finger. "A moon maiden's collar? That wouldn't buy a decent bottle of wine. Don't be so insulting, Mara. I want you. A single woman like myself needs a good servant. I'll keep you safe, and you get a life free of that floating barge of trash and whores."

"You want me to be a—your slave?"

"Doesn't it sound glamorous? I'll dress you in clean robes every day. You will never get on your knees or back for another patron. You will sleep with a full belly, and once I trust you enough, I may even allow you to leave our home to walk the streets of Upper Sollan. We might even visit the temples in Hightable if you're a good girl. The king will certainly destroy them soon, and I'm sure you'll want to see them before he does."

Mara eyed Vibian's still-hidden hand. "What are you holding behind your back?"

Vibiana rolled her eyes and revealed her hand, flashing a long, sharp knife in her grip. "Let's not make this a messy affair. You have nowhere else to go. Give me the child, and I'll dispose of it. Forget this ashwalk. It is a doomed quest. The king does not want you to complete it. If he doesn't wish it, you will never make it. This is his city. His eyes are always upon it."

Mara stiffened. "Let me out. I will not be your slave. If the Six protect me—"

"Hah!" the woman's cheeks reddened as she laughed. "The Six wouldn't spit on a whore if they wouldn't help my husband, a loyal acolyte to the Coin Counter. Their power fades from Urum, even as the king's rises. It's no secret magic fizzles on the fingers of the Six's priests. The serpents say it will be sooner than later before the last one casts their spell, and then, the Six are nothing and the Serpent Sun is everything."

"Let me go!"

The woman's lips puckered into an angry point. "So you won't stay with me? You won't even consider it?"

"I will not be your slave if it means giving up my child. I will finish this ashwalk, and no king with his greedy eyes on heaven will keep me from the Mother's temple." Mara lifted her chin. "Neither will a lonely widow with sweet tea and salted pork!"

Vibiana brandished the knife and charged. Mara gasped, sprinting to the other side of the table as the woman wildly slashed at the air.

Mara stood at the head of the table next to the crackling hearth. Vibiana stood at the opposite end, eyes glittering with a dark and determined anger. "Fine then, whore. I'll drive a knife through you and drag your body to the king myself. I offered you everything. Remember that as you lay dying. I offered you everything!"

I never should have tried to remove my burlap, Mara thought.

Vibiana darted around the table. Mara twisted around for the door leading into the rest of the woman's home, but like the exit, a lock secured it. Cursing, she spun and lurched toward the hearth.

The woman's strong grip clenched Mara's burlap. She yanked the robe, spinning Mara so her back turned to the hot flames.

Vibiana held the shiny knife before her. She twisted her wrist, and the blade glimmered in the light. "This is the end of your journey, Mara."

The woman thrust the knife at Mara's chest. She grit her teeth. At the last possible moment, Mara twisted to the side.

Horror ignited in Vibiana's eyes. Her momentum carried her stumbling forward, the knife slashing through empty air, and she toppled headfirst into the yawning hearth.

Embers and ash belched from the flames. Vibiana shrieked. Mara winced. The fine oils in Vibiana's hair ignited as sparks coated her in a cloud of ash.

Mara watched in horror as Vibiana yanked herself from the flames. Her knife clattered to the ground. Her hair was a single, twisting flame. She writhed, eyes burnt closed, skin blistering, clawing blindly toward Mara.

"I'll kill you!" she wailed. "You cursed bitch. I'll kill you!"

The necklace fell out of the woman's dress and dangled loosely from the chain. Mara lanced out quick as a bolt of lightning and snapped the key from its chord. Vibiana lashed out, her sharpened nails missing Mara's hand by a hair. The woman stumbled into an apron and ripped it from the counter. She buried her head in the thick cloth, wailing and sobbing with the pain of her burn.

Waiting any longer would doom Mara to the soldiers she had no doubt raced toward the shrieking cries coming from the apartment. She sprinted for the door and unlocked the bolt. She glanced over her shoulder and watched Vibiana sob, the remnants of her hair curled and smoking wisps, her scalp a scarlet mess of burns and blisters.

Mara wanted nothing more than to run to her, to comfort her and call for help even though the widow tried to kill her. No one deserved that pain. No one deserved that suffering.

She turned away and rested her head against the door, inhaling the air rife with the reek of burnt hair and skin. Her eyes watered as she choked down her sob.

"All because I did not want my burlap," she said, shoving the key into the lock and twisting.

Mara kicked the door, and cool air rushed into the room. She stepped out and closed the door behind her, hanging the key over the knob. She turned and slipped into the lane, Vibiana's sobs ringing in her head like the remnants of a nightmare. The heavy march of boots echoing around the labyrinthine avenues grew louder and louder.

12

EYES BENEATH THE STAIRS

Just beyond the clusters of apartments, Mara heard the harried shouts of Sollan's soldiers as they swarmed around the packed homes. She searched the shadows, the corners, the lonely nooks and tranquil alleys for any place to flee, to hide until the storm of honed steel passed.

A sharp turn led her to a narrow lane devoid of any soldiers. Without a second thought, she darted into it, speeding past curtained windows and elegant façades. Vibiana's wails pierced the night sky, adding to the soldiers' shouts and heavy footfalls echoing on the city's stones.

"Quick men, search the area!" a booming voice echoed.

"Oh gods. Six, save me!" Mara spun around a corner. Maybe ahead she could find a quiet place where they would not spot her.

Shadows of a patrol bobbed against the walls, distorting and growing in length as they neared the corner. Mara cursed, twisting the opposite direction. A jolt of panic raced through her veins when she saw yet another patrol's dark shadows bouncing against the wall from just around the bend.

"This way, don't let the sorceress escape!" a soldier roared.

Precious few seconds remained before they had her trapped. Her panicked gaze darted around the lane, looking for any place that might keep her and her child hidden from their eyes.

A marble stairwell protruded from the second floor of an apartment and angled sharply to the road. A single low arch supported the stairs, each side lined by reed baskets and pots of aloe plants and fiery poppies.

Without another breath of hesitation, she dove between two tall baskets. Her knees hit the stones, a few loose rocks digging into her skin. She grimaced at the piercing pain lancing up her leg and steadied the baskets with one hand while she gripped her son in the other.

Mara hunched. She scooted within the small arch, her back angled awkwardly against the slanted stairwell. She twisted her legs from under her and pressed herself into the lowest portion of the stairs while tucking her son tightly in her lap.

No sooner had the wobbling baskets she dove through stilled than a line of ten soldiers marched into view. Mara glanced over her shoulder and spotted the second patrol rounding the opposite corner, a line of gleaming breastplates and deadly swords.

The lead soldier of each line held a long pole of bobbing lanterns. They nodded to one another and brought their lines to a halt just where Mara could see both men through the thick leaves of an aloe.

"Hail, Kogamon. Have you see her?" one asked. He wore a long beard curled by oils and braided at his chin.

The other man called Kogamon shook his head. He gripped his lantern pole with a hand covered in a patchwork of tiny scars. "The sorceress? No. Vibiana? Yes. It was a horror like no other, Jost."

Jost grimaced and clutched the braid of his beard. "How bad was it?"

"She'll be wearing a mask the rest of her days, however long those are. I've no doubt the poor woman will take her own life now that she's been so disfigured by the witch's sorcery. Damn that demon and her magic. Vibiana is a good woman." Kogamon leaned to Jost, eyes darting up the alley. "Her husband Decimus was a good man. His loyalty to the Coin Counter was misplaced, but he did not deserve that fate. Now she shares a similar one."

Mara clenched her jaw. She rested her back against the angled wall of the stairwell and stared into the sloping ceiling.

It wasn't my fault, she mouthed to the Six, *please, forgive me. And forgive Vibiana for what she's done.*

Mara noticed the conversation had grown strangely quiet. Part curious, part terrified, she looked down from the ceiling and leaned forward so the world beyond the plants and baskets appeared once again.

Both captains had turned the same direction, and so had their lines. The men faced down the lane opposite where Mara looked. They stood stiff as boards. She recognized the fear in their eyes. She had seen it glimmer in the eyes of the men guarding the entrance to Upper Sollan. Soft as a flower petal carried on the wind, Mara turned and peered down the lane where their sweaty gazes had locked.

Two figures calmly approached the patrols. One she recognized as Sister Ialane Donra. Her mask scowled at the men. Her pale cloak billowed around her. Her swords hung loosely at her side, and her serpent's eyes of jeweled blood glittered just beneath her chin.

A man, or at least Mara thought it might be a man, accompanied Ialane. He walked with the calm rhythm of a practiced acrobat. Ivory leathers wrapped around him from his fingers to his toes, concealing his body. He wore a loose wrap over his shoulders that coiled like a snake up his face and hid his features deep within a masked hood hemmed by gold embroidery. Mara could see no weapons on the man, but a tickling splinter of dread in her belly told her they were there.

Ialane and her companion came to the first line of soldiers. The men split and let them pass. They strolled to the base of the stairs and disappeared from Mara's sight. She twisted to the two captains, but the priestess and her companion did not appear.

They stand on just the other side of these stairs, Mara thought. *One sound and they will know I'm here.*

Jost and Kogamon shifted nervously. Mara's heart thundered. Sweat coated her palms. She wiped them on her burlap and clutched her son. She feared Ialane and whoever walked with her, but more so did she feel the fears ebbing from the two men's pores.

"You did not see the sorceress?" Ialane asked.

"No—no—no Sister Ialane." Kogamon shook his head enthusiastically. "Patrols are scouring Upper Sollan as we speak. We will find her soon. We will not let her reach the Blooming Ring."

"Praise be to the Serpent Sun," Jost added. "May Good King Sol raise the Fourth Sun and burn the Six to cinders!"

"Spoken like a true believer," a voice said, thin, wispy, and edged by sarcasm.

Ialane chuckled lightly. "You doubt his faith, Brother Caspran?"

Caspran? That must be her companion, Mara surmised.

"I doubt the faith of all men," Caspran said. "No doubt these two licked the feet of the Mother's shrine last Harvest Festival. They only bend to the king because he chokes the old gods' power from the world to make his own. A sliver of their soul will always be in the Mother's arms."

"You are as much a poet as a priest, Caspran."

Jost swallowed. Kogamon lifted his bearded chin. Neither said a word.

Ialane's sigh was audible even from Mara's hiding place. "How is it we have practically an entire army in Sollan, and yet a single, filthy ashwalk pilgrim can still evade you? Are you men that incompetent?"

Kogamon lifted his chin higher. His beard reflected the lantern's light. "No, Sister Ialane. It's just…"

He glanced nervously at Jost. His fellow captain tightened his jaw, his eyes flashing a sign that begged the other captain to keep his mouth shut, but if Kogamon saw it, he ignored it.

"…You say she is a powerful sorceress," Kogamon said, his eyes once again fixing ahead. "Perhaps she has used her magic to keep herself hidden? And even then, we have no idea what she looks like. She could be any woman in the streets cloaked in any number of disguises. What fool would keep cloaked in burlap when the whole city would know her now?"

"What fool?" Ialane asked, poison dripping in her voice. "Do you want a description? Should I have the king's best artisan sculpt you a likeness from marble? The witch still wears her burlap. I would have her by now if she did not."

Mara frowned. Her gaze drifted to her cloak. The soot had sunk deep within its rough threads.

Kogamon leaned back. "You, ah, say she is a moon maiden? Perhaps you know more? From which pleasure barge? What might her eyes look like?"

"You know the barges well?" Ialane asked, the poison in her tone turning lethal. "I wouldn't be surprised if your coin paid for the whore's meals. Tell me, Kogamon, how well would you sleep at night knowing your coin lined the pockets of our king's assassin?"

The man's cheeks reddened above his dark beard. His high chin slowly dipped.

Captain Jost's grip flexed on his lamppost, the scars on his skin whitening with his tightened fingers. The man took the smallest step back from Kogamon. Behind them, the line of soldiers also gave the outspoken captain room. Kogamon stared ahead. His breaths came out like a caged bull's. His nostrils expanded with each exhale. Mara could almost smell the panic coming from him.

"Sis—Sister Ialane, I—I—I would never contribute to Good King Sol's death. I would give my life for him—"

"Would you?" she snapped. "Brother Caspran, Do you think he would give his life for the king?"

"I'm not quite sure," Caspran said. An eagerness edged his voice, a hunger that chilled Mara. "But I do love a good test of faith."

"So then, would you die for your king?" Ialane asked. "Would you give your life for Good King Sol?"

The captain struggled with the words wrestling behind the wall of his lips.

No, Mara thought. *Don't tell her what she wants to hear!*

Mara's heart ached for the man who would probably happily clap her in irons and cart her to the wicked priestess if he found her beneath the stairs. Still, she couldn't help but pity Kogamon as Ialane's trap slowly closed around him.

"Speak up, my good soldier," Ialane cooed.

"I would give my life for the king," he said, tears wetting his eyes.

"I am so glad you would. You are a *good soldier*."

The man blinked. He looked up, a smile creeping up his lips. "Yes, Sister Ialane, I serve the king faithfully."

Kogamon's eyes widened until Mara could see the wet whites surrounding his pupils. He stumbled back, palms raised before his face.

"No...no!"

A serpent slithered into view, its sandy scales glistening in the lamplight. Kogamon fell into the line of the men he once commanded.

"Keep him still!" Ialane ordered. "He has given his word that he will die for his king, so let him do it."

"Or we may have to test the faith of all you good soldiers tonight," Caspran added.

The soldiers grabbed the flailing captain, holding his arms wide and pinning his feet to the cobbled road. The man cried and writhed, his wide eyes locked onto the slowly slithering snake. "Please, I don't want to die like this! I've done nothing, Sister Ialane. I serve the king faithfully!"

"Then you will die faithfully for him."

The snake paused at the man's feet. Its tongue flicked out, striking the captain's polished greaves.

"I don't understand! What have I done?"

The snake coiled around his ankle. Kogamon sobbed. Mara grimaced, sending a prayer to the Six.

"What have you done?" Mara heard Ialane take a deep breath. "'Decimus was a good man,' you said. 'His loyalty to the Coin Counter was misplaced, but he did not deserve that fate.' These were your words, uttered from your lips, infecting the men you so dutifully commanded."

Kogamon choked on his sob as Ialane Donra repeated the words he'd spoken to Jost. "I said his faith was misplaced…" he murmured. "I did not mean to anger you, the king, or the Serpent Sun with my words."

"Kogamon, I have given you a simple task. I have sent the king's men throughout Upper Sollan. You were to find one girl. One girl. Yet, you cannot. And then I find not one but two patrols idling in an empty lane, gossiping like hens when our king's life hangs in the balance. And when it is abundantly clear I wish you to continue your search, what do you do ?"

She laughed, and the sound sent a shiver down Mara's spine. "You stand there like a fool and say you want a description, that a fucking ashwalk pilgrim is not enough for you."

"They always need more," Caspran said. "They are never satisfied. It is in their blood to hunger, to beg like a dog that's eaten from the master's table."

The serpent slithered up Kogamon's leg. The man bit his trembling lip. He shook his head, his braided beard swaying over his breastplate. "Please…"

"This man, this captain of yours, he is no stranger to the pleasure barges," Ialane said. "I can see in his eyes he knows the soft touch of a moon maiden. I can almost hear his thoughts as he stares at my serpent, the regrets of his many nights full of sin and naked flesh and glimmer tingling down his throat. He claims his coin did not support our enemy. But he cannot say for certain. He doubts!"

"I do not doubt," the captain rasped. "Mercy, please."

The snake twisted around the man's breastplate. It reached his shoulder, its ruby eyes glittering as its tongue lapped at the soft, sweaty flesh at the base of his neck.

"But I will show you mercy, good soldier," Ialane said. Jost and the soldiers holding Kogamon exchanged confused looks.

"Oh thank you, Sister Ialane." The man slumped, tears staining his cheeks and disappearing into his beard. "Thank you. I swear it will never happen again."

"Just answer me this."

The relief vanished from the man's face as the other soldiers' features hardened. Mara cupped her son's head in her hands and pressed him against her collar. Although he drew no breath and his eyes would never open, she made sure he did not face what she suspected would soon happen to poor Kogamon.

"What would you ask me?" the captain asked.

"Can you tell me with all certainty that not a single coin of yours ever helped that whore? Say the words, soldier, say them, and if they are true, then they will save your life."

The serpent coiled around the man's neck. It faced him, its tongue flicking his nose.

For a moment, not a breath slipped from the lips of any in the lane. Not even Mara risked a taste of air.

Kogamon looked up. His head shook so lightly Mara almost missed the motion.

He clenched his jaw, and his face twisted in a snarl. "I'm dead no matter what words I say. So I spit on you and spit on our heretic king. He is no god. He will never defeat the Six. The serpent you worship and the one you screw at night can starve in the ash fields of hell for all eternity. Blessed is the Burning Mother, for all who bleed for her will dine at her table for eternity!"

"How disappointing," Ialane murmured.

"Yet not unexpected," Caspran added.

Kogamon spit in the snake's face. "Long live the Six!"

Ialane's serpent hissed. It bared its fangs and struck, burying them deep in his throat. Rich, crimson lines gushed from the wounds as the creature sunk its poison into his blood. He twisted and writhed. Blood ran down his breastplate and dripped onto the stone. His face reddened as his veins turned into black lines like rivers on a map.

His eyes clouded. His mouth foamed. He seized, and then he slumped.

The snake uncoiled from Kogamon and slithered to the ground. It disappeared behind the stairs, returning to Sister Ialane standing just out of Mara's sight. The soldiers who held the captain dropped him unceremoniously on the street. Beneath his body, a pool of burgundy blossomed like a rose opening for spring.

Ialane Donra cleared her throat. "Now that the good soldier is finished with his rather childish heresy, we have pressing matters to address. Find me that girl. She is a moon maiden. She is an ashwalk pilgrim. You do not need any other description than this. Any guard who captures her will receive her weight in gold. Kill her where she stands, and bring the corpse she carries to me."

Mara swallowed the sharp cry in her throat. She turned from the grisly scene and pressed her back against the stairwell. She gripped her son. Her angry tears stained his burlap. She grit her teeth into a granite wall and lightly stroked his tiny temple.

My son will never be a serpent's feast, she thought. *I don't know why they want you, Son, but I promise you that no serpent will sink its fangs into you tonight.*

Mara closed her eyes and listened to her pounding heart. The patrols split and headed to opposite ends of the lane, leaving Kogamon's corpse rotting on the road.

13

SILENT SONS

Mara struggled from the stairwell's shadow. Aloe leaves poked and prodded her cheeks as she swept through the verdant curtain that had kept her hidden from Sister Ialane and Brother Caspran. She'd scraped her knees when she slid beneath the stairs, and each time they pressed against the cobbled road a flare of fire shot up her legs.

With her child tucked in the crook of her arm, she crawled into the lane and lurched to her feet, gaze darting down each end of the avenue. After some hesitation, her eyes landed on the poor captain's corpse. Kogamon stared dully into Harvest Festival's starry sky. Blood stained his throat and matted his dark hair. The serpent's poison blackened his veins and opened his mouth in a silent scream.

No longer did Mara think of him as a man. He had more in common with the discarded oyster shells she tossed to the coral sharks than a soldier in the king's army.

She knelt before the body and closed her eyes. "Burning Mother, receive his spirit. May he dine at your table under the endless suns in the heavens."

Gently, she closed his eyes and pressed her fingers beneath his jaw so his lips sealed. "You were not an evil man, Kogamon," she whispered. "King Sol and this serpent god of his, Ialane and Caspran, they'll pay for this evil. The Six will not stand for it. Their power will return, and then...then there will be peace."

Mara had never truly prayed to the Six for much of anything. But standing before the mangled corpse, his body alone and abandoned after what was probably a life of service to his king, it twisted her heart. Captain Kogamon had a mother. She had held him as a babe as Mara held her son that very moment. His mother had once closed her eyes and dreamt of the wonderful things her son would do. Now, his mother may never even know the child she bore into the world lay dead in a pool of his own blood, the only funeral he would receive a quick prayer from the woman who caused his death.

"He is no good king, the one who rules this city." Mara scowled, coming to her feet. The king—her king—took advantage of the Six's waning powers. He had his eyes on heaven, and if the rumors were true, he would ride a great serpent to reach it. Whatever the Serpent Sun cult might be, whoever its priests were who spread its words like a pox through the kingdom, they all had to be stopped.

She gave the dead man a parting look of respect as she darted past his corpse. The road gently sloped upward. Twist after bend greeted her harried steps. Always she climbed. Always the buildings thickened.

After a few tense moments of darting and dodging and ducking the patrols filtering like ants through the streets, she came upon a set of stairs built into a tall rock wall. Lanterns drilled into the wall lit the stairs in a citrine glow. Long stalks of ivy and brilliant blossoms of dragon's breath the color of richest wine spilled over the top like foam from a frothy beer. The stairs rose high above her, but unlike the wall that separated Lower and Upper Sollan, this one lifted the city higher. It was more a platform than a wall.

"No, more like a table," Mara said, a grin slowly splitting her lips. "A very high table!"

She knew this place. She'd heard it before. It was the line between the rich and the elite. Upper Sollan housed the rich. Upper Sollan glittered with wealth. Still, it did not compare to those whose wealth was as old and vast as the Sapphire Sea. Beyond the stairs curling up the wall, she would find herself in the Blooming Ring outside the mighty wall of Hightable.

Mara swallowed. Her gaze drifted to her loose burlap sleeve. Hunted in a land so close to her heart yet so very strange, and there she stood at the edge of the city's heart. Her arms began to tremble.

Giving up now? Olessa's voice whispered in her mind.

Mara spun away and rocked her son. "I should never have made it this far."

Take the step, Mara. Gia's voice was a soft tickle down her neck. *You must take this step. The night will not last forever.*

"Don't be afraid," Mara said, although she meant her words more for herself than her son. "What would you do, Gia? You would stride up these stairs like the king himself owed you coin. Olessa would have already been banging on his bedroom doors and threatening to feed him his chamber pot."

Mara faced the stairs. She placed her foot upon the first step. Then, she climbed them. The air cleared with each step higher. Halfway up, the narrow stairs rose above the last tiled roofs of Upper Sollan.

Wind whistled in her ears and kissed her dry lips with its cool caress. She tightened her grip on her son and darted up the last steep flight.

She reached the top and twisted around as a gust billowed through her cloak. Below her, Sollan spilled out like a forest of brick and stone and tile. The city stretched into the distance, lanes upon lanes, homes upon homes, until the Sapphire Sea met the shore and slowed the city's spread. Although the sea sought to stop the city, Sollan's docks still thrust their long fingers over the water as if in defiance of the place where men were never meant to tread.

"And the Floatwaif," she whispered.

Mara's heart skipped a beat. She leaned onto the balls of her feet and squinted. In the distance, beneath the shadow of the mighty titan set upon the horizon, she spied the bobbing grid of Floatwaif, the barges flecked with swaying lanterns dancing like fairies over the Sapphire Sea's waters.

She waved like a little girl at the lights. Even if a thousand people surrounded her, she still would have giggled like a toddler at the sight of her home. Mara looked to her son and smiled. "Has it really only been hours since we left them? I feel like we've crossed half of Urum tonight."

The lights of Floatwaif glittered on the waves. Mara slowly shook her head and let the vision sink into her memory. "And yet I already feel a stranger. I miss you, Gia. Even you, Olessa, with your hard lessons and silk glove. I wish you could be here now. I wish you could see our home. We are not poor from a distance. We are a field of stars floating on the waves. It is so beautiful."

Tears welled in Mara's lids. She wiped them on her sleeve and turned from the world she knew. Atop the raised table she scaled, a vast park full of tall palms, aromatic junipers, and massive olive trees sprouted. Between the trees, the tall grasses were filled with poppies every color of a brilliant flame. Long, placid ponds held Ellan swans purer white than the belly of a fresh cloud. Athe peacocks squawked amongst the grasses. Their feathers shimmered slate and sapphire in the starlight, crowning their thin heads in brilliant, feathery halos.

"And this is the Blooming Ring," she said.

The park she faced, the beautiful, serene picture of heaven she saw, it all ended at the high wall surrounding Sollan's heart. Mara thought the stairs she had just scaled tall. She thought the wall separating the upper and lower city mighty. The one she faced dwarfed them both. The park stretched toward it. It encircled the wall like a moat of blossoms and ponds.

If something lay beyond the barrier, she could not see it. Hightable's wall towered over her world. Whatever it guarded would not be given up easily.

"Hightable," she whispered. "They built you to turn back the titans themselves."

"Men, did you hear something?" a man called from the base of the stairs.

Mara recoiled, shuffling away from the top steps. She clutched her son and stared at the stairs, the only sound disturbing the night the wind tossing her robe around her legs like a playful patron.

No other call rang from below. Slowly, Mara leaned forward, peeking down the flight. A familiar pole with lanterns fastened to its upper end appeared, bobbing with the footsteps of the soldier who carried it.

Mara spun around and sprinted into the park. She passed beneath long, looping boughs and enormous, knotted trunks. Tall grasses tickled her knuckles and lapped at her son's burlap.

She reached a pond that came nearly to the high wall. The barrier's shadow blanketed everything around her in a tranquil black filled with chirping crickets. Her breaths labored, her lungs burning, she hobbled to the water and crouched at the sloping shoreline.

The soldier's patrol appeared at the steps. She watched the leader of the patrol scan the park, pointing his lantern like it might reveal Mara hiding at the water's edge.

But the park was so large and the grasses so high that the man's meager light couldn't hope to chase away the shadows enveloping her. The lantern pointed away, and the soldier disappeared back down the steps.

Alone in the structure's shadow, she lifted her chin, gazing at its imposing height. "I'd need wings to climb that. It really was built to keep a titan at bay."

Her vision flicked to the enchanting sea and the black silhouette of the titan at the bay's mouth. *They built this entire city expecting your return.*

Mara stalked to the wall and placed a hand upon its stones. Her palm couldn't find so much as a single imperfection or handhold in a single brick. She pressed her brow against its face and savored its cool kiss against her sweaty skin.

"What am I to do?" she wondered.

A gentle hand clasped her shoulder and squeezed. She recoiled, spinning around, her arm soldier-straight toward her attacker.

"Don't touch me!" she hissed. "I'm—I'm an evil sorceress, and I'll turn you into a moth and smash you against the wall!"

She pressed her back against the stones. At first, nothing appeared in the darkness. Then, a milky mask melted from the black like the moon revealed from a passing thunderhead. The silent son's expressionless mask nodded, angling to a side.

The adrenaline flooded from Mara's veins on her sigh. "You really should be a little better about how you approach someone. What if I had a knife? I might have run you through."

The silent son bowed. He calmly motioned down the curving wall. Mara peered in the direction he pointed. "But I don't see anything."

He dropped his arm and floated like a ghost down the base of the barrier. Mara followed in his footsteps, her eye ever on the park separating Hightable from the rest of the city.

"Why do they build the walls so high?" she asked the priest. "And why did you build your temples behind them? No army of men will ever scale Hightable."

Of course, he did not answer. Mara scrunched her nose. "What is the Burning Mother's temple like?"

The silent son continued on his quiet course. Mara rolled her eyes. "I need to find her temple. I don't know why you help me, and I don't know why the king and his awful serpents hunt me. Can you tell me anything? Anything at all?"

The silent son continued on his annoyingly silent way.

"You are very frustrating. I am a moon maiden, and I have lived my life doing nothing but pleasing others. This is my first time in the city that I can remember, and I come with my dead child in my arms because the Six demand it. What happens when I get here? Everyone in this city spits on me. They throw rocks at me. They hunt me. They want me dead! And for what?"

Her words lit a fire in her heart. She squeezed her son and picked up her pace. "And for what? Why are you here? Why am I here?"

While the silent son did not reply with words, he did halt. The priest of the Loyal Father stiffened. He whirled around, his soft black robe fluttering around him yet still not revealing a hint of the man beneath it.

His unblinking, emotionless mask stared over her shoulder. He leaned forward, the dark pits of his eyes scanning the park behind them.

He reached out and grabbed her arm. He ushered her onward, but this time Mara had to run to keep up with the man.

"What is it?" she asked.

The silent son raised a hand, his palm inches from the wall. He never slowed, he never looked any direction but forward. He kept flying ever on with Mara in tow, his fingers caressing the stone face like a child might toy with a waterfall as they ran past its rushing waters.

Mara frowned at the man's extended hand. She glanced at the wall, its face hidden beneath an impenetrable blanket of darkness. "What did you see?" she asked, her voice soft despite their frantic pace. "Who is chasing us? Those soldiers?"

Eyes weighed upon her back. Mara glanced behind her as the wall's shadow peeled away like the petals of a flower peeling from a bud. The living black became other silent sons, their pale masks smiling, laughing, crying, and scowling behind her.

So the one helping me has been the same priest all along.

The other priests formed a wall behind her and herded her along the Blooming Ring. Her footsteps pounded against the soft earth. She hoisted her babe higher and tried ignoring her burning lungs.

"Why are they here?" she asked. "What is wrong? I know something's wrong. Please, you must tell me."

The silent son broke into a full run, and so did Mara. The priests behind her nipped at her heels like hounds chasing a rabbit.

A long, thin structure like an arched walkway appeared along the curve of the wall. It jutted from the barrier's top and spanned the distance of the Blooming Ring. Spindly arches supported it, and from its mouth a ribbon of water spilled in a snaking line into Upper Sollan.

"An aqueduct!" Mara exclaimed. "Then that is the way to climb this cursed wall?"

The silent son motioned frantically. He slowed, grabbing her wrist and keeping her momentum moving forward. He spun her past him, his brothers lining up beside him to form a barrier against the quiet shadows.

"Why are you stopping?" Mara looked frantically at the line of priests.

They turned to her, their masks a spectrum of every human emotion. They pointed over her shoulder at the massive aqueduct or pleaded with their pale fingers. While Mara couldn't see their faces, their fear and anxiety washed over her like the waterfall spilling from the high channel.

"You're not going to show me how to climb it?" she asked.

The silent sons frantically stuck their fingers toward the aqueduct. Slowly, Mara nodded. "I—I understand."

She stepped back, turning to face the precarious path into Hightable. "Thank you," she called, running toward the aqueduct. "I hope the Six bless all of you for your kindness!"

Mara darted into the thick grasses flowing toward the aqueduct. She knelt within them, their tall, tawny stalks closing over her.

The silent sons wanted her to climb the structure. She knew they risked much to get her there, but she would not leave until she knew what they feared. Maybe, just maybe, she would discover something important.

14

IN TALL GRASS

Shadows and soft grass enveloped Mara. Long, thin stalks swayed before her vision like dancers on a stage.

Mara watched from her hiding spot, close to the silent sons yet far enough away to remain hidden. The Mara from the House of Sin and Silk would never have stayed to see who or what the priests of the Loyal Father faced. But Mara no longer stood on the long, flat deck of the pleasure barge. Olessa would not be there to scold her. The strong boys would not be there to crack their knuckles. Gia would not be there to stand by her side.

Then again, Gia would have stayed to discover the truth. Gia would not have been afraid to see. If Mara wanted to save her son's soul, she needed to be more like Gia and less like herself.

She glanced quickly at the sky. The stars still dazzled against the blackish field. The night was deep and dawn would sleep beneath the horizon for awhile yet. Mara had time enough.

She cradled her son close to her chest. She glanced down and smiled at his closed eyes and puckered lips. He would have been such a handsome man when he was grown. Moon maidens would have jumped to serve him.

Her heart twisted and hardened into a shard of coral. *No*, she thought, *he would not be one take moon maidens as patrons.*

Movement interrupted her idle thoughts. A form that could have been sculpted from moonlight melted from the shadows before the silent sons.

Mara's fingers tightened on her son. An ember of anger inflamed her heart.

The man wore pale wrappings that hid him head to toe. His hood cloaked his face in darkness. His fingers danced with anticipation.

Her eyes narrowed. "Brother Caspran," she whispered.

Unlike her first encounter with the priest, Mara noticed that with moonlight framing his form, daggers tucked into his garments glinted in the silvery light.

He squeezed his fists and rolled his shoulders. A breeze whipped through the park and sent the silent sons' black robes flapping. They stood before the man without a word passing from their lips. As always, their masks revealed nothing of the men behind them.

Brother Caspran slipped his fingers into the folds of his clothes. He pulled his fingers out and brought with them a slender blade he danced over his knuckles. "Good evening, kindly priests. Did you by chance miss Good King Sol's proclamation that all who've sworn oaths to the Six must confine their flesh to their houses of worship until Harvest Festival ends?"

The silent sons stiffened. The man flipped his dagger into the air, and it rose a glimmering shard against the wall. He caught it between his fingers and continued bouncing the razor over his knuckles.

"She is here, is she not? You're hiding the whore somewhere in the pretty grasses of the Blooming Ring, are you not?" His shadowed gaze scanned the park. "There is only one who would bring you fools out from your dying god's hovel tonight. You cluster together like a bunch of old hags watching their wigs being braided. There is of course no other reason you'd be in this place on this night other than for Mara."

Mara's eyes widened as he spoke her name. She'd never met him once in her life, yet he spoke her name like they'd been common enemies for ages.

"You're desperate to save the whore, aren't you?" he asked.

The silent sons did not reply.

Caspran smirked and flipped his palm so the dagger would land within it. He closed his fist on the blade and held it before the priests. Drops of crimson oozed from his wraps and dripped onto the grass. "I know a thing or two about desperation. Your Loyal Father happily visited it upon me. He turned his back on me. He spit on me. I remember holding my daughter's body in my arms. I remember looking into her dead eyes and wondering why the Six would do such a thing. We were their children, too, just like you!"

The man's hand shook. Mara tightened her grip on her son. She looked for any reaction in the silent sons, but they might as well have been statues. No matter the painful devastation that darkened Caspran's past, he would hear no apology from men who had sworn their voices would never ride the breeze as long as their bones walked the land.

Brother Caspran seemed to acknowledge the same thought as Mara. He lifted his fist, opening the palm wrapped in leathers to the world. Blood dulled the little dagger's glimmer and soaked his glove.

"We will find her. Nothing can stop the serpents from rising. The King will bury your sun and raise his own, and then the stain of the Six will be forever crushed. Unless, of course, your Loyal Father will bestow some of his mighty power upon his faithful? Perhaps he'll bless you with his strength? Perhaps he'll save those who swore their life to him? Perhaps his magic isn't really dying, and all the fears that make your skinny little bones shake beneath those flapping robes of yours will finally disappear? If you have true faith in a true god, then you will be protected, will you not?"

Caspran flicked his wrist, and the bloody blade spun slowly around his hand. It floated over his stained wrappings like a moth might flutter around a flame.

Loyal Father, Mara prayed, protect them. *They are your silent sons. Don't let another die for me.*

One of the silent sons raised a hand draped in black. His pale fingers protruded from the dark robe. Lightly he touched them to the brow of his mask, its expression one of tearful sorrow. He motioned at Caspran with the same fingers and bowed.

"Forgive me?" Caspran asked in a shaking tone. "How dare you offer me forgiveness! I need no forgiveness. I need no compassion from the likes of you. You should be begging forgiveness from *me*. You should be on your knees, hoping I show mercy on you for the sins your gods committed."

Another silent son mirrored the first's gesture. And so did another. And so did yet another. The silent sons all at once forgave the priest of the Serpent Sun, bowing their heads in respect to the man.

"Filth and vermin! *Filth and vermin!*" Caspran flicked his wrist, and the dagger whistled from its orbit around his hand. It zipped through the silent sons, bursting in and out of their flapping robes, moving so fast Mara's eyes had to work to catch the flashing glints of silver.

"What's wrong, silent sons?" he asked with a cackling laugh. "Did your Loyal Father abandon you in your time of need? Did the magic that once burned through your veins whither like a flower beneath the power of the Serpent Sun? How does it feel to know he abandoned you? Tell me...*How does it feel!*"

The man bellowed harder as his dagger tore fabric and flesh. The line of silent sons trembled. A gloss wet their dark robes and splattered red over the grass. Mara shuddered. She closed her eyes and pressed her sleeve against her lips to smother her cry. She had never seen such violence, never thought living beings capable of taking such pleasure in such a horrible act.

"Take this blade for a tithe, priests," Caspran continued. "Your dedication to the Loyal Father is commendable even if misguided. He has abandoned you, and now you die. For what? A whore and her dead bastard?"

Mara cursed herself for being weak. She cursed herself for not knowing what to do, for not having the power to stop the madman from slaughtering the only people in Sollan who showed her kindness.

"Stop!" Mara screamed, jumping to her feet.

The dagger paused above a pile of black robes and white masks dripping blood from their eyes and noses. His dagger hovered over his open palm. Like the masks, it soaked in the blood of its victims.

She'd doomed herself. She'd stood and doomed herself. The silent sons died for nothing. They all died for nothing.

Caspran's shadowed gaze drifted in the direction of Mara's voice. He snapped his fingers, and any remaining blood on his dagger turned to scarlet smoke and vanished on the wind.

Wind flipped through Mara's ashen cloak. She stared at Caspran, a statue frozen by fear and hardened by anger.

He took a step forward. Mara's lip trembled. Her knuckles whitened on her son.

"We'll find you!" Caspran shouted. "We'll gut you like a pig and take your son. You won't succeed, Mara. You will never make it to the Mother's temple by sunrise. You are not as close as you might think."

Caspran's chest heaved. His dagger flipped madly around his body. He thrust his palm forward, and the razor whistled toward Mara. She sucked in her breath and closed her eyes, twisting to protect her child's body. All around her, the blade hacked away at grass and flower. Thin stems flew into the air.

And then, silence. Mara slowly opened her eyes. She stared at her son, cradled as he was in her arms. Nothing cut her skin. Nothing tore her burlap.

Mara faced Brother Caspran. The man's gaze swept across the park. He shook his head and twisted on his heel, marching through the grass until the shadows entombed him. "There is no way in to Hightable but through its gate. I will find you there."

Mara swallowed the knot twisting her throat. *He didn't see us. No, he couldn't see us. We stood before him, and still he could not find us.*

I told you, Olessa's voice whispered. *Ash and burlap keep you safe. But that's not important at the moment. He let some other bit of knowledge slip. If you weren't such a glimmer-clouded fool you'd have caught it. Your son is a bastard, and he called him one.*

Mara squeezed her eyes shut to drown Olessa's voice. "My son would have been more than that."

You stupid girl, her madame hissed. *Think!*

"He…" Mara opened her eyes and stared at the murderous stranger. "He knows my child is a boy."

No one knew Mara's child. No one had seen him in the city. If this mysterious man had gone to the House of Sin and Silk with his flying dagger…

Mara blinked the tears from her eyes. She bit hard on her lip and wrapped her son in her arms. Visions of Olessa and Gia screaming as the dagger buried in their flesh over and over and over again flared across her thoughts. They died for her. Caspran had gone to her home and tortured the only people she ever knew or loved, and they had died for her. No one would be left to bury Olessa. No one would be left to send Gia's spirit to the Six.

"Murderer!" she rasped. "I don't care if you hear me. You're a monster! Monster!"

Mara tried calming her frantic heart. She scanned the park, but from the aqueduct behind her to the gently curving wall ahead, no sign of the man remained.

Rustling from the pile of bodies tore her from her thoughts. Trembling fingers long and pale appeared within the bloody garbs.

The painful knot she swallowed leapt back into her throat. Mara hurried to the bodies. She grimaced, trying as gently as she could to shift the dead priests off the living one. Blood stained her burlap sleeve clear to her elbow. It wet her fingers and seeped beneath her nails.

The priest's hand clasped hers. She planted her feet and grunted, pulling him from his deceased brothers.

He made a muffled sound behind his cracked mask. Mara glanced behind her, half expecting the silent son's murderer to melt out of the wall's shadow, but Caspran did not.

Mara swallowed. She faced the priest and clenched his hand. "It's okay, I'm here, I'm here."

He squeezed her hand before releasing it. His fingers moved to his expressionless mask, the mask of the silent son who had been her savior since the beginning. He clasped the mask's chin and lifted, and both false face and robe fell away.

Blood trickled from his thinning hair and slid down his smooth, milky temples. His eyes were gleaming pools of polished brown, and when he saw her, he smiled like one might smile at a wayward child cresting the last hill before returning home.

"I'm so sorry," Mara said. Her trembling fingers caressed his jaw.

She placed his head into her lap and gently rocked him. "This is my fault. You and your brothers didn't have to die. I should have done something. I should have said something sooner. I thought I was strong. I—I thought I could face the king." She choked down a sob. "I'm sorry, but I can't. I don't know why you help me, but I'm not who you think I am. I'm nothing. I will never stop the king. His serpent priests will kill me."

"Mara, Mara," the silent son whispered. He reached into her hood and caressed her jaw. "You are so much more than nothing."

"You know my name?" Mara's tears filled her eyes and dripped onto his bloody cheeks. "You spoke! You are a silent son. Your vows keep you from speaking. Please, don't forsake them for me."

The silent son smiled and pinched her chin. "I forsake nothing. For you, every silent son would throw off his mask and sing until the stars died."

"But why? Why do you care about me? Why do they want me dead and my child's body?"

"They are an old enemy, Mara, and they will destroy the Six if you fail. The rest of man will follow after. They…" he grimaced, his nose distorting into a wrinkled wedge.

He coughed, and blood wet his lips. The silent son grabbed her wrist. He looked into her eyes. Tears poured from his. "I am afraid. If there are no gods in the heavens, where will my soul go when I die?"

She bent over and pressed her brow to his, closing her eyes. "Do not worry, my friend. The Six will receive you with open arms. You died for me. If I could, I would see you safely there myself, and if any god thought to cast you out, they would answer to me."

The priest laughed, and his cheeks swelled. His tears wet her skin, and hers wet his. His hand left her wrist as his fingers caressed her temples. "I am honored to have met you. When the time comes when we meet again, I hope you'll share a glass of wine with me at the Six's table and speak of brighter days."

"If the Six will have me, I swear it."

"They will. Now go, Mara. Climb. *Climb*." His hands lightly squeezed her cheeks. She opened her eyes and saw all the words he had yet to say swirling within his dark orbs, carried on the tide of memories welling within him.

The silent son's mouth opened. He tried speaking, but only a long sigh escaped his lips. The light in his eyes faded, and his hands fell from her.

Mara kissed his brow and closed his eyes. She stood and said a prayer for all the fallen priests. Ahead, the aqueduct waited.

15

THE CLIMB

If eternity was a measurable distance, Mara thought it would stand as tall as the aqueduct towering overhead. She stood at the base of what one might laughably call steps snaking around the arch's base in steep flights.

"Steps…" Mara shook her head and rolled her eyes.

She prodded a step with her foot. The stair would barely fit both her small feet. "These aren't steps. These are misplaced bricks."

Each flight scaled at a sharp angle up one side of the square pillar before turning sharply to the next side and climbing higher. The breeze she once welcomed for its cool, crisp caress now seemed more a taunting gale that eagerly waited to fling her from a great height.

No rail kept the fool who dared scale the pillar safe. "I suppose I'll be an acrobat too tonight. I've lived so many lives in so few hours. Who knows what title I'll wear when I reach the Mother's steps?"

Mara tightened the burlap wrapped around her son. She tucked him deep into her robe so she could use both hands on the perilous climb. His weight tugged her forward. He would keep her off balance as she ascended, but she could only hope the Six guided her steps well enough to keep them both from harm.

Her teeth clenched, her back pressed firmly against the pillar, she placed her foot upon the first step, and then she placed the next. The movement repeated, achingly slowly at first, more quickly once her confidence increased.

Mara tried not to think about the dizzying height. Instead, she let her mind drift to other things. She imagined her son playing in the House of Sin and Silk's kitchen. Chef Faratta scolded him for sneaking a scoop of stew, but he flashed his round eyes, and the old woman melted like ice in boiling water. He sucked the butter and garlic glistening on his fingers, licking his little lips as he grinned at his mother.

He came no higher than her knee then, and kitchen grease matted his hair and stained his clothes. She would try to bathe him at night, but he hated bath time even though he loved diving into the Sapphire Sea. Her son was a natural swimmer and didn't fear the coral sharks like she did, but even then, she never quite felt comfortable watching him paddling alone in the dark and briny waters.

Sometimes, she would bend and cup his chin in her hand. She'd call him her little coral shark and say he couldn't swim because she feared he would forget to come back to her.

Her son would giggle and wrap his arms around her leg. He would tell her how silly she was, that he knew he wasn't a coral shark and would never forget his mom no matter how much fun the sharks promised or the forgotten ruins of lost kingdoms they begged to show him.

Mara stifled her own chuckle at the fantasy scrolling through her thoughts. She reached another corner in the pillar and grasped it for support, quickly turning the sharp angle. Hightable towered over the rest of Sollan, and so the world she knew slowly shrank into tiny points of light and miniature roofs topped by chimney whiskers.

Her foot found another brick. She leaned onto the step. It cracked and sent a line of dust trailing to the ground.

Cold sweat rolled down her back. It glimmered on her chest. It wet her palm and stained her son's burlap a deep shade of brown.

Looking down at him, she glimpsed the ground below. The broken step crumbled and fell away, leaving a gap like an old man's smile, his throat the deadly drop looming beneath her.

Mara forced her eyes straight ahead. Her fingers clawed for a handhold that did not exist. She pressed her back against the arch and inhaled, looking to the stars.

"Gia," she whispered, "I've never been this high before. I'm not so sure if I like it. I think I might prefer a bite from a coral shark to cracking my neck after a long fall."

Mara inhaled. She stretched her foot over the gap. Thankfully, the next step held tight against the pillar. Mara exhaled and continued on her way.

Once again, her thoughts drifted. Her son had grown and stood just above her belly. She had to remind herself every time she saw him how far he'd come from a babe wrapped in burlap in her arms.

He spoke often of going on adventures in lands far from the House of Sin and Silk. He had dreams of hunting for titan relics and discovering the lost kingdoms of the Second Sun. He fashioned swords out of broomsticks and fought imaginary alp demons. He crafted spell books out of Olessa's discarded ledgers and worked miracles in his imagination not seen since the Six first waged their war against the titans. All the while, Mara would watch from her station in the kitchen, patiently peeling shrimp and cutting soft fin bass for hungry patrons.

He loved spells and stories of magic. His jaw would go slack and eyes wide whenever Gia snuck into the kitchen and whispered stories of the miracles the

Six's priests worked throughout Urum. He wanted to serve them one day. He wanted to work miracles people would remember, and not just the people in Eloia. Eloia was just a kingdom to him. He wanted the whole world to know his name.

Mara reached the middle of the stairs. The wind was an endless howl in her ears, and her heartbeat a pounding war drum with it. She turned to the next flight, and her stomach dropped. Most of the steps on that side of the arch had crumbled away, leaving a dangerous breach for her to cross.

If she wanted to reach the top, it would require a great leap.

"Gods, this is awful."

She peeled her back from the wall and came to her knees, both of which barely fit onto a step. One hand cradled her robe where she'd tucked her son. The other hand gripped the broken step before her.

Mara leaned forward. The drop seemed to stretch ten leagues more as she stared down the length of the aqueduct's arch.

"I can do this," she said. "The silent sons believed in me. They are gone now, and if I do not do this, I will join them."

She gripped the stair. Her muscles tensed. She leaned forward and froze, eyes still glued to the ground.

"Come on, Mara, you can do this." Mara clenched her teeth. "Do this!"

With a deep inhale, Mara leaned onto the balls of her feet. Her toes dangled from step's broken edge. She sprung, and her body flew from the laughable safety of the stairs.

The chasm of empty space loomed beneath her. She leaned forward, flailing for the broken step across the gap, realizing in a moment of horror her jump wouldn't take her completely there.

Mara wrapped her arm around her child as her ribs slammed against the jagged brick. Air rushed from her lungs. Her feet dangled over the deadly drop. Her weight and the uneven steps threatened to tug her to her death.

"*Nnnn*…no! No!"

Mara clawed at the stair. She dug an elbow into the stone and pressed her weight onto her arm. A single, deep grunt rumbled from deep within her.

Using her elbow as leverage and her free hand to keep her steady, Mara heaved herself higher. Her body inched up. Her arm strained and trembled. Her slick palm threatened to slide from beneath her any moment.

She lifted a leg, straining to pull her knee to the broken stair. It raked against the rock, and she winced at the hot flash of pain it scraped against her shin.

Her knee planted on the bottom step. The tears from her pain turned to a wide smile, and she pulled the rest of her body onto the stairs.

Mara twisted to her side. She kissed her son's brow and turned so her back pressed firmly against the pillar.

Laughter bubbled from her lips. If she had more room, she would have danced for joy. As it was, with her luck, dancing would have brought the steps crashing down and alerted a serpent priest or simply sent her plummeting to her death. She had no desire to turn a corner and come face to face with Ial-ane's snake or break her neck on the flowers of the Blooming Ring.

Mara licked the sweat collecting on her lip and came to her feet. She continued on, trying her best to ignore her throbbing shin.

"Let's see," she murmured. "How old is he now?"

Her son had grown closer to manhood and stood just as tall as his mother. His voice cracked awkwardly at times, and the hair on his lip and chin made him look as if he'd been eating soot from a brazier.

One of the strong boys offered to teach him how to shave his face, but he refused. It was a sign of him becoming a man, and he wore his soft beard like a badge of honor bestowed by a high priest of the Six. So too he brandished a wandering eye. He tried little to hide it, seeing how the barge's patrons cared little to hide their own gazes from washing up and down the maidens.

Mara often caught him gazing at the younger girls. She warned him that Olessa would beat him silly if she caught him drooling over one of her assets, but it soon became clear the boy pondered if a beating might be worth a way-ward glance or three.

It would be around then that he finally gathered enough courage to tell her he would leave the House of Sin and Silk. Mara fought him at first, but she knew in her heart there would come a time when her child would want to see the world beyond Olessa's floating kingdom. Growing up with Gia's stories and eavesdropping on sailors' drunken, boastful tales had addicted his heart to whatever might lay beyond the horizon. He would never be truly happy unless he struck out on his own so he could find his way.

Mara's heart twisted. She didn't know if she could let him go.

Her gaze drifted to the pouch of her cloak where he rested. Her arms clasped around his body. Her dirty arms. The arms beneath the old burlap. The arms stained by sweat and blood and her dark travels.

"What that I would give to have these dreams come to pass," she said.

Mara turned to the arch. She placed her palm against the cool brick and pressed her brow onto the stone. "You are a fool, Mara. He will never know steaming stew or Faratta's scoldings. He will never defy you and swim without fear of the coral sharks. He will never make swords from broomsticks and spells from ledgers. He will never look longingly at moon maidens and twist your heart into a worried knot by sailing the Sapphire Sea for relics of lost ages."

She clenched her fist and rapped it softly on the stone. With a heavy sigh, she continued on her way, turning yet another corner. Only then did she realize the top of the aqueduct waited one short flight away.

Mara steadied her steps despite the excitement racing through her veins. She climbed the lest steps. She hoisted herself onto the aqueduct with a smile.

A river rushed through through a deep channel carved down the middle of the structure. Water dumped out the aqueduct's mouth and careened like a crystal ribbon into Upper Sollan. A stone walkway bordered each side of the channel leading toward Hightable's wall and the heart of the city beyond.

She nearly strode toward Hightable without another thought but hesitated instead of marching onward. Mara turned. She walked to the edge of the aqueduct. She straightened at the overlook and smiled at the city.

First came the fine apartments and estates of Upper Sollan. Lanterns lit its walls and gardens in soft blues and golds, glittering off the glass windows of the buildings around them. Smoke curled from slender chimneys and drifted toward the stars. The avenues sloped like rivers on a mountain toward Lower Sollan. There, she barely made out the cramped shops and homes, the streets bustling with bobbing lanterns and revelers dancing with full cups of wine as drums and cymbals played happy tunes.

Lower Sollan halted at the shoreline. The docks formed long, thin lines, like the fingers of a dead silent son reaching for the horizon. Beside a stretch of empty water that led to the open sea, the faint lights of the Floatwaif glittered on the waters. She could barely see the barges from where she stood, yet she swore she could smell the rich scent of coral shark stew and fried shrimp seasoned with a hint of salt ever-present on the breeze.

Mara had never stood so high above the world. She looked down at her son and smiled.

"Do you think this is how a god sees Urum?" she wondered. "No wonder Good King Sol wishes to ride his great serpent to the stars. He has outgrown this world of men and titans' bones and lusts for higher things."

Mara held her son before her. She lifted him high and turned him to the city. "This is Sollan, my son, the grandest city of Eloia, and even if it is only for a moment, know that you rise higher than all others in it."

A gust of wind roared around her. It threw back her hood and sent her burlap flapping around her legs. Mara closed her eyes and committed the city and the moment she shared with her son to her to memory. She may never rise so high again, and it would be a shame to forget such a view.

16

LIKE A THIEF IN THE NIGHT

Mara had successfully scaled the ungodly wall that protected Hightable, the beating heart of Sollan and jewel of the kingdom of Eloia. She thought it odd that the past kings of Eloia would build a wall so high it hid the kingdom they ruled from their eyes. If she could have woken every day to see the world from so high, every home and tower in Hightable would have had walls of polished glass.

Yet the residents within Hightable viewed the world much differently than Mara. None of their buildings eclipsed Hightable's towering barrier. They lived in a garden world all their own and desired not to look upon anything beyond their gilded cage.

Squat towers dotted the wall at even spaces like the spokes on a king's crown. Midway between each tower, an aqueduct like the one Mara scaled struck out over the Blooming Ring and sent water careening into Upper Sollan.

Within the wall's massive circumference, beautiful lawns brimming with blooming flowers and willows cloaked in white and scarlet blossoms snaked in curling patterns around sprawling estates. Channels of crystalline water ran throughout the neighborhood. Gentle arches formed causeways over the rivers and connected gardens and estates to one another like veins and arteries might keep a titan's heart pumping blood to the giant's body.

Deep within Hightable, beyond the gardens and the mansions, clustered like the soul within the city's heart, Mara spied a mass of buildings scaling a hill crowned by Good King Sol's gleaming gold palace. One of those temples housed the statue of the Mother, and at her feet, the Ever-Burning Flame.

She shook her head, pulling her hood higher over her brow. "The priests are prisoners in houses of worship. The nobles are prisoners of Hightable. The fortunate are prisoners in Upper Sollan. These people, they live in beauty, but really, only the poor are free to come and go. I would risk a beggar boy with a knife clutched behind his back over living in Good King Sol's shadow any day. For all its beauty, this city is one prison built around another."

Mara looked to her son and adjusted his burlap. "And tonight blood will stain those prison walls," she whispered. "I know it. Before this night is done, we will witness more of the Serpent Sun's insanity."

The aqueduct disappeared within the barrier. She stepped onto the wide wall and peered into the noble district. A dizzying drop greeted her, ending in a labyrinth of thorny bushes and ponds brimming with lanterns floating on crystal lilies.

She peered to the side along the long curve of the structure. Far from where she stood, a few estates dared to grow to the height of the wall. Their tiled roofs rested at gentle angles against the barrier's smooth stone side. If she could make it to one of the estates unseen, she could perhaps leap to the roof and descend without breaking both her legs.

Mara glanced behind her. In the distance, bobbing lanterns slowly worked their way around the top of the wall. No doubt a patrol followed behind those lights, searching for any sign of the ashwalk pilgrim.

She darted in the opposite direction, but her legs wobbled and protested, so she slowed her pace. The arm supporting her son ached and trembled. Her shin throbbed from the bloody scrape the aqueduct stairs gifted her. Her vision lost some of its clarity, a sign Olessa's glimmer faded from her blood. The deep blue of the night paled against the horizon. Her climb had gobbled much of her time. Dawn waited in the wings, ready to seal her fate.

Mara reached the first tower and crouched within its shadow. Dark windows spanned the side facing the lower city. The tower was capped with a flagpole proudly waving the flapping banner of Good King Sol like a feather in a cap. Rolling her eyes at his crest, she ducked beneath the windows and darted across the wall's walkway. Voices from within drifted to her ears, grumbling guards complaining about missing Harvest Festival's boisterous parties and smiling women.

With the tower behind her, she strode quietly along the wall's curve. As she approached the high roofs, her excitement brought new energy to her weary eyes. She was so close. Once inside Hightable, the temple would only be a walk through a manicured gardens. Soon, the long night and her ashwalk would end, and her son's spirit would fly to the Six to be received by the Burning Mother's open arms.

Mara came to the section of the wall near the high roofs. She stared at their ruddy tiles, the excitement and hope bubbling in her heart cooling as she grimaced at the gap she must leap to make it to across.

A crumbling stairwell on a thin aqueduct pillar was one thing. The space between her and the estate was another. The breach laughed at her. It mocked her. It told her she'd come so far, but now it would turn her back because the treasures of Hightable were never meant for her filthy feet to trample.

"Maybe a tower is empty," she mused, giving up on her plan to leap like a grasshopper from wall to roof.

She turned to the tower she passed moments before. A bobbing lantern wandered into view around it. Behind the lantern light, a line of guards marched like insects following a flame.

Cursing, Mara whipped around and scanned the next tower. Another patrol melted from its walls, led by the ominous, bobbing lantern. There she stood, cloaked in burlap and ash and stained by her blood and the blood of others. The two patrols closed around her like a hare with a broken leg between two wolves.

"No, no, no!"

She ran toward one patrol, searching for a way down the wall. Seeing nothing, she turned and ran a short distance the other direction. Unfortunately for her, the city kept the wall clear.

Mara crouched, trying desperately to shrink as small as possible. In a few moments, not even that would save her. She gripped her son and shivered under the piercing whistle of a chill wind.

"I've come so far," Mara said as she closed her eyes. "I can't fail now. Not now."

A shadow slid over her. Mara clenched her jaw and lurched blindly toward what she had no doubt was a soldier with his sword drawn, her nails ready to rake the man's face before he ran her through.

A weight hit her body. Mara twisted and spun toward the edge.

She tumbled forward. She opened her mouth to scream, but a hand clapped over her lips before her wail could pierce the night.

"Are you trying to get us both killed?" a man asked. "Scream and my ass'll be the rug for one of those serpent priest's bedrooms. That's if I'm lucky. I hear our king's little pet likes dining on the Six's holy men and women. I swear, you common thieves make the more talented among us look like fools with your bumbling about like a—wait, are you wearing burlap?"

The man's hand left her mouth and spun her around. He wore tight black garments and boots trimmed in black that came to his knees. His fingers wagged like peachy caterpillars from his fingerless black gloves. His face lay mostly hidden within a loose hood, but his hooked nose defied the shadows and framed thin lips that wore the constant, faintest grin despite the thin scar running alongside his smile.

He leapt back farther than any normal human and considered her from a distance. "An ashwalk pilgrim, then? Are you the sorceress Good King Sol is tearing the lower city apart for and sending his soldiers into Hightable to stop?"

"I am, but I'm no sorceress."

The man smirked. "And he is certainly no good king. I have to admit, you don't help your case with all that blood staining your arms and legs. You look like you clawed your way out of some child's nightmare."

"I doubt you would look any better after what I've gone through tonight. Are you—are you going to call the soldiers?"

His lips split into a full grin that framed his long teeth. "I'd be a fool with a death wish if I did."

"So you won't turn me in?"

He shrugged. "Didn't have any plans on it. Don't know why I didn't see you balled up on the wall, either. It was like you weren't there until I was on top of you. You practically had both of us falling over the side. Here I was just minding my own business, off to Hightable on this happiest of nights to cut the pursestrings of Sollan's wealthiest when I come upon an ashwalk pilgrim. The ashwalk pilgrim, more precisely. The sorceress from the Second Sun with a thirst for Good King Sol's blood, if you would believe his pompous little criers and those masked heretics of his."

Mara glanced behind her. How the guards did not see them, she had no idea. "Please, show me where you cross. They will recognize me. They will kill me and take my child. I—I don't know why they haven't said something already. I can almost see their faces in their helmets!"

"It is oh so very dark outside," he said slyly.

She charged toward him, halting barely an arm's length from the man. She peered into his hood, locking stares with the eyes glittering from within its shadow. "You are a thief?"

"Uh, yes, I believe that is the term. Now good evening, oh mighty sorceress of the Second Sun. I leave you to your ashwalk and pray to the Slippery Sinner we never meet again."

The thief flashed a mischievous grin and clicked his heels. His body burst into wisps of inky smoke and drifted over the gap. He reformed on the estate's roof and stretched like a cat freshly woken from its nap.

"Wait!" Mara hissed.

He glanced over his shoulder and pinched his hood. "I'm kind of busy. The nobles should be good and drunk by now. Easiest pickings of the year, you know."

"You can't just leave me here. The patrols…they'll see me!"

"That's my problem because…?"

Mara looked frantically to either side. The shadows keeping Mara hidden would flee beneath the light of the lanterns, and the lanterns drew closer in a terrifyingly steady beat. "Please, sir. I've got nowhere to go. I've come so far. I can see the temples. I just—I just want my son's soul to reach the Mother. It's trapped inside him."

Her lips trembled while the thief's pressed into a flat line. "I'm a man of the Slippery Sinner, not the Burning Mother. I've got to pay respects to my god tonight, and he demands the coin of the pigs in Hightable. If the Mother truly is on your side, she'll see you out of this mess."

"Maybe she brought you to me." The footsteps of the patrol echoed on the stones. Mara inched to the edge of the wall. "Maybe the Sinner helps her. The silent sons helped me. They died to save me."

"Their bodies outside the wall…you witnessed their murder?"

"Yes, and now the Sinner brought you here to play your part to save us. Please. In the name of all the Six, have mercy on me!"

She heard the low voices of the soldiers as they exchanged words. The thief clenched and unclenched his fists. "Damnable woman, tossing my soul in a vat of guilt like shrimp in hot oil."

He snapped his fingers, and his body disbursed into a dark cloud. The smoke raced across the gap and swelled around Mara. The man reappeared, but a veil of grey mist surrounded him. He wrapped an arm around her and placed a finger to his mouth. "Not a word from those sad little lips of yours my lady, unless you'd like a soldier's sword through those perky melons."

Mara stood still and silent as if she was carved from the wall itself. The bobbing lanterns came within a stone's throw, their light illuminating the line of marching soldiers behind them.

She squirmed, but the thief's strong arm held her still. He clapped his hand over her mouth, and together they watched as the patrols crossed paths not more than an arm's length from where Mara and her companion stood within the mist.

The captain of one patrol nodded at the other. "Captain Balthel," he said.

Balthel adjusted the tall lantern pole and mirrored the first captain's nod. "Captain Isseus. No sign of the sorceress?"

The two patrols came to a halt with both captains dead center before Mara and the thief. Captain Balthel shook his head. "None at all, but best keep your eyes sharp. I've got word that the witch murdered a bunch of silent sons in Blooming Ring. Pretty gruesome scene, they say."

An angry pit burned in Mara's chest. She clenched her teeth to keep her tongue behind them.

"Really?" Captain Isseus shook his head. "I thought the Six's priestly dogs were suckling from her breasts. Why would she murder them?"

"Sister Ialane said those priests were heretics among their order, that they tried saving the king from the woman. Don't let their deaths fool you on the other silent sons. Every priest of the Six has a little taint inside them, especially the ones holed up in their temples."

Isseus puckered his lips. He tightened his grip on the lantern pole and straightened. "Best keep at it then. Signal if you see anything."

Captain Balthel saluted. He adjusted the lantern pole on his shoulder and led his patrol down the curve of the wall while Captain Isseus led his in the opposite direction. Mara and the thief waited silently until the boots of both patrols faded into the night.

Mara pulled the man's hand from her mouth. "I didn't kill those silent sons. A man in white named Caspran did, and he is friends with that Ialane Donra of the Serpent Sun. He has a blade that needs no hand to find flesh. He ripped the priests apart. I watched as he slaughtered them!"

"*Shhh…*" The thief looked with concern to either side of the wall. "Let's get off this thing and somewhere where we can talk."

He turned to the estate roof and gently wrapped his arm around Mara's waist. She stepped back, but his arm kept her from going far.

"I can't cross that. I barely made it up the aqueduct stairs."

The thief laughed and looked at Mara with wide, glittering eyes. "You climbed the Waterstair? I doubt I'd even make it up that thing without some of the Sinner's magic in my fingers. There's a running joke among thieving circles that if a fellow rogue's gone missing, check the Waterstair for their bones. More than one cocky vagabond has met a grisly fate from a fall from those steps. You really are a sorceress, aren't you?"

"I'm not—no!"

The thief laughed as he tightened his grip around Mara's waist and leapt in a graceful arc over the gap. She watched in horror as the solid safety of the wall slipped away, replaced by the empty, churning air. The wind strengthened and sent her cloak flapping like moth's wings around her waist. The wind pushed her, prodded her farther than she ever should have been able to jump.

They landed light as feathers on the manor's clay tiles. Mara's stomach lurched, but she swallowed the burning bile and let her world steady.

"Easy there," the thief said. He pointed to a chimney poking above the roof. "Let's have a chat in the chimney's shadow. It'll keep us out of sight. There are a few questions I'd like to ask a very peculiar ashwalk pilgrim I met tonight."

17

SHADOW PLAY

"Sander Hale, Priest of the Slippery Sinner, Collector of Gold Curiosities and Patron of Pious Reminders." The thief took a deep bow.

Mara leaned against the chimney. She adjusted her son against her neck and smiled weakly. "Mara, moon maiden of the House of Sin and Silk."

"A moon maiden?" Sander smirked. His eyes glittered beneath his hood, the only feature illuminated by light his hooked nose and scarred, impish smile. "Everyone in Sollan knows about the House of Sin and Silk. How is old Olessa? She still using that same awful wig everybody knows is fake but nobody has the balls to tell her? I was just a boy when I saw her last and snuck aboard the barge, but I'll never forget the whooping she could give with that damnable silk glove."

Mara's head dipped, her gaze drifting to the filthy body of her son. "I pray she still lives, but Caspran knew my son was a boy. Only she and two others knew I had a son and not a daughter. One of those died before me. I fear the same fate has met the other two. They...they were my family."

"Chin up, Mara." Sander gently lifted her chin until her eyes meet his eyes. He gripped her shoulder and squeezed. "The priests of the Serpent Sun have a way of knowing secrets. That doesn't mean your friends are dead. You've met Sister Ialane Donra and that hound of hers Brother Caspran Bilshabal. They're both priests of the Serpent Sun, and they serve Good King Sol faithfully. The evil they stain this world with, it is a reflection of the darkness festering in our monarch's soul."

"Why does he hate the Six? Why does he hunt me?"

Sander shrugged. He crossed his arms and stared toward the king's palace and the great temples surrounding it. "I've only just returned to Sollan from that frozen shit hole affectionately called Skaard. When my parents took me from the warm fields of Eloia, Sol's father sat on the throne and called the city Thean. Imagine my surprise when I return to the place of my birth only to discover the Six who have protected our kingdom since man clawed his way from the mud are now spit and cursed like tyrants and murderers. The fools turn their back to the gods and walk willingly into a serpent's maw."

"Then this cult of the Serpent Sun is as much a mystery to you as me."

"Somewhat." He cradled his chin and pursed his thin lips. "I have a few theories, but I won't burden you with them because theories are all they are and you clearly have enough on your mind."

"This great serpent god they serve, it has power." Mara kissed her son's head. "Ialane's serpent is no ordinary snake, and the way Caspran commands that razor…"

She shuddered, closing her eyes as the murders she witnessed flared in her mind. Magic came from the gods. All people on Urum knew that much. If the priests of the Serpent Sun did not worship one of the Six, then they must bend a knee to some undiscovered—or forgotten—god.

"The Six are still the true gods," Sander said. "Don't forget that. Whatever power it is this serpent brings, it can't defeat the power of the Six."

"But their power fades, Sander. The silent sons, they could barely help me, and when Caspran attacked them, they fell like wheat to a scythe's blade."

Sander grunted. He lowered his hand from his chin and squeezed his fist. His fingerless glove cracked as his knuckles whitened. "I feel it too. It's like someone soaked a rag in pepper oil and shoved it so far down my throat it's doused the fire of my soul. Those silent sons, they were men of Sollan. The corruption here has extinguished their flame. The Serpent Sun chokes the light of the Six. It is here the sickness started. It is here it will spread through all Urum if it's not stopped."

He raised his fist. He opened his palm, and within it held a swirling flame made of shifting cobalt smoke. "It won't be long before I'm the wheat staring down a sharpened scythe. It seems not even the Slippery Sinner can escape every judgement. That's rather a disappointing thought. It's why I joined up in the first place."

"What do you plan to do then? You can't stay in Sollan. This city isn't safe for a priest of the Six. They've imprisoned them in their temples. The serpents—they'll kill you if they find you wandering Hightable."

"Says the ashwalk pilgrim every soldier and loyal convert of the Serpent Sun hunts tonight," he said with a chuckle. "You're some kind of brave and many kinds of foolish for undertaking this journey. Let's hope your son's soul is worth the trouble."

"There's not enough gold to weight a scale large enough to tempt me. The Six protect me. They brought me to you, didn't they?" she gently touched the crook of his arm, her finger running down his forearm until it lingered lightly on his knuckles. "They brought you here to guide me to the Mother's temple, to help me complete my ashwalk."

Sander yanked his arm from her. He slipped on a tile and nearly tumbled down the roof but bent and caught his balance before he could topple over. Clearing his throat, he stood and wiped his fingers on his dark tunic.

"Oh, no, no, no, no. You really are a moon maiden, trying to rile my blood with that gentle touch of yours. Listen, Mara, I helped you get into Hightable. I know you're on a dangerous journey. But I, ah…" he shook his head. "…I don't do things like that. Men of the Slippery Sinner don't skip like happy fools into a shit storm like the one you're about to find yourself drowning in. We're survivors. We keep the histories. We sing the tales as we travel long roads. We tithe for the rich that are too selfish to do it themselves. None of that we would successfully accomplish if we went parading into some heretic's arms or farted around the battlefield with a bunch of soldiers."

Heat rose in Mara's cheeks. She balanced on the roof, looking down at the man who should have been her savior. "Why even come to Hightable then? The Serpent Sun will know I'm here soon enough, and they'll be looking in the shadows where you'll be hiding. You think you're safe? Your power wanes, priest. Yet I am an ashwalk pilgrim, and somehow I have been blessed enough to avoid them."

"Hey, I'm only here to pick up a few gold coins and hopefully a gem or two from a drunk noble. As soon as I have enough to make my way north, I'll be back in Skaard reminding rich and poor alike sin casts a long shadow and none are safe from the Sinner's touch."

"You coward."

"I prefer battle savvy. Has a nice ring to it, doesn't it?"

"Fine. Leave. Thank you for your help, brave priest of the Slippery Sinner. I pray he doesn't judge you when you face him. Cowardice is a sin when it's shown to an innocent in need."

"Ah, but the Sinner never judges. He knows how weakly a human's heart beats when faced with the trials of this world. Isn't that a happy dogma?"

Mara turned her back to Sander. Her lips contorted in a frustrated line. No one in that cursed city would help her. She looked down at her son and forced a smile, pecking his soft brow. "We've made it this far, my love. We can make it to the temples, you and I."

Sander's shadow slipped over her shoulder. "The temples will be crawling with soldiers, and I'll bet every coin I steal tonight you'll find those wicked priests slithering all over them, too. Ialane and Caspran are the most powerful, but there are many more serpents like them in Sollan."

"I will make it to the Mother's steps." She rocked her son as if he might simply be sleep tucked as he was in her arms. "I have only known one life, one place, and yet I know when I look upon his face, no soldiers, no serpent priests, no king, and no heretic god will keep me from the temple. Olessa tells me the Six used a piece of themselves to make the first men and that a little of the gods burns in all of us. I believe her. I really do. I know them. I feel them, and they will light the way."

A long silence settled over them. A heavy tear slipped from her eye and rolled down her cheek. It fell from her jaw and splashed on her son's brow. "I have to believe her. If I don't have the Six, then I have nothing else but a dead child in my arms and a bounty on my head."

Sander's hand gently rested on her shoulder. "Mara, you have no weapon." His voice slipped into a sad and silken whisper. "You're covered in blood and filth and cloaked with burlap. You literally have no defense against the snakes. Those priests are powerful, and they say the king even has a great serpent of his own, a monster brought to life not seen since the old ages of Urum."

"I don't care. My son will rest in the Burning Mother's arms tonight. I swear on the Six and every other god that might be hiding in the stars that he will see her face in the Ever-Burning Flame, and he will dine with those at the long table who died for him on Harvest Festival."

"Oddly enough, I believe you." His hand left her shoulder and pinched her son's burlap hood, pulling it from the infant's face. "He would have been a handsome man."

"Yes, yes he would have."

She heard Sander's exasperated sigh quickly roll into a low groan. "You kill me. You really kill me. Sinner save me from this poor woman because she's got me in her grasp. It's the fucking bloody burlap. It'll get you every time."

Mara glanced over her shoulder. Sander reached into his collar and produced a small orb fastened to a silver chain. He yanked the chain from his neck and held the orb before Mara.

Within the round crystal, an odd bluish glow pulsed like a fairy's heart, surrounded by tiny pinpricks of light swirling around the crystal's center. He held it closer to her. "Go ahead, take it."

"It's magic?"

"Yes, it is. An artifact hard to come by and now probably impossible to make. I suppose it's fitting a woman worth a kingly ransom carries a priceless treasure. Wouldn't you agree?"

Gingerly, Mara took his gift. She fastened the chain around her neck and tucked the orb between her breasts. She expected to shiver from the cool glass, but when it touched her skin, warmth washed through her chest. "What does it do?"

"When you find yourself in that shit storm I mentioned, break it, and it will summon me to you. Sinner save us both from drowning in the sewage."

Her heart dropped, and so did her chin. "Then you really won't take me to the temple."

He clasped her chin and lifted it up. "I would that I could, but Sollan's not safe for either of us any longer. I need to gather coin for the journey to Skaard, and now I think I'll need to gather twice as much if I'll have a moon maiden as my companion."

Her eyes lit up as her mouth formed an o of surprise. "Take me across the sea? I've never been to Skaard. What about the House of Sin and Silk and Olessa and—and Gia? What about Gia?"

"Mara, the serpents will discover where you come from. That place is not safe for you. You can't go home, but maybe you can go on. This damned conscience of mine won't let me live with myself knowing I didn't do what I could to save you."

"I've never been across the sea. I don't know what Skaard is like."

"You'll wear furs instead of silks because it's colder than an ice titan's balls, but you'll have a life. I don't think I need to tell you that your life under Good King Sol's rule will be measured by hours and not years if you stay."

"I...I don't know..." Mara closed her eyes. "Gia, what should I do? Would you leave for Skaard, or would you return for me?"

"Gia would leave," Sander whispered. "I can tell you that much. I have to go now, Mara, but I will return to you before sunrise. Break the orb before then if you feel your life's in danger."

Mara nodded, her eyes still shut tight. "Thank you, Sander Hale. I'm glad you had a change of heart, although I do not know what made it beat again."

Sander chuckled. "Because, Mara, every son had a mother once."

18

A WEARY WOMAN

An ivy arch greeted Mara at the entrance to the garden labyrinth. She stood at the base of the tall estate, its shadow keeping her comfortably cloaked in darkness. She would need to traverse the verdant, blossom-speckled maze to get anywhere near the temples, but peering into the labyrinth's deathly quiet entrance sent a shudder down her spine. Something about the dark leaves, the pale grass, the flower petals hanging lazily from the ivy like snakes' hungry tongues—they were all mired in tranquil neglect. The confined air of Hightable let them grow, but their imprisonment suffocated their spirits.

She stepped into the maze and slowly traipsed through its sharp turns and shadowy lanes. Mara closed her eyes and imagined Gia walking with her.

"This is an odd place, Gia."

"This is how the others live. These are the ones who own the world and all the beautiful things within it."

Mara squeezed Gia's hand. "They don't own you."

"No," Gia said with a laugh, "our madame is the one with that claim."

"Are you okay?" Mara asked, opening her eyes. "I worry about you. I fear the worst for you and Faratta. I'm even afraid for Olessa. Good King Sol and his serpents wish to raise a sun by snuffing ours, I fear. They are wicked. They kill and take joy in it like they are patrons of a deathly maiden. I don't know how I could live with myself knowing they hurt you because of me."

They turned a corner in the labyrinth to face yet another long wall of ivy peppered with silky, sickly-sweet blossoms. "You must stop blaming yourself for the pain of others," Gia said. "You did nothing. You caused nothing. The serpents, the king, they are the ones to blame for this dark night. Never forget that, Mara. You are good in all of this, no matter what happens. The Six favor you. They always have. I've seen it for myself many times. So did Olessa, that is why she kept you safe. That is why she kept her promise to her brother. There is something about you the Six want, something they need, and King Sol knows and fears this."

"But I have nothing, Gia. I don't even have my collar anymore. A boy stole it to feed himself for a few days."

"Mara, Mara, it's not about what you own. It's about what you offer. Remember that when you stare into the Mother's flames."

Mara paused, her brows knitting together. "What I offer?"

She looked beside her, but her eyes met only a wall of ivy. Of course Gia had never been walking with her. Olessa's glimmer faded, and with its last bit of strength, it would trick her with illusions.

If Gia still lived, she was serving patrons, most of whom would be so drunk by then they could hardly stand. An image of Gia reclining in a corner, cleaning her nails while a patron emptied out his stomach in a chamber pot flashed through her mind. Mara grinned and stifled a snicker with her hand.

With her child cradled in her arm, she struck deeper into the maze. Her feet padded softly on the grass. Her free hand toyed with the ivy as she passed, and the leaves responded by tickling her palm.

Mara rounded a corner and came to a small square courtyard in the labyrinth with a marble fountain in its center. The fountain's glassy waters reminded Mara of her dry, burning throat. She licked lips plastered with dried skin and approached the fount. Resting against its smooth marble side, she massaged her ankles and exhaled as the soreness ebbed from her feet.

"I could almost sleep here for the night."

Mara dipped her hand into the waters. She tried not to grimace at her horrible reflection. The face peeking from the burlap hood turned her stomach. "Olessa would say I look like a rat that's somehow survived a swim with the sharks."

She dipped her face and scooped water into her mouth. The crisp liquid flowed down her throat and collected in a satisfying pool deep in her belly. She smiled and took another drink, water dripping from her knuckles.

"Pinne? Pinne is that you I hear splashing around in the fountain?" a woman called.

Mara froze. Water continued dripping from her knuckles and splashed into the pool. Not seconds ago, the drops barely made a sound. Hearing them then, each drop might as well have been a crack of thunder during a funeral prayer.

"Pinne?" the woman repeated, her tone notching up. "Get over here or I'll have the guards drag you myself. Your master is suffering so. Come!"

Mara lurched from the fountain. She darted in the opposite direction of the woman's voice and sprinted into an ivy-walled channel. It turned and twisted much like the lanes and avenues of Upper and Lower Sollan. She wiped the water dripping from her lips and smiled.

Once again, she'd avoided being caught. The Six truly did protect her.

She whipped around a corner and skidded to a halt. She'd reached the opposite end of the garden labyrinth, and before her stood a gazebo with delicate arches wrapped in hydrangeas with blooms every heavenly shade of pale.

Oil lamps lit the gazebo's interior with a flickering gold light while burning incense trailed the sultry perfume of sandalwood into the still air.

In the gazebo's center, a long table draped in ivory linens waited. On that table, a woman rested on her stomach. She draped a linen over her waist, but her back was bare and glimmering like polished wood.

"There you are, Pinne," the woman said without looking up, her tone tinged with an air of disappointment. "Come, give your master a massage. It's been such a dreadful night hosting my husband's silly Harvest Festival parties. I had to oversee the cleanup while he left with his friends for the lower city. No doubt looking for a whore to bed. Like he thinks I don't know the little adventures he has beyond the wall. I swear, men are all the same. If you'd lose just a tad more weight, Pinne, you might discover this secret for yourself. Your swelling waist has been so unseemly as of late. It fits so poorly set amongst the blossoms of my little garden, and I must say I've asked the kitchen staff to be on the lookout for you nabbing nibbles while they cook."

Fear froze Mara's feet. She stared at the woman, knowing that at any moment the noble might glance up and see that Mara was not the servant named Pinne, but the ashwalk pilgrim the entire city hunted. Mara could practically hear the woman's scream split the air.

"Well?" the woman asked, her disappointment edging on frustration. "Did I not order you to rub the weary from my back? Quit standing there like a dumbstruck glimmer fiend and get to work before I dock your rations."

The woman snorted a laugh. Mara fought the urge to spit in her hair.

Instead, Mara swallowed. She squeezed her son and edged to the gazebo. "Y—Yes. As you command."

"Good girl, Pinne."

A pitcher of oil rested on a pedestal by the massage table. Mara grabbed its silver handle and dribbled the gleaming liquid on the woman's porcelain skin. She frowned at the oiled hourglass of the noble's figure and her soft shoulders. Mara had dealt with worse at the House of Sin and Silk from both men and women, but somehow that night, she would have paid a handsome sum to treat a filthy beggar over a body with its edges worn smooth by a life of luxury.

While Mara shuddered, the noble shivered with delight. "The oil's still warm. It feels good. Don't go sparingly with it, Pinne. We've got plenty more."

"Yes, ma'am." Mara poured more oil onto the noble's glistening back. It streamed in thick lines onto the linen.

"Now work it in, and don't be shy. You know I like a little push."

Mara bit her lip and put her free hand into the oily slop. She worked her fingers into the doughy layers of the woman's shoulders.

"Harder, Pinne. You usually do better than this. I hope you haven't snuck any wine for Harvest Festival. You told me you don't drink, but one can never trust servants these days. Their stock is just so low, you see. And use both hands!"

Mara squeezed her son. *I would never let you go for the likes of her.*

"One-handed is a new technique," Mara said as she forced a smile. "The other ladies of Hightable all rave about it."

"They do?"

"Yes, ma'am. It is the newest fashion amongst the highborn, so the other household servants say. They say…Good King Sol prefers it."

"He does? Interesting. I—I do feel a certain loosening of the muscles I had not experienced before when you used two hands. Yes, it is very nice indeed. Very smooth. Very calming. This singlehanded massage is not so bad after all. Good King Sol knows what's best. I shall make sure to tell the other ladies how I enjoyed it."

Mara rolled her eyes. "Indeed, ma'am."

As she worked on her massage, her thoughts drifted to escape. She had no idea where the real Pinne might linger, but Mara doubted it wouldn't be much longer before the servant checked on her lady.

"Tell me, Pinne," the woman said, "have you heard anything of this sorceress stalking the lower city? I do hope she's burning some of the filth and flotsam down there. It could do with a good fiery cleansing before the king's men gut her."

Mara swallowed the glasslike lump in her throat and hoped her teeth wouldn't crack she clenched them so hard. "I've only heard she is an ashwalk pilgrim and that the priests of the Serpent Sun hunt her. Do you—do you know anything else?"

"I only know what the other ladies whisper. They say she's out to kill the king. Good luck with that, I say. I hear Good King Sol has already assumed a throne in heaven, riding on his glorious serpent, and we all know no god can be killed, even if it is a sorceress flinging spells."

"But is there room for another throne among the Six?"

The woman sucked in her breath. "Dear me, you stupid girl. Servants are so blissfully ignorant. You're property of House Iona. You wait on the most esteemed Lady Rin Iona. Don't go spouting off about the Six around anyone else if you'd like to keep your head. Some highborn still bend a knee at night when no one looks, but I'll not tempt my house with a serpent's wrath. Understand?"

"I do. Please forgive me."

"You are forgiven. You are from the lower city, after all. Children of your stock just do not have the mental capacity of the nobility. It is a fact you should know quite well by now." Lady Rin turned her head to the side. She smiled with her eyes closed while Mara's eyes shot wide as full moons.

"It won't matter much after tonight anyway," Lady Rin continued. "They say Good King Sol will purge our city of the Six soon enough. Once the cleansing begins—"

"Cleansing? Tonight?"

"Yes, tonight, or did that hollow head of yours think the king would stand to have those temples surrounding his home for all eternity? Why do you think he ordered every priest and acolyte into them? Not to keep them safe. Not to keep him safe. He's gathering them under his heel, so when the time is right, he can bring it crashing down on their little heads like a soldier's boot on roaches. What better time than Harvest Festival to wipe the stain of the Six from Sollan than when the city is drunk on wine and saltwater gin and bedding maidens on barges?"

"All those most loyal to the Six are in the lower city," Mara murmured. "There will be no one to hear the priests' screams."

"No one but those of us faithful to the Serpent Sun, and I for one will enjoy a nice glass of wine while I watch from my balcony as the Mother's temple burns. Oh—Pinne, you're massaging a little too hard. You'll leave a bruise!"

Mara caught her breath and softened her palm against the woman's shoulder even though she wanted nothing more than to break it and strangle her with a strip of burlap. Mara's gaze caught the flickering oil lamp, and for the briefest moment, she considered ripping it from the arch and tossing the flame on Lady Rin's oiled back.

Mara blinked away the dark thoughts. She remembered Vibiana's screams, and the wicked burns from the widow's hearth fire. Even though Lady Rin was more serpent than a snake, Mara's will lacked the hunger to visit that cruelty on another living being.

Instead, she would have to be satisfied that the blood of the silent sons who died protecting Mara covered Lady Rin's back. Ash from her cloak clogged the noblewoman's pores. Threads of burlap seasoned the woman's skin like peeled chives.

Mara straightened. "Lady Rin?"

"Yes, Pinne?"

"I'm afraid the oil's run low, and I have another new technique I'd like to use that the other servants rave about. They say the king himself created the technique, and it has yet to filter down to the others in Hightable. It is a secret, and one I have kept so close to my heart because I loved you so I wanted you to be the first in Hightable to experience it."

"Oh dear, really? Be a good girl and fetch some more oil, then. Don't take too long. I would hate to be forced to beat you on such a pretty night, and after you give me such a…gift as your, ah, love."

"Of course, Lady Rin. I'll return as quickly as I can."

She spun on her heel and darted from the gazebo. Her heartbeat thundered in her ears. Her oil-soaked fingers trembled. She apologized to Pinne the servant girl, who would probably get a beating when Lady Rin discovered that the ashwalk pilgrim had treated her that night and not her loyal servant.

Then again, perhaps the woman's status would keep her lips sealed. Mara could only imagine how the other ladies of Hightable would shun the one who let the king's would-be assassin and evil sorceress of the Six give her a back massage.

Mara grinned. Poor Lady Rin wouldn't sleep for a week, and best of all, she wouldn't dare tell another soul.

19

MARA'S CHOICE

Mara wove through one frustratingly beautiful garden after another. She hid in the shadows of unlit gazebos and pressed her back against the marble pools of glorious fountains. Always she kept the temples and grand palace in sight. Slowly she worked her way toward them, the infant's body growing heavier with each breath she took, the stars in the night sky beginning to fade with the creeping dawn.

No alarms rang from Lady Rin's home. No soldiers came marching through the wide streets, flooding into the woman's tall, sprawling estate. Mara had been right to think the noble's humiliation at the hands of the ashwalk pilgrim had kept her mouth shut. With any luck, the servant named Pinne also escaped a beating.

Few soldiers patrolled the streets of Hightable. Apparently, not even the king thought Mara would penetrate Sollan's heart. She couldn't blame them for thinking so. Even she surprised herself by making it that far, by skirting the sickening violence that fell everywhere around her like leaves in autumn.

She flitted like a burlap wraith behind an estate with darkened windows. A garden of trimmed hedges and round pools capped by miniature titan skeletons sprawled before her. Opposite the mansion and clear on the other side of the garden, a simple servant's quarters sat amongst a throng of weeping willows with soft, curving branches weighed by countless pink and white blossoms.

A gold lamplight illuminated the second floor of the mansion. It melted from one window to another, slowly moving through the estate as its carrier made their way through the sprawling home. Mara narrowed her eyes and watched as the light drifted window to window.

"It could be a servant like Pinne," she said.

The light paused before a window.

Mara chewed on the corner of her lip. "Or it could be a noble like Lady Rin..."

She didn't have the time to spare on detours away from the temples, yet some part of her knew the safest path and the quickest one diverged before her. She spun on her heel and sprinted into the manicured yard.

Pool after pool she passed. Her breaths came hot and heavy. The wind pulled her hood from her head. Her dirty, matted hair bounced over her shoulders. Mara glanced behind her. The gold light had drifted from the second floor to the first like a hungry demon searching for its prey.

Ahead, the blooming willows loomed large. She leaned forward and sprinted harder. She took a last, fleeing look behind her. The light illuminated the crack beneath a door and the ground. The handle twisted, and the door parted.

Mara leapt into a curtain of blossoms. The soft petals kissed her cheeks and caressed her arms as she barreled through the silken veil. She twisted around a trunk and pressed her back against its rough bark, panting like a fox freshly escaped from a hungry wolf.

She closed her eyes and inhaled. Only her heartbeat kept her company beneath the willow's boughs.

Exhaling, she peeked around the trunk. Across the garden, the door swung wide. A nobleman appeared with an oil lamp in hand, glaring down the length of his lawn.

"He can't see you," Mara told herself. "You're safe."

Her eyes locked onto the man. His gaze centered on the tree where she hid. Mara tightened her jaw. The willow branches swayed. His eyes narrowed, but he never called for soldiers. He never stepped beyond the comfort of his doorway. The nobleman retreated into his mansion, and the door swung quietly shut behind him.

Mara breathed a sigh of relief. She pinched her brow, rubbing her temples with her thumb and middle finger. She had precious little time to reach the temple before Olessa's glimmer completely faded from her blood.

"Look at where your son would have lived," she heard Olessa say. "Look at the luxury afforded to those in Hightable. It is the pearl of the shitty oyster that is Sollan. I see you still wear the ashen burlap. Good girl."

"It's what the ashwalk demands. I nearly changed earlier and it almost got me killed. The Six want me in burlap." Mara closed her eyes so she could better picture her madame.

"Then you really do want to save that little bastard's soul? This wasn't about having an adventure for a night?"

Mara's gaze drifted to her lifeless son. She smiled at his plump cheeks even though their blue hue brought tears to her eyes. "I do. It's not."

"If he had lived, I would have sold him to one of these highborns. This would have been his world."

"I believe you," Mara murmured. She brushed her finger through his wispy hair. "But that is not the life he would have lived."

"And what life do you think that would have been? You are no longer faced with death on the Waterstair. Tell me what you see. Tell me what you believe, Mara."

Mara leaned against the willow's trunk. Around her, blossoms pale as fresh milk weighed the tree's branches. They formed a cocoon for Mara and her thoughts. In her mind's eye, she parted the branches, and beyond, the play of her son's life spread out before her like an epic tale told for generations.

"Tell me," Olessa repeated.

"This king of ours, many think he is a man with vision. But he has more than just vision. He has hunger. He has rage. Those that willingly bow before him will regret the act before long. Those that love him now will fear him later. They will give up hope."

The words spilled from her like she'd rehearsed them. "But my son? He would never give up hope. He would have seen Good King Sol for the monster he truly is. My son would have stopped this king. As a boy he would have hidden in shadow. As a man, he would have stepped into the light and raised armies to slay the king and his flying serpent and squelched the Serpent Sun before it rose. If a heart beat in the lands of Urum, they would know my son's name."

Mara stalked forward. She stared into the willow blooms. Olessa joined her, and together they watched the play of her son's life unfold before them.

"Do you see him, Mara?" Olessa asked.

Mara smiled and pointed through the petals. "Look, Olessa, right there! He walks with five others. The days are dark and the world full of fear, but wherever he goes, a light shines. They follow him, Olessa, they follow him to the ends of Urum, to kingdoms I have only ever dreamed of and places long forgotten by men."

Olessa pursed her lips and nodded. "He's searching for something. But does he find it?"

"I'll help him if he cannot find the way. I will always be there for him."

"However you can, I'm sure you will." Mara's madame crossed her arms over her fiery silks. "And when he faces the king, what do you see for this son who should have been no more than a highborn's servant?"

"I see..." Tears stained Mara's vision as a vice slowly closed around her heart. "...It isn't clear."

"Look harder."

Mara wiped her tears on a sleeve and squinted. "I see pain. I see fire. I see darkness, and...and..."

"Death," Olessa stated flatly. "You have made your son a legend in your dreams, but you forget times of peace and prosperity do not heroes make. It is only through a bloodletting that a name is remembered beyond a generation. Knowing that, would you still want this life for him? Would you suffer his blood upon the sands to know his name would weigh a poet's verses until the winds wore the mountains into valleys?"

"I don't wish him harm. I don't wish him suffering."

"Then don't dream of great things he could have done. Dream of him living a comfortable life, tucked away in servant's quarters much like the ones beyond this willow, trimming hedges and pressing clothes for people who believe their shit is worth its weight in gold. He will never hunger. He will never thirst. No harm or suffering will come to him, just as you wish."

"But he will never truly live," Mara whispered.

"What does it matter? He doesn't live now. Isn't it easier to give up on the dream when you know it could never happen?"

Mara pressed her fingertip onto her son's nose and smiled. "No. It's much, much harder, because you think it just might have."

"Then what do you say, girl? The night is late and dawn approaches."

Two choices lay before her like the first fork in a very long road that would determine the course of countless lives. Her better half knew she should dream of a quiet, peaceful life for her son. Her better half knew living as a servant would be a thousand times over more peaceful than living as the king's mortal enemy.

She lifted her chin and glared through the branches. Her better half never could have brought her so close to the Mother's temple. Her better half could never have come so far and survived so much.

"I choose to dream of a legend. I choose to dream of a savior who is no saint. I choose to dream of a boy who will become a man who would deliver the world from darkness. This is what I choose to dream, because I know in the deepest parts of my beating heart that should he have lived, it would have been the path he walked."

Olessa turned to Mara. Her madame cupped Mara's cheek and smiled. For the first time, Mara realized the vision of Olessa was not the one she remembered from the House of Sin and Silk. The Olessa standing before her no longer sported a burgundy bush of a wig but waves of russet hair running like polished agate down to her breasts. The deep fan of wrinkles around her eyes had smoothed, the dark rings beneath her lashes now pink-kissed cream.

Mara leaned closer to her madame's face. "Olessa, you look so young!"

Olessa chuckled and tapped Mara's cheek. "I feel much better than I have in ages, my dear."

Mara's throat thickened. "There is no going home, is there?"

"I am so, so sorry, my child, but no, you will never return to the House of Sin and Silk. I came to you to know for sure that—" Olessa fought her words, her dark eyes glassy with tears. "What am I saying? I came to you to ask forgiveness. I was harsh on you from the first day my brother brought you to me. But in truth, Mara, you were more my daughter than my moon maiden. I loved the little girl my brother brought to my barge. Please forgive me for the bruises, for the poisonous words and broken wine glasses. I never told you how I truly felt even as the skiff took you from our home, and now it is the painful burden I will bear until the last sun sets on the horizon."

"I knew what you felt for me," Mara placed her hand over the one Olessa used to cup Mara's cheek and smiled. "You never needed to say the words. I saw the truth in your eyes. I knew, and it was all I ever wanted."

Olessa cried. Her tears were glass pearls melting down her cheeks. "When you left my—our home, it broke my heart. I went into my room and wept. I wanted to go with you. I wanted to take you to the temple steps myself. I was such a coward, Mara. I will never forgive myself for not turning to you while Tolstes rowed you toward the shore. I raised you. I loved you. And when you needed me, I gave you glimmer and kicked you from our home. Forgive me, my child. Forgive me."

"I forgive you. I forgive you a thousand times. You are my mother, Olessa. You always were."

Madame Olessa's form cracked and peeled, her smooth skin becoming the silk petals of the willow around them. "Gia was right. You are stronger than you know and so, so much more."

Mara's mother dipped her head and folded her arms across her chest. Her dress fluttered in the wind and dispersed into countless pale petals. Her arms and legs followed after.

"Never stop dreaming," Olessa whispered, her voice fading on the wind. "And quit dawdling here like some glimmer fiend looking for a high. The king's serpents slither through Hightable for their meal. Are you just going to sit around and pick flowers like a fool? Get to the temple, Mara. I love you, child. Now go!"

Mara took a last, fleeting look at her madame as what remained of the woman disappeared in a flurry of willow flowers. Mara turned on her heel and dashed from beneath the confines of the tree, her eyes set on the temples looming in the distance. Around the perimeter of Hightable, bells echoed in low tones, sending their deep notes vibrating through the still air.

20

A NOBLE SACRIFICE

Until the moment Mara heard the first bell ring, Hightable felt relatively safe even so close to the palace. But when the alarms cast their deep calls into the night, she knew they realized the ashwalk pilgrim no longer stalked the lower city.

Olessa had been right. The king's serpents would slither through the district, looking for their meal.

She dodged and darted through manicured lawns and labyrinthine gardens. She hid beneath bloom-laden willows and peered around slender pillars. Nobles once retiring to their comfortable beds lit lanterns and lamps as the bells rang their siren song. Dark windows glowed with fresh lights, illuminating silhouettes of Sollan's wealthiest.

Marching lines of armed men streamed into Hightable from its single grand gate leading to the Blooming Ring and beyond. The soldiers went from estate to sprawling estate. They hacked at willow branches, knocked over urns and toppled ivy-covered statues.

Somehow, she always just barely avoided them. They would flood a garden or lawn, stomping into the grounds and tearing up grass and flower alike, but they would always miss her by a moment.

She reached a mansion comprising two tall wings walled by marble pillars. An archway connected the wings to one another. Beyond the arch, she spotted a small manicured lawn that ended at a wide plaza. On the other end of the plaza, a temple teased her hopes.

Mara glanced behind her. The wide eye of the moon pierced itself on one of the towers overlooking the district. Paling skies drowned all but the brightest stars. Soon, a new sun would rise. Harvest Festival would be a memory, and Mara would be…

She turned from the moon and pressed her son against her chest. She blinked, her legs suddenly wobbling like she stood on a skiff beneath a summer storm.

Nausea twisted her stomach, and she nearly spilled its contents on the grass. Then, as quickly as the queasiness came, it vanished. Her legs solidified, and her stomach uncurled and hardened.

"The glimmer," she said. "It's—it's almost gone. It's leaving me. The sun is rising. We don't have much time, my love!"

The arch waited in a mix of silver and shadow. Mara swallowed and closed her eyes, inhaling the honeyed scents of flowers that pervaded Hightable's stifling air.

Mara crossed the remaining flower-speckled greenery. She slipped beneath the grand archway and halted. The temple lay beyond the grand plaza, each mighty column supporting its tall roof dotted with brilliant lanterns. The words scrawled into its marble told the world the Shining Child lived within its walls, welcoming all who wished to cleanse themselves of sin.

A line of soldiers marched through the plaza. Their knuckles whitened on their swords' grips. The temple's lanterns reflected against their steel breastplates. A captain did not lead them. A serpent priestess did.

Sister Ialane's white cloak billowed around her despite the bare breeze penetrating Hightable's wall. She halted in the plaza and craned her neck. Her scowling mask's gaze zeroed on the estate where Mara hid. Slowly, the woman's body turned in the direction her mask faced.

Mara twisted into the shadows. With her back against the wall, she peeked into the plaza.

The soldiers turned and formed a steely barrier between Mara and the temple. Ialane tickled her serpent's jaw and motioned toward the estate. "Three of you to that one," she called. "The rest take the neighbors."

Soldiers swarmed like angry hornets toward the neighboring estates while three men charged the one where Mara hid. They formed a tide of sharpened steel and shadowed eyes. The three soldiers poured into one of the wings, and in moments, dragged a husband and wife screaming into the yard.

"Please," the woman wailed, "we've done nothing. We are loyal to Good King Sol!"

The three soldiers bearing swords and torches towered over the noblewoman and her husband. The pair kneeled before the king's men in tattered and dirty silks, their eyes wide and brimmed with panicked tears. A necklace slipped from the woman's nightgown and hung loose around her neck. On the necklace, a polished gold circle held a star with six points within it. The golden symbol glittered in the torchlight.

Sister Ialane floated like a porcelain phantom before the soldiers and their prisoners. She tilted her head to the woman and bent forward, her fingers flicking the symbol hung around the noble's neck.

"You are loyal to Good King Sol?" Ialane asked.

The woman's eyes widened at the sight of her necklace. She interlaced her fingers and scooted on her knees toward Ialane. "Y—yes, Sister Ialane. We are loyal to him in every way."

"Really. In every way? *Every way?*"

She nodded enthusiastically. Her husband's eye caught the symbol flashing in the torchlight, and the color drained from his smooth features.

"Nialle, take it off," he whispered, his fingers shakily moving to the necklace.

"Quiet!" Ialane Donra backhanded the man. His head spun to the side, and he collapsed onto the ground.

The priestess clasped Nialle's necklace. Her thumb rubbed the holy star that represented the Six major gods of Urum. "You say you are loyal to our king, yet you wear the symbol of the Six around your neck. Did you think they would protect your dreams? Did you think the Serpent Sun would be blind to your apostasy?"

A tear slipped down Nialle's cheek, and her chin began trembling violently. "Please, Sister Ialane, I meant no disrespect. I am loyal to the king, but my family has prayed to the Six for generations. I—I did not think merely a prayer to them was illegal when their temples lay beyond my very doors."

"You are a noble of Hightable. You stand here groveling like some beggar from the Floatwaif, thinking I'm such a fool I would believe you had no idea of the king's wishes for his purest peoples?" Ialane straightened. "All in Hightable know the priests of the Six have plotted our king's death. All in Hightable know a sorceress they summoned seeks his soul tonight. Yet you claim ignorance? I should run you and your husband through here and now and burn this home to the ground and all within it."

She will die because of me, Mara thought. *She has been nothing but faithful, but because of me, she will die.*

So many had already died for her. So many had suffered because of the ashwalk. She looked down upon her son. Sickly blue tinged his cheeks and painted his lips. For the first time that night, he began to look less a boy and more a body.

"I can not let another suffer for me," she said. "I'm so, so sorry my darling love, but I know you would never forgive me knowing I let them suffer."

She kissed his brow and took a deep breath. Gripping her son, she slid from the shadows and stepped beyond the arch.

"Wait," a child hissed. A small hand grasped her arm and yanked her back beneath the relative safety of the breezeway.

Mara whipped around to face the child. Her eyes met his, and she nearly fell flat on her back. Mara caught herself and leaned forward, searching the boy's familiar features, his little narrow nose and ashen cheeks. He gripped her arm with a hand that lacked a finger, and his eyes glimmered with the adventurous light of youth.

"Tag?" Mara pressed a hand against his cheek. "Tag, how did you come to Hightable? Did you climb the aqueduct? What did Sander call it? The Waterstair?"

He grinned and flashed his broken-toothed smile. "You're silly, Mara. You've come so far, and you'd give it all up for a noble? I don't think I'll ever really understand you."

Mara swallowed and licked her rough, chapped lips. "She is going to be hurt because of me. Ialane will murder her and her husband. They will die, all because of me. I won't have it anymore."

Tag wrinkled his nose and pulled her down to his level. "Mara, you know nothing of the world. They won't suffer because of you. No one suffers because of you. She suffers because an evil man has his eyes on heaven and he will do anything and kill anyone if it means getting a little closer to the stars. A serpent kills them, not an ashwalk pilgrim."

"But if I didn't have my child—"

"There would be no hope. But you do have your son, and there's some hope…although the night's fading and your time's getting shorter than I am. I should've taken you. The meal wasn't worth what I lost."

Mara clenched her jaw. She straightened, pulling away from Tag. "Why are you here, Tag? You betrayed me when I needed you. You left me in an alley. Yet now you come here speaking words of encouragement to continue my ashwalk when I could save a woman and her husband's lives."

His gaze drifted to his feet as his hands went to his shrunken chest. His fingers fiddled with one another as he pressed his foot hard against the stone patio. "I didn't know then what I know now. I was hungry, Mara. In the streets, you take what you can get because you never know how long it will be before you eat again. And then you wonder, will I really ever eat again?" He looked into her eyes. "Will they catch me next time? Will I lose another finger?"

All the hardness in her heart melted. She kneeled and smiled. "Tag, I forgive you. I have lived on my madame's barge all my life and never went without a meal. I could not even know the dark things you faced in your short years."

"I was afraid," he whispered.

"I know."

"I hated myself for leaving you in the alley, Mara. I cried when I left. I cried and cried and knew my momma saw everything I did from the heavens and turned her head in shame. I wish I had been stronger. I wish I would have taken you to the steps."

"I know."

"You can't give yourself up. You've got to know your life's beyond whatever happens in front of this house."

Mara hesitated. Her gaze drifted to the ground, searching for an answer. "I still don't understand what this is all about. I still don't know why they want my child so badly. I'm afraid. I'm afraid because I don't know what this is or why I have a part in it."

"Things will become clear before long. You're nearly to the Mother's temple. Make it to the steps. Don't give up. If you care about me and all others from Hightable to the Floatwaif and all the many kingdoms of Urum, you just can't give up no matter what happens."

"Will you take me to the temple this time?"

Tag grinned, his pink wedge of a tongue sticking through his broken tooth. "You'll find your way. I would lead you if I could, but I can't. I'm not leaving you, though, I promise I'll never do that again. I'll always be here with you, even if you can't see me."

She blinked, shaking her head. "What? Are you a priestly magician now?"

The boy bowed. He backed into the shadows, his body melting into the darkness of the arch. "Stay strong, Mara. You're nearly there."

His voice tumbled into a whisper, and he vanished. Mara leaned forward. She reached into the darkness. Her hand found the wall and searched its face for any nook or hiding spot the boy might have slipped within.

She found no hiding spots, and neither did she find the beggar boy who lacked a finger. Mara whipped around. She knelt by the arch and peered into the courtyard. The noblewoman Nialle still crouched before Sister Ialane as if the world had held its breath while Tag spoke with Mara.

The creeping crawl of time resumed, and Nialle fell before the priestess. "Please, mercy, Sister Ialane. My husband and I are good people."

The soldiers lorded over the woman like hungry vultures. Ialane Donra ripped Nialle's necklace off and threw it into the yard. "Then do you pledge fealty to the Serpent Sun? Will you cast off all faith to the Six and let the Serpent Sun rise?"

The woman peered into the sister's mask. Her own eyes fought with the bargain. Olessa once told Mara faith was a soul's most precious currency, and one did not tithe it to a different god lightly. Seeing Nialle struggle, Mara finally understood the words.

Nialle's husband still lay unconscious on the ground. The soldiers focused fully on his wife, and she focused fully on Ialane.

"Now," Tag's scratchy voice whispered in her ear. "Go now!"

Mara bounded from the arch. She moved swift as the wind whistling from the open sea and soft as a lover's kiss upon the neck. If she could just reach the plaza, she could find her way to the Mother's temple. The temples were close, so very, painfully close.

Her toe struck an upturned rock. A fiery, blistering pain shot through her foot and raced up her leg. Her knee twisted, and she fell onto the grass. She caught herself with her free hand, her son held in a death grip with the other.

She sucked in the tears threatening to spill from her eyes. She glanced behind her. Nialle's bleary gaze caught hers. Ialane began turning toward the sound.

The noblewoman swallowed, her throat glistening with sweat. The dark curls of her locks clung like polished hooks to her pale cheeks.

I have doomed us both, Mara thought.

Nialle's wet eyes hardened, her jaw flexing with a snarl. She grabbed a soldier's sword and pointed it at his throat.

"There is no place for a serpent among the Six," Nialle cried, the blade tearing in a silvery arc toward the startled man.

The weapon scraped against the his breastplate. Its sharpened tip found the soft flesh beneath his jaw. Crimson coated silver as the man's blood snaked down the blade. Sister Ialane hissed as the other soldiers threw their torches aside and swung their weapons.

Nialle glanced at Mara one last time. She smiled and closed her eyes like a priest was about to bestow a blessing. "Praise the Six, for they will endure all suns!"

Mara turned and sprinted onto the plaza. Behind her, steel tore flesh and silenced the noblewoman.

21

HOPE CHAINED

After the longest, darkest night of her life on the most blessed day of the year, Mara had finally reached her destination. At the base of the hill in the heart of Hightable stood the mighty houses of Six, the heart of the faith that spread throughout all Urum.

No monument in the city was as grand as the temples. Not even the mighty titan standing guard in the shallows could ever hold a candle to the majesty of the temples of the Six.

Braziers shaped like men and women held brass bowls flickering mighty flames. Firelight washed against the tall temple walls. Ivory pillars crowned by sculptures of blooming orchids, roses, and trails of ivy supported their roofs. Murals lining the temple walls told the story of the god within them.

At that moment, she faced the temple of the Silent Father. Two braziers of brass silent sons illuminated the towering doors at the top of the marble steps leading to its interior.

Mara did not know much of the Six, but she knew the Mother and Father were opposite pillars supporting the same arch. The Mother's temple would be placed on the other side of the palace hill.

She closed her eyes and whispered a fleeting prayer of thanks to the Silent Father for all his sons had done for her that night. Keeping to the perimeter of the vast, circular plaza where the shadows were longest and both highborn and soldier were few and far between, Mara made her way around the hill.

Wailing nobles dragged from their homes punctuated a dying night of soldier's boots stomping on smoothed stones and gruff shouts from steel hoods. Mara kept to the long shadows and graceful arches bordering the plaza, her feet moving along the gentle curve of the grand courtyard as quickly as her heartbeat.

A bead of sweat rolled down her back in a frigid line. She shuddered, blowing a lock of dark hair from her vision as the temples slowly scrolled by.

As she bounded like a lioness toward her goal, she noticed the crowds filtering into the plaza from various lanes. They swarmed like a plague of locusts into the courtyard, gathering around the tall lampposts illuminating the open and staring at the king's legions standing between the world and the temples.

There were so many people. So many whispering lips. So many shouting soldiers. So many poisonous eyes fixed upon the gods' temples. Yet none of them saw her. All looked for her, but none of them saw.

She smiled. The Six saved her. The Six cloaked her in shadow. They would deliver her to the Mother, and all would be made right. A moon maiden, a whore, a mother with a cursed womb would evade the full might of the king and save her son's soul. The thought swelled a heart used to timid beats with the rocking thrum of pride.

The plaza encasing the temples rounded with the hill. A roof appeared. Mara's heart skipped a beat. Her smile spread into a toothy crescent.

Although she had never seen the Mother's temple, she knew she had arrived at it. Her hands tightened on her son's body as tears brimmed her weary eyes. "We've done it. We've done it, my son!"

Crowds gathered in ever-growing throngs within the plaza. So thick they became that Mara struggled to keep hidden, even on the edge.

Eventually she came face to face with the temple. She lingered on the far side of the cobbled stretch and stared at the building where she'd buried all her hopes.

Two giant maidens held burning braziers toward the brightening sky. They surrounded a massive door closed tight, its iron bound planks belying it would not give up its treasures easily.

If only she could reach the building. The highborn swarming the temple clumped like fungus in its shadow, and the soldiers stood in strong and steady lines as a barrier to any who might dare approach the steps. The people spouted obscenities, curses, and longwinded soliloquies at the Mother. Among the shouts, praises of Good King Sol coated the hate like honey dripping from a poisoned peach.

Mara took a deep breath. She sank into a mass of tall marble pots overflowing with silky vermillion daffodils and smooth, spongy tongues of aloe. Alone in the shadows, she waited until something of a gap grew in the crowd.

She looked at her son, and his features twisted her heart into a thousand knots. The last of his hale skin had faded into ash-tinged blues, and his lips took on a sickly grey.

"All will be well soon," she said. "Your soul will be free, and you will be nestled in the Burning Mother's arms. I will find a way through the king's soldiers, my love."

"I'm sure you will," a rough voice said.

Mara jumped, twisting to the sound. She backed into an urn and barely grasped its marble lip before it crashed to the ground. A man as foreign to Hightable as a moon maiden sat against the wall behind the vases.

His milky eyes betrayed their uselessness. His sunken skin sagged over once proud cheeks. His teeth might have been mistaken for an old hound's fangs so bent and broken they appeared. Filthy rags clad his thin arms. His long, bony finger toyed with the rusted tin cup set beside him.

"Galladus?" Mara asked.

The beggar she had met in Lower Sollan grinned. One of his broken teeth caught his lip and warped his smile. "You remember my name, little moon maiden? I haven't felt so blessed in quite a while."

"You're in Hightable!" For the moment, Mara forgot her mission and fell to her knees beside her friend. She clasped his hand, feeling its rough callouses weighing the thin, liver-spotted skin, and the subtle shake he couldn't control.

"I suppose you could say as much." His teeth slid behind his lips. He squeezed her hand and looked over her shoulder at the crowd gathering before the Mother's temple.

"But how did you get up here? I have seen so many things tonight that I am…" Mara looked to her knees and frowned. "What was in Olessa's glimmer? Has it addled my brain? Am I seeing ghosts like they say happens to glimmer addicts, or…"

She stumbled back. "Are you an alp? Are you a vision of the demons of the Second Sun? They are said to swarm around the ashwalk pilgrim and her child's unsaved soul. Olessa said as much and Gia warned it true. Have you come to keep me from saving him?"

"Shh, child." Galladus gently clapped her hand. "I am no demon alp returned, and you can be assured I have not come to keep you from saving the boy."

Mara instinctively tightened her grip on her son. She glanced over her shoulder. The gap she would have taken had closed, and now the crowd was a wall that might as well have been three times as tall as the one she scaled to Hightable.

"Yet you stalled me! You kept me from the temple. I was so close, Galladus! Why?"

"Not all paths are clear that appear to be. A canny hunter will lay a trap no lioness could ever hope to see. The Six threw shadows to keep you hidden, but not even they can turn a serpent's eye when blood is in the air."

"I don't know what to do. I am here. I am here! Where am I to go but through the highborn and the soldiers to the Mother's steps? I have no wings. I have no silent sons to make holes in walls and shadows."

Galladus puckered his lips. His dull eyes slipped toward his tin cup. He angled the broken mug's mouth and stared sadly into its empty belly. "It was the busiest night of the year. Still, none gave their coin. The city has soured. As hearts turned from the Six, they fled like barbarians beneath the blades of Eloia's armies. I knew soon after you left I would not eat tonight."

"So you braved the way to Hightable despite your lame leg and bad vision? I would have brought you with me if you wanted. We could have walked this together."

A clunking cackle tumbled from his lips. He slapped his knee and looked to the side, his smile quickly fading. "No, my braving days were over when I grew too weak to wield a sword."

His deep breath swelled his chest, and his clouded eyes locked on hers. "Tell me, Mara, what is your value?"

The beggar's question utterly disarmed her. She slumped, grabbing the rough edge of her cloak. "I don't understand."

"It is not a riddle, little moon maiden. Tell me your value."

She bit her lip and stared dully at her son. All her life, Olessa had dictated her worth. Olessa set the price Mara's patrons paid, and even then she hardly ever knew the count of coins.

"Three, maybe four silver? Perhaps a gold on a busy night? We were not allowed to know the count. Olessa said we profited through a comfortable life."

"Dear, I wish to know your value, not your worth. I need to know if the price I paid was worth it."

"The price…" Mara's brows knitted together. "You died. They killed you, didn't they?"

Galladus had no answer for her, but his eyes said all she needed. Mara was not sure if the beggar before him was a specter or some glimmer-born ghost, but her heart ached for the poor man nonetheless.

"Your value, Mara," he repeated. "What do you believe it is?"

"I do not know."

"Yes you do. I know you do. Think a little harder."

She hoisted her son against the base of her neck and bit her lip. No one had ever asked such a question. Truth be told, Mara never really considered what her value might be beyond a few coins for a night of pleasure in the House of Sin and Silk.

Or have I?

Mara's chin dipped as she thought. "They say I am the Maiden of the Moon who serves patrons for coin, the Ashwalk Pilgrim cloaked in ashen burlap, the Sorceress of the Second Sun, and the Killer of Kings who reach for the heavens. But really, I am none of them. They are titles given by others, and depending on the one I'm wearing, my value changes."

Mara lifted her chin. Despite the milky cloud curtaining his eyes, Galladus focused intently on her. "Go on…"

She pursed her lips and pulled the burlap from her son's face. "Yet none of them are me, and none I wish to be. I am a mother; that is all, and that is everything I'll be. That is the title I wear and the one that can never be taken from me. You ask my value, but it is not a question I can answer. Ask my son's spirit when this night is done. He will tell you a mother's worth by the sacrifices she made for him."

Galladus reached for her. His rough hand clasped around her wrist. He smiled, a tear sliding down the weathered cracks of his cheek. "Yes, you are a true mother. Thank you, Mara. I thought I had seen all the wonders of the world. I did not know that all my life the greatest treasure Urum had to offer lived within my horizon. There is no doubt in my mind you will reach the Ever-Burning Flame."

"I hope so."

"You will, you will. A new sun will rise soon, my child. Stay strong, and do not forget what we have given to give you hope."

The cracks lining his cheeks deepened. They spread and multiplied like mud drying beneath a relentless sun.

Mara caught her breath. She backed away from the man and watched his skin crack and peel. His flesh and bones flaked to the ground and gathered in shifting piles. Galladus turned to ash before her, the last thing remaining his bleary eyes and bright smile.

A breeze pierced the protective wall of urns and teased the pile of ash that seconds before had been her friend. The ash took flight, each flake turning into the silky wing of a pale moth fluttering skyward.

"Goodbye, Galladus. May you dine with the Six tonight and ever after."

She turned from the wall and faced the perimeter of flowery urns. Beyond the marble vases, the crowd was thick as coral shark soup. Soldiers had erected a platform at the base of the Mother's temple. They surrounded the building with tall lampposts studded with glowing orbs.

Mara hid behind an aloe plant's broad leaves. The soldiers planned something. They had erected a stage, but for what, she could only guess. None of her guesses brought any comfort.

All sounds in the crowd quieted. Movement disturbed the mob. A path opened like some horrible beast disturbed the calm quiet of the ocean's surface.

Two familiar figures appeared in the path. One wore a mask pale as milk crowned by gold and a serpent coiled loosely around her neck. She led the cult of the Serpent Sun and called herself Sister Ialane Donra.

The other hid his form behind straps wrapped around his body like some half-made mummy. The daggers glinting from his straps sent a sickly shudder down Mara's spine. He called himself Brother Caspran Bilshabel.

A third figure trudged behind them, dragging heavy chains in their wake. The links clinked against the plaza's stones. Noble and soldier alike looked with disgust at the prisoner. Mara leaned into the curtain of leaves, but so hunched was the poor prisoner that she could not make the figure out through the crowd.

The two priests of the Serpent Sun reached the platform. They scaled it, strolling casually to its center. Brother Caspran twisted to the prisoner. He snapped his fingers, and the chains wrapped around the figure lurched toward the priest like snakes lurching for a mouse.

The prisoner tumbled onstage with a sharp cry. The figure huddled there, hunched like a frightened, trembling child at the feet of the king's priests. A sickening feeling gurgled in Mara's stomach, and she began to tremble.

Ialane motioned at the lampposts, and their lights blazed brighter. They washed the stage in brilliant gold, chasing every shadow beneath them to the edges of the crowd.

The serpents had captured a woman. Blood stained her temple. A cut scarred her lip. Her left eye was a swollen plum that freely shed its tears. Around her neck hung a brass collar, and she wore loose silks that bore many tears and bloody stains. Like all women from the East, she wore her hair in oiled braids.

Mara stumbled back. Her own tears coursed down her cheeks. "No, Gia!"

The Mother's steps suddenly seemed so very far away.

22

BLOOD ON THE BLADE

Never before had Mara seen her one and only friend gripped in brutal torture. It twisted Mara's heart into a painful, throbbing stump. Behind the two serpent priests and their captive, the Mother's temple rose like some unassuming lord above the heresy before it.

Only a precious few stars shined in the deathly sky. Soon the sun would rise and bring light to the dying embers of Harvest Festival. With its rise, her son's fortunes would fall. His soul would be forever trapped within his lifeless body, a feast for the alp demons and a curse for whatever few moments remained of Mara's life before the king clapped irons around her wrists or shoved a blade through her heart.

Ialane Donra surveyed the crowd through her pale and angry mask. Her two swords hung loosely at her side while the snake around her neck flicked its pink, forked tongue toward the people beneath it.

The priestess grabbed Gia's chains. Sister Ialane yanked the irons, throwing Gia to the ground. "Moon maiden Mara, we know you cower in the shadows."

Mara stepped back, and the aloe leaves swept like a quiet curtain over her face. Glittering eyes glanced her direction, searching for the sorceress the people of Sollan believed came to kill their king.

"You are a heretic and a whore," Ialane continued, "you are nothing. You seek to slay Good King Sol. You seek to bring an end to his peaceful reign. You will fail. The Serpent Sun stands against you. The people of Sollan stand against you. The kingdom of Eloia stands against you. All the lands of Urum stand against you. You are alone."

I am not alone, Mara thought. *I have never been alone.*

Gia lifted her chin, her dark eyes searching the crowd. "Don't listen to her, Mara! You've made it. You've made it!" She laughed, a tear running from the unbruised eye. "We are at the Mother's steps, just like I said. Just like I dreamed. Don't let this serpent witch draw you out when you're so close. She's nothing to us. She's nothing to you!"

Gia's smile darkened. She turned to the priestess and spit. A glistening glob lopped against Ialane's mask. It dripped from the porcelain visage and landed on her snake's pale scales.

Brother Caspran balled his fist. He whipped around, striking Gia in the jaw. She screamed, her head flying backward.

Mara pressed her cloak against her mouth to mute her sobs. Tears wet her cheeks and stained the burlap. Gia suffered for her. Gia bled for her.

Ialane wiped the spit from her mask and flicked it at Gia. "Your kind are all the same. You think yourself special. You think yourself strong. You are neither. You are cattle that escaped the pen and think you rule this world for it. Look at your friend. You are the cause of her pain. We could end it at any time…"

The priestess opened her palm. Her serpent slid its head over her fingers, its beady, ruby eyes observing the crowd. "…Or we could make her scream until her hair grays and her teeth have all rotted out of that pretty mouth. Is this what you want, Mara? I will make her beg for death. I will bring her to the edge of oblivion, and just as she stares gratefully into the void, I will yank her back into the light. Every day will be a new torment. Every sunrise a new lesson in pain. Give yourself up, or this will be the whore's fate."

Gia struggled to lift herself. She glared at Ialane with a swirling cyclone of hate in her eyes. "I don't care what you visit on me. Make me suffer until I am a thousand times on the edge of death. Torment me. Torture me. Mara will not give herself up to you, you serpent. We may be moon maidens, but you are the whore."

Ialane tickled her serpent's jaw and turned her back to Gia. "It wasn't difficult finding the House of Sin and Silk. Men's mouths flap so easily, you see. Word of a woman on her ashwalk spread quickly through the streets. First, I came to a beggar…"

The priestess reached inside the folds of her robe. She produced a tin cup stained with dried blood. "Galladus was his name if I recall correctly. He was some poor, broken soul who belonged to the old king. Once, he may have even been a mighty warrior. No longer. To think, his years of service earned him nothing more than a grave in a puddle of piss and shit in a dark alley."

Mara's jaw tightened. She glared at the woman from behind the curtain of leaves.

Ialane crushed the tin and tossed it to the platform. "He refused to cooperate as well, so I cut his manhood from him and fed it to my serpent. I thought it a fitting end for such a dedicated warrior. He died screaming. His body rots in an alley as we speak, a feast for rats and feral cats. Now I ask you again, give yourself up. Do not let your friend suffer. It is pointless, and she will suffer greatly if you don't do as I command."

Mara squeezed her eyes shut. The image of Galladus burned in her mind. He lay in a pool of his own blood, flea-infested rats gnawing at his dead eyes.

She opened her eyes and bit her lip, shaking her head. *No, I will remember him better.*

"Don't let her sway you, Mara!" Gia searched the crowd with her good eye. Her braided hair fell over her shoulder and swung beside her bruised and battered arm. "You are strong, I know you are. Remember that."

Ialane laughed a light, tinkling chuckle. "You are not strong, Mara. You never were. You were obedient. You were pampered. You even let a little beggar boy trick you out of the one possession you had worth any coin."

Sister Ialane prodded her robe. Her fingers clasped an object. She produced Mara's collar. Dried blood stained the plated brass, and the ring bent in an odd direction. "I took another finger from the boy before I took his life. It's an awful thing when one so young is snuffed from Urum, don't you think? Luckily, he was scum of the lower city, a parentless thief who deserved the punishment I awarded him. But unlike your steely friend Galladus, the boy squealed like a stuck pig. He told me everything I asked. He told me of a beautiful moon maiden on her ashwalk. He told me of her home, a place on the Floatwaif called the House of Sin and Silk. His death came quickly for his compliant words."

"No, Tag, not you, too." Mara bit her lip to keep from crying. She cupped her son's head and shook her head. "I am so sorry. You should not have died because of me."

Mara's heartbeat quickened. Her eyes shot straight to the priestess. "The House of Sin and Silk," she rasped. "No…"

"I crossed the calm waters of the bay," Ialane continued. "I made my way to Floatwaif. Filthy place, those rotted barges overflowing with wart-riddled whores and eunuchs. It has always been a disgusting mark upon this city. For what reason Good King Sol let it persist, I will not know. But tonight is a new night, Mara, and tomorrow we will be in a new Sollan, a clean Sollan. It will be a Sollan without the Six, and it will be a Sollan without the Floatwaif."

Ialane reached into her robes. Mara's tears poured down her cheeks as her arms wrapped tighter around her son. The priestess produced a thin net of gold chains. In it, bits of burgundy hair shimmered in the links. Mara knew the hairnet well. It had crowned her madame's head for most of Mara's life.

The woman flung the hairnet to the platform and flicked her fingers as if they had been dripping muck. "The House of Sin and Silk. What an appropriate name for a den of caged whores. Olessa built quite a kingdom for herself on the Floatwaif. Her barge was its beating heart."

Slowly, Sister Ialane raised her hand. She balled her hand into a tight fist. "And then I ripped that heart out. I burned it. I sent that den to the bottom of the Sapphire Sea and cut your madame into bits and fed her to the coral sharks. The rest of the Floatwaif burned with her. The thousands of better off forgotten filth of Sollan burned, Mara. They burned for you! How many more will burn because you do not show yourself to me. Throw off that disgusting cloak and show yourself!"

They killed everyone. They burned her home. So many thousands lived in Floatwaif, all dead because of Mara. Olessa dead because of Mara. Tag dead because of Mara. Galladus dead because of Mara.

She looked at her son, and a glimmer caught her eye. An orb tucked between her breasts shone with a faint, pulsing light the color of a calm sea. The thief Sander Hale had given the odd artifact to her just in case she needed him, just in case she found herself facing impossible odds.

Maybe if she broke it, maybe he would come. Maybe he could use his magic to rescue Gia.

Mara plucked the orb from her breasts and held it before her. "Sander, I pray you really were a priest of the Slipper Sinner. Help me. I need you."

She crushed the orb. Warmth flared in her fist. She opened her hand, and a tiny, swirling cyclone of glittering blue dust swirled within her palm.

The cyclone spun faster and faster. It swelled. It burst. It evaporated.

Mara stared at her empty palm. She lowered her hand and searched the shadows for the man. She peered between the vases and scanned the crowd. She glanced to the temple roofs and searched their tiles.

Sander did not appear. No priest of the Slippery Sinner bounded from the darkness to bring Gia to safety.

Mara clenched her teeth. *Of course he would not come. There is no easy path from this.*

She faced the crowd. Ialane and Caspran surrounded Gia. Ialane shook her head. She gripped one of her swords, strumming it impatiently. "Very well, Mara."

With a flick of her wrist, the priestess unsheathed the sword. Its long, curving blade glimmered in the lamplight. She brought the razor edge to Gia's tanned and sweaty arm, slowly sliding it down the woman's flesh. "Perhaps a cut or two will draw you out?"

Mara's eyes widened. She stepped into the curtain of leaves. She lifted her chin and braced herself for the reveal. "I cannot let you suffer, Gia. Not another. Not for me. The Six will guide us both to safety, I know it."

Somehow, whether through dumb luck or a last, fleeting blessing from the Six, Gia's good eye fixed on Mara. They connected, two souls shining in a crowd of violent darkness. Gia's lips trembled in a sad smile.

You made it, she mouthed. *Remember me.*

Gia spun lightning fast. Her knee connected with the back of the Caspran's leg, and he went flying to ground. She whipped her braid around Ialane's sword and used it as a cushion for her hand, thrusting the blade away.

Caspran buckled. The priestess stumbled back. Gia leapt to her feet with all the practiced grace of a dancer. "My name is Gia Winn. I lived a moon maiden for the House of Sin and Silk."

Mara's friend balled her hand into a shaking fist of pale knuckles. "But I die a priestess of the Burning Mother, a loyal servant to the true gods!"

Caspran bounded to his feet as Ialane regained her balance. Gia's fist snapped like wound spring and slammed straight between Ialane's masked eyes. The woman's head jerked back. The pale mask cracked like thunder and split. It shattered and dropped in alabaster shards to the ground.

A collective gasp slipped from the crowd, and the mob stepped back.

Sister Ialane straightened. Her hair fell in ivory waves over her shoulders. Her skin was pale as frost, her smooth jaw hard as iron. Her full lips twisted in a sneer that bared two sharp fangs, and she scowled at the crowd with dark pupils rimmed by polished gold.

Gia stumbled back. "Gods, what are you?"

Ialane's nostrils flared. She swallowed, surveying the crowd that gazed dumbstruck at her as if she were a some sort of freakish animal carted from an unknown land. The woman's lip trembled. Her sword arm shook. Her perfect, porcelain nose wrinkled in a snarl.

She turned to Gia and shrieked. The serpent around her neck uncoiled and buried its fangs in Gia's arm.

Gia seized. Ialane thrust her blade through Gia's chest. Mara's friend crumpled over the blade.

Ialane shoved the sword deeper and leaned into the dying woman. "Tell the Six we're coming for them."

Mara lurched through the plants. "*Gia, No!*"

An urn tipped and burst on the tiles in a mess of shattered marble, black soil, and spongy leaves. The crowd turned. Caspran flicked his wrist, a tiny, silver blade glinting in the light. Ialane kicked Gia's lifeless body from her blade and rotated toward Mara, flipping the waves of her ivory hair behind her.

The priestess smiled. Terror froze Mara's veins.

Ialane Donra wiped the blood from her sword as her serpent wound its way back up her leg and around her neck. The priestess pointed the tip of her blade in Mara's direction, the woman's odd eyes searching the area by the fallen vase. "Ashwalk pilgrim, tonight you die."

23

CHAOS AND CRIES

Ialane Donra's fanged smile glittered hungrily over Gia's body. Brother Caspran snapped his fingers, and the dagger in his hand whistled toward Mara.

Mara couldn't move. She couldn't breathe. Ialane's cold grin held her in its hungry grasp. It was a smile born of eons of hate, a smile born of endless hunger. Yet, her eyes did not focus on Mara.

She cannot see me, Mara thought. *How can she not see me?*

A black form swelled before Mara and wiped away the world. She blinked, her body finally released from its unnatural hold. Mara stared at the dark wall. A mask appeared within the black, calm and smiling like an old friend seen after a long trip across the sea.

"Silent son!" Mara stepped forward, cupping the mask. "You've saved me."

The priest of the Loyal Father heaved. Blood trickled from his mask. "Go…" he whispered in a voice racked with pain and panic. "To the steps, Mara. To the Mother's steps!"

A dagger's bloody, pointed edge appeared beneath his mask. It twisted, tip first, toward Mara as it tunneled through his flesh.

The silent son fell, and like a falling curtain he revealed the highborn crowd, the soldiers, the stage, and the two priests of the Serpent Sun standing upon it.

Mara tucked her son into her arm and leapt over the silent son's body. Her feet pounded on the plaza tiles. Wind threw her burlap in flapping wings around her shins. Her dark, waving locks unfurled and flew behind her.

"Kill her," Ialane roared. "Soldiers, kill the woman! Slay her where she stands and any who aid her!"

Chaos erupted amongst the crowd. Soldiers peppered in its midst unsheathed their swords and barreled through the panicked highborns.

Mara angled around the mob. Soldiers and swords trampled toward her, swinging their blades wildly. Ialane and Caspran bounded unnaturally high from the platform, their weapons gleaming in the light.

Oh gods, I will not let them take me. They will never take me!

An inferno lit her heart. Her eyes focused on the Mother's steps even as the line of soldiers before it barreled to meet the other soldiers hacking their way toward Mara. Her feet bounded like a mighty antelope. She couldn't slow, she couldn't stop. One misstep, and she would tumble. Somehow, she did not.

An arrow whistled past her. Another struck the plaza stones and shattered.

A gale wind bellowed through the plaza. With it, the shadows lurking beyond the lamplights raced across the smooth stones and swirled around her feet.

The shadows coalesced. They thickened. They grew into a mighty river rushing with churning black waves.

A soldier flung his sword at Mara's head. The shadows swirled and rose. A silent son's mask appeared in the cresting wave, and the sword buried in his back.

Another soldier leapt toward Mara. The shadows lurched as another mask appeared and caught the blade. The silent son twisted out of the black and flapped like a dead fish atop the startled man.

The shadows swirled and roiled, rising and falling like the waves of a river spewed from the mouth of a god. "Protect her!" the black river roared in a thousand mighty voices. "We are silent no longer. We speak with one voice. We pray with one soul. We are the silent sons of the Loyal Father. We speak, and we summon the Six. *Loyal Father, protect the pilgrim.*"

Thunder cracked like no other thunder Mara had ever heard. It shook the plaza. It rocked the temples. High above the hill, a column holding up the palace cracked and crumbled.

"*Shining Child, protect the pilgrim.*"

Clouds laced with violet lightning birthed in a once starry sky. Ialane's piercing shriek sliced through the air like a razor through parchment.

"*Gentle Lover, protect the pilgrim.*"

Lightning blasted the plaza, flinging guard and noble alike. Masked and hooded priests of the Serpent Sun bounded from rooftops and sped from shadows like a hive of pale spiders. They cut down all in their path on their murderous flight toward Mara.

"*Coin Counter, protect the pilgrim.*"

Mara clenched her teeth. Her throat burned from her heavy breaths. Her legs had long since numbed, but a warmth welled within her and increased her speed. Arrows and swords buried in the river of silent sons. Masks appeared and fell away.

"*Slippery Sinner, protect the pilgrim.*"

A hail of black arrows crested from the palace behind the temples. Mara looked in horror as they blotted the stormy sky and rained like hell from a demon's mouth. The river of silent sons crested over her, their shadows swelling into a raging tunnel whose end opened to the Mother's steps.

The arrows thudded into the priests, and the river faded as the last of the holy men died. The shadows thinned, and the wind embraced her.

A sharp pain lanced into her shoulder. She screamed at the burning point digging into her flesh. She glanced over her shoulder. Caspran's dagger buried in her arm. It twisted and dug like the fang of a hungry snake.

Tears blurred her vision. She bit her lip so hard she tasted the tin of blood.

The steps loomed large through her watery vision. Crying out, she leapt toward them. Her feet left the ground. An arrow whistled beneath her. One passed a finger's width from her face and broke on the stairs.

Mara landed hard on the marble steps. She fell forward and caught herself. Her wrist twisted and bent. The bone cracked, and she screamed at the fiery pain. Her toe hit a step. She collapsed, her knee slamming against the stone.

A wicked laugh pierced the chaos of the battle. Mara twisted around. Sister Ialane stood at the base of the stairs. The priestess brandished both swords. Her serpent's ruby eyes locked on Mara's son. Its forked tongue flicked from its jaw and tasted the air.

"So close, ashwalk pilgrim," Ialane said. "But I see you now that Caspran's dagger found its mark. It looks as if the Six did not have the strength to save you. Their sun sets on Urum, girl. The Serpent Sun rises, and with it the loyal will feast on the old gods' flesh and take the Six's power for our own."

"You will never defeat the Six." Mara struggled up a stair using her elbow.

Ialane casually climbed a step. "You are a fool. You have always been a fool. You will always be a fool. You will die tonight. You were born to die tonight. You never understood the truth, and it is a great pleasure of mine to send you to oblivion knowing you will never discover it for yourself."

The priestess raised her blade. Mara grappled with climbing another step. She cradled her son and pressed her broken wrist against him as a shield against Ialane's hungry serpent.

It flicked its tongue and uncoiled from the woman's neck. The creature slithered down her body and up the steps. It rose before Mara and slowly opened its wide jaw with a dripping hiss. Two pale fangs coated with poison gleamed in the light of the temple's burning braziers.

"Time to end this," Ialane said.

"Not quite," boomed a familiar voice. A small orb whistled past Mara and slapped inside the snake's jaw. The creature snapped its mouth shut and gagged and writhed. It spit the dark orb onto the steps and hissed.

"No!" Ialane swung her sword in a silver arc at Mara. "You won't be saved this time!"

The orb exploded in a plume of inky smoke. Popping sparks erupted within the black like fireworks bursting in a cloudy sky. The smoke stung Mara's eyes and disoriented her with its bright flashes.

Ialane's sword sliced through the smokescreen. A hand wrapped around Mara's neck and yanked her flat against the steps. The sword swished over her head, cutting air instead of flesh.

The strong hand jerked Mara up the last steps and snatched her to her feet. She twisted around as a the hand pulled her toward the Mother's doors, and she finally saw her savior. He wore tight black garments and boots trimmed in black. A dark hood hid most his features, but Mara instantly recognized his hooked nose and faint scar running beside his lips.

"Sander, you came!"

"Took me awhile. I never said I'd be there that instant, you know. So imagine my surprise when I try and come save the silly pilgrim woman and I see this bloody battlefield with silent son corpses and damn near half of Hightable bleeding out at the Mother's temple."

"We must get inside!"

"Eh?" He glanced down the steps.

Ialane tore through the smoke, coughing and wheezing. Her serpent had slithered up her leg and coiled around her neck. It glared at Sander, bearing its fangs with a piercing hiss.

Sander's face lost its color. "Fuck me, the Serpent Sun priests are alp? So there was a demon sorceress from the Second Sun in Sollan after all. It's just not hunting our king. It's working for him."

"That's an alp?" Mara stumbled back. "But all the alp are dead. All living things died when the Second Sun fell."

"The stories they tell common folk are often laced with lies. If you're smart, you might discover a different truth. Or rich. The rich can always buy the truth. There's a fancy saying for both, but I'll be damned if I can remember it. Don't you hate that? I wanted to sound all wise and priestly, but ah well, maybe the next brush with death, it'll come. At least we know why you were so good at keeping out of their sights. There's a reason the Mother makes her ashwalk pilgrims wear ash and burlap."

Sander pulled Mara against the temple door. Brother Caspran swatted through the remaining smoke and stood by Ialane's side. The priestess tightened her grip on the sword and pointed the tip at Mara. "No matter. The door is sealed and the faithful trapped within it. They will listen to your screams as we kill you both and my snake devours that child. Then, the temple will become their grave."

Mara pressed her son tight against her chest. Sander clucked and shook his head. He threw back his hood and bowed before the two priests of the Serpent Sun. "That's the thing about dealing with a man of the Slippery Sinner. No doors bar us, and we're just so damn hard to catch."

He twisted and slammed his palm against the door. An odd sensation racked Mara's body. She fell backward, her flesh warping through the crack in the doors as if she was water down a drain.

Sander smiled, his breath washing over his face as his form twisted with her. "I'm sorry it took so long."

Mara looked to the steps as the world faded. Ialane screamed and flung her sword. Brother Caspran flung his daggers.

The outside world blinked out. The weapons thudded against something solid.

The world reappeared. Instead of a Harvest Festival Sky, she looked upon a set of doors. She placed a palm on the thick wood and slid to her knees.

Her heart pounded. The wood and wrought iron muffled the alps' screams.

Sander threaded his arm beneath Mara's and hoisted her up. "Welcome to the temple of the Burning Mother, oh ashwalk pilgrim."

24

BLESSED IS THE MOTHER

Countless eyes glittered in the firelight of the Mother's temple, each one brimming with hope and edged by red-rimmed fear. Only a moment ago, Mara had faced the greatest crowd she'd ever seen. In the massive temple, the numbers gathered counted easily twice as many.

The temple itself spanned enough space to swallow a whole neighborhood. Pillars carved in the likeness of women supported a high roof. Olive and emerald ivy leaves dotted with honeysuckle blossoms coiled up their bellies and filled the room with their rich, honeyed scent.

The crowd parted and formed a path to the opposite end of the temple. In the back, towering above all others within the house of worship, stood the statue of a woman. The statue clasped her hands beneath her swollen belly and dipped her chin to gaze upon her unborn child. At her feet burned a white fire tinged by scarlet.

Mara swallowed, tucking her son a little deeper in her arms. "There are so many people."

"Bless the Six, they are all here." Sander tensed, his foot sliding back. "They have all come to face their doom beneath the king's shadow, the faithful fools."

"All of them?" she asked.

Her gaze swept over the crowd. A few silent sons stood taller than the rest, their pale masks stark against their black robes. A few others wore the crimson flame of the Burning Mother on their brow. Still others painted glittering gold beneath their eyes, a sign of the stalwart Coin Counter. Priests and acolytes of the Shining Child gazed upon her from within the myriad of tattoos scrawled over their skin, each intricate design a symbol of a sin committed. Those that worshipped the Gentle Lover nodded with respect, ornate nets of gold and silver woven in their oiled hair. There too she recognized men and women clad in the black and grey of the Slippery Sinner.

Mara stepped back and bumped into the temple's doors. "Why have they come here? Why are they staring, Sander? I—I don't like this. I'm so tired of not knowing."

Sander shook his head. He licked his lips, and his gaze slowly settled on her. "Who in all the hells are you?"

"I just want to send my son's soul to rest. That's all I've ever wanted."

"Then let's take you to the flame." He gripped her broken wrist.

She cried out, falling to her knees.

Sander's eyes shot wide open and he followed her to the ground. "Fuck, fuck, I'm so sorry. I had no idea it was broken. You've really swam through a shark's jaws tonight, haven't you? Damn me to every burning layer of every hell there ever was and will be. I did not mean to hurt you. I'm just—I'm new at this priest thing. If I'd been a little more experienced maybe but…Gods, I'm so sorry, Mara."

Mara sucked the snot back into her nose and looked at her son. No trace of pink colored his body. His sickly blue tinge had spread over his skin. The filth and blood from her womb dried and cracked in patches on his brow like a leper's wounds. Even then, not even Upper Sollan, not even Hightable, not even the Mother's temple could ever hope to match his beauty.

Still, she knew his soul faded. Mara shuddered. She bent over his tiny body and pulled him close, her wounded wrist crooked like a sailor's hook beneath him. She cried, and the tears splashed against the temple's marble tile. Her body heaved, the last of her energy drowned by her frustrations.

"Why have they done this to me? I have done nothing." She clenched her teeth and stared at the smooth stone. "I have done nothing! My son is dead, Sander. Oh gods, my beautiful son is dead and I never knew him. I've never said the words until now, but he is dead. I—I—I always saw him as alive, but he is dead. He is dead."

A great tide of emotions washed out from her shuddering spine, and she inhaled. Mara tightened her jaw and shook her head. "No, every dream I had, every vision I saw, you lived the life I pictured for you. You may not have breathed in my world, but you have always lived within my heart."

She smiled at her son. A shadow washed over his face. She kissed his brow and lifted her gaze.

A woman stood over her. A crimson veil mostly masked her features. Within her auburn hair piled high upon her head, stones with simmering hearts glimmered with their own light. She wore a necklace of wide, gold discs, the firelight revealing dimples wrought by tiny hammers on the metal.

Her crimson dress billowed around her as if she stood upon a high hill and opened her arms to the wind, yet no hint of a breeze disturbed the temple's placid air. Mara could not see the woman's eyes, but she felt them nonetheless. They embraced her. They warmed her. They knew her better than she knew herself.

Not a single word broke the stillness of the temple. Only the crackling fire at the statue's feet gave life to the quiet.

Mara found it difficult to meet the woman's gaze. She felt like a little girl again, caught by Olessa trying to sneak a sip of wine or drop of saltwater gin. Her ash-ridden cloak of burlap screamed poverty in a field of luxury, and the sickly green stain her moon maiden collar left behind let the world know how little it valued her.

The veiled woman bent. Her hand slipped from the rolling scarlet waves of her dress. "May I help you? You are a weary ashwalk pilgrim, and you have suffered much for us tonight."

Mara stared at the woman's perfect hand. She bit her lip and looked away. "My wrist is broken, and my other arm holds my son. I cannot take your hand, even if I wanted."

The woman's hand lingered in Mara's periphery. A moment later, it disappeared, and the stranger in scarlet straightened. "You are close to knowing your own strength, and you are close to the end of this long night." Her red silks whirled in a pool around her ankles. "Would you at least walk with me then?"

"Where?" Mara struggled to her feet, shooing Sander's helpful hands away. Too many helped her that tonight. Too many helped her and paid a price far higher than they deserved.

The woman extended a hand toward the statue and the flame at its feet. "To the end. To the beginning. To the place you seek that has sought you for so, so long."

Flames so white they burned Mara's eyes danced at the Mother's feet. Despite the burn, Mara couldn't turn away. She wouldn't turn away. She knew them. Somehow, she remembered them.

Mara took a step. Her knee wobbled and began to buckle. Sander gently clasped her shoulders and supported her until her strength returned. He leaned to her ear, his warm breath washing across her neck. "Do not fear them. I will follow you. I will not leave you here at the end, my ashwalk pilgrim."

Rolling crimson silks swelled around the mysterious woman as she glided down the path. Mara followed, the long, weary night pulling on her steps like lead weights around a swimmer's ankles.

"My name is Cassandra," the woman said. "I will guide you to the flames."

"I have been walking a long way tonight. They told me the Mother could save my son's soul before the alp devoured it. I—I almost didn't make it, but I had help along the way."

"The flames can do much." Cassandra paused and motioned for Mara to lead. "But it is you who will save his soul."

Mara licked her lips and took the lead. She tried her best to ignore the faces in the crowd, but all eyes bore down on her and followed her every movement.

"Traditionally, the ashwalk pilgrim speaks of her life," Cassandra said.

Mara rubbed her fingers down the rough threads of her son's burlap.

"Which part?"

"Everything you think might matter."

"I don't remember much…" the throbbing ache in her broken wrist flared. She paused and glanced to the side, closing her eyes until it passed. "But I do know a man of the Burning Mother brought me to the House of Sin and Silk. His name was Laedon, and he convinced Madame Olessa to raise me despite the cost and burden. I worked very hard for my madame. I never complained. I served my patrons even if I hated myself for doing so."

The woman nodded as they walked. "Blessed is the mother who toils in fields to feed another, for her soul will never hunger."

Mara shook her head. "I drank the ebon orchid draught. I swear I did. Still, I was with child. I tried, the Six know I tried. It should have worked. Olessa told me it would. It didn't, and then I was with a child—a son."

"Blessed is the mother who overcomes impossible odds, for her every breath is a miracle for all the world to see."

Mara glanced into the crowd. A line of silent sons stood above the rest. They each wore a mask with a different emotion and looked the same as any other in their order, but she knew those men. Somehow, she recognized them. One saved her from Kard and showed her a path into Upper Sollan. The rest fell with him in the Blooming Ring to save her from Brother Caspran and his flying dagger.

Their pale masks bowed in respect. Mara reached for them, but they swiftly retreated into the crowd. She turned away, continuing her unsteady pace toward the flames.

"I had my son just a sunset. I dreamt a bright future for him, but he never took a breath. I gave birth. I bled on the barge's deck. I cried. I held his body in my arms. They feared him when they saw him. Then, they feared me. They thought my son and I cursed. I saw it in their eyes. It hurt more than any beating."

Cassandra nodded. "Blessed is the mother who stands against injustice, for she will rise above eternity."

"They told me that demons would eat my son's soul." She looked to her son's body and swallowed her angry sob. "They said he would suffer if I did not take him to the Ever-Burning Flame before sunrise. They wrapped us both in burlap stained by ash. They would not help. They would not risk. I—I thought they loved me. I thought someone loved me. I thought if one of them did, they did not love enough. I was bitter at first, I think. But now, I understand their fear. I hope—think they loved me in the end."

A man muscled out of the crowd and stood like an eager boy at the edge of the path. His blond hair was cut short and trimmed to perfection, and his round, blue eyes carried an innocence that melted hearts. The last time Mara saw him, a sailor's dagger stuck in his throat. In the Mother's temple, no scar marred his neck.

Mara faced the man with a smile of recognition. "Tolstes? I saw you float. Kard killed you. Did he not? Did I leave you?"

Olessa's strong boy smiled. He took a deep bow and melted into the crowd.

Cassandra paused beside Mara and waited, hands clasped at her waist. "What happened next?"

"A man called Tolstes took me from my home, but he could never follow me into Sollan because he was murdered by a glimmer fiend. A silent son brought my boat ashore, and I ran through revelers. I found a boy missing a finger. He said he could help. He promised he would."

"And did he?"

Mara gave up her search for Tolstes with a sigh and continued down the path. "I gave the boy my brass collar. He said he could buy us meals with it. I learned later he stole it to feed himself. I wish I could see him. I wish I could hold him. I wish I could whisper in his ear everything would be okay. I was angry he lied, but I am glad he had a meal. I would give him a thousand brass collars if I could."

"Blessed is the mother who freely gives, for the world will gift her an undying love."

Mara looked into the crowd. A small boy darted into view and lingered on the path's edge. He looked up at Mara and smiled, the little arrow of his nose wrinkling with his cracked-tooth grin.

She smiled and reached for him. He reached for her with a hand that sported all five fingers. His small arm couldn't quite reach her, so he pulled away. Tag bowed and slipped into the crowd, disappearing within the robes of the faithful.

"And what happened next on your pilgrimage?" the priestess asked.

"A kindly warrior showed me the way." Mara grinned despite her pain and weariness. "Most saw him as a beggar, but really he was a mighty warrior. He loved the Six. He served them well. He served his king well, too, even though the king's son tossed him aside. He was a good man. I wish more people saw that in him."

"Blessed is the mother with vision, for she will see the good in every soul."

A polished glimmer distracted Mara's eye. She caught a man standing amongst the faithful. He towered above the others and brandished a breastplate polished as a fresh coin. Their eyes met.

"Galladus? You look so young and healthy!"

He flashed his perfect teeth and bowed, quickly fading into the throng. By then Mara had almost reached the flame at the statue's feet, and only a few remained on either side.

Two women filtered from the crowd and stood beside the fire. One she recognized as her madame looking young and vibrant and overflowing with joy. The other was Gia, unharmed and cleaned and polished like a bride who wore the garments of one of the Mother's priestesses. A red flame marked her brow. Tears glimmered with Gia's pride as joy spread her smile.

"They are all here," Mara said. "Everyone is here."

Sander gently squeezed her elbow. "I am glad to know you, Mara."

She turned to him. "Why? I think I might be the unluckiest woman in Urum tonight."

The priest of the Slippery Sinner smirked and backed away. The man stood still in the empty path, the great doors framing his body.

"Why aren't you coming?" she asked.

He closed his eyes and bowed. "I am so sorry, my ashwalk pilgrim. I would have taken a hundred thousand blades had I known. You felt abandoned. You felt alone. Trust me when I swear to you that you never walked alone. You are loved more and by a greater number than any other on Urum."

Nothing made any sense. She whirled around to face the flames. Olessa and Gia had disappeared. Only Cassandra stood before her, the Mother's marble statue towering over the woman's flowing silks.

"Who are you? Are you the Mother?"

"My name is Cassandra, Mara, and I am the High Priestess of the Mother's temple, but I am not the Mother. I served the goddess since the earliest days of my memory. I worshipped her in my darkest and brightest hours. I prayed to her as others came and went. I brought her wisdom to Sollan with the High Priestess who came before me. I listened when a young acolyte named Laedon told the old High Priestess how a little girl stepped from the Ever-Burning Flame with a warning that a war is coming, that the Six will fade beneath an old enemy's power, and that one day she would return home with a savior in her arms."

"But my son is dead." Mara stepped back, shaking her head. "This is impossible. I—I did not step from the flames. I...I came to save his soul..."

"And you will. You will save his soul. You will raise a hero who will stand against the raging serpents. The Six will fade. The Third Sun will set. It will be your son who determines what Fourth Sun rises and if the Six have a place in it."

"It can't be..." Mara turned to the crowd. The sea of glimmering eyes held so much fear, so much pain. The children of the Six would die tonight—all of them. She knew they knew this. She knew they accepted it for the dead savior she brought to them.

"It's not fair. None of this is fair. If the Third Sun sets, many will die."

"Countless innocents."

Their eyes she couldn't take. They shamed her. They pelted her with their hope and tarred her with their innocence. She stared at her son, her brows knitting together.

"What have I done, my son?" Mara fell to her knees. "Why did I step from the flames? Why did I bring these awful omens?"

A strong hand grasped her arm. Cassandra smiled through her veil and lifted Mara to her feet. "Never again will you kneel to another. Never again will you bow."

The priestess backed to the edge of the crowd. Mara pressed her child against her chest and cleared her throat. "I…I am sorry. I do not know why the king hunts me. I do not know why his demon priests want my son. I did not wish to bring this on you. On any of you. I'm just a moon maiden…or I was. I think my home is gone, so now I am a homeless nothing."

Slowly, Cassandra lifted her veil. The dark, round discs of her eyes shone with the firelight glittering within them. She smiled, tears running in glittering lines down her cheeks. "Mara, you are so, so much more than that."

Cassandra clutched her robes and kneeled. Her silks pooled around her frame like a fountain of rich wine.

The priestess lifted her arms. Every priest, every acolyte, every man, woman, and child in the enormous room fell to their knees. Sander stood last, shaking his head in awe. He smiled when their eyes met, and then he, too, went to his knees.

Cassandra crossed her hands over her chest. "You have journeyed far, but you have found your way, as you always do."

Mara shook her head. "I…I'm not…"

"It is here we worship you. It is here we sing your praises. It is here we have loved you. It is here you watched the faithful. It is here you heard their prayers. It is here you mourned as the king you protected turned against you. It is here you sent your spirit into the world and became flesh. It is here you journeyed with your son, the Heir of the Six and Last Light of Magic."

Mara's grip tightened on her son. "That's impossible. I…"

"It is here all bow to you, for this is your house, and in it your fire burns. Blessed is the Burning Mother, for all bow to her, and she bows to none!"

Cassandra bent and prostrated, pressing her palms and forehead flat against the floor. Every soul within the temple did the same, a sea of faithful, bent in respect toward highest goddess of the Six.

25

THE EVER-BURNING FLAME

"I can't do this."

Mara spun from the crowd. She faced the red-rimmed flames swirling like tongues at the Mother's feet.

"This isn't me." She looked to the statue's bowed head. "I'm not you. I'm not! I'm…I'm a whore! I don't even have a last name because I never deserved one, and now I'm supposed to be you? Everyone I know will die if they haven't already, and for what? To save his soul?"

"It was a price worth paying," Olessa said, walking out from the fire.

Her madame stood beside her, hair flowing in waves down her shoulders, face radiant with her youthful beauty.

"You came back," Mara said with a sniffle.

Olessa motioned to the other side of Mara. "We both did."

Excitement raced through her blood. She whipped around and saw her friend nod with respect.

"Gia!"

Gia's long, dark braids were so perfect and polished they could have been made of onyx. Her strong eyes shone with pride. She held her chin high and cocked a smile. On her brow, she wore the fiery symbol of the Mother's loyal clergy. No longer did she wear the brass collar of a moon maiden. Instead, she wore the fiery, flowing silks of a priestess of the Mother's temple.

"You are a priestess?" Mara asked.

"I did not live as one, but I died as one. It was the least the Six could give me."

Thunder rocked the temple. The floor trembled as trails of dust filtered from the ceiling. "They're coming for us," Mara said. "I'm afraid, Gia. What will they do to me after I give my child to the flames?"

Mara looked at her son. "Oh gods, I have to give him up. I don't want to give him up. I don't want to see him burn. I can't. I can't! I want to leave. Let me leave."

Gia smiled sadly. "There are only two ways out of this temple. Through the doors or through the flames."

"Then the serpents will have me no matter what I do?"

Gia looked over Mara's shoulder at Olessa. Mara spun around, gripping her son tighter. "What? What is it? Is it a way out?"

Madame Olessa turned on her heel until the the firelight washed over her cheeks. "You cannot let them have you, Mara. They will do unspeakable things. Their power—it is a power of the old ages. If they take you, they will kill you, and the Six will become the Five, and we will all burn beneath the Serpent Sun."

A sinking pit of dread opened in Mara's stomach. She turned to the flames as another thunderous blast shook the temple. "It is not just my son who will feel the flames tonight, is it?"

"It is not."

"I will die tonight. I have done all this, risked so much, and it has always been my destiny to die. Ialane was right when she spoke those words."

"It is the destiny of all living things to die." Olessa turned from the fire. Her ghostly hand caressed Mara's cheek. "But we are more than just a living thing. Gia and I stand before you as proof of the thereafter."

A third blast smashed against the temple. Mara glanced behind her. Long cracks spread across the doors. The multitudes backed away, tightly packing against one another.

"I don't know…" Mara faced the flames. "I'm scared. I don't know if I can do this."

"What is his name?" Gia asked. She drew close to Mara and gazed at Mara's son's pale, lifeless form tucked within the ashen burlap.

"I haven't given him one. I wanted to wait to see if he was a boy or girl, but then he never drew breath and it seemed pointless."

"Tell me the story of his life," Gia said.

"I dreamt of it on the Waterstair, and I told Olessa when she came to me in Hightable. Don't you spirits catch each other up?"

Gia and Olessa shared a laugh. They walked toward the fire, taking a position on either side. Gia clasped her hands before her. "You told Olessa what you hope, but now a crowd of living souls bears witness. Tell us what you see. Speak the prophecy, Burning Mother. Speak and let it be."

Mara looked again at her infant soon. She edged toward the flame, its heat washing over her in waves. "He will be a great man. Not a perfect one, but a great one. When the magic of the Six fades and the Serpent Sun spreads throughout Urum, he will be the only one strong enough to stop it, because in him I pour all my hope, all my strength, and all my love. In him I give every godly spark within me. In him I give my immortal soul."

Mara stepped closer to the fire. Another crashing crack of thunder rocked the temple.

"Go on," Gia said. "What next?"

"The Six will fade, but he will remain. He will gather their disciples to him, and through him they will work wonders. Through him they will stand against the Serpent Sun. Through him they will battle King Sol and the glittering dragon he rides. Through him they will stop…" Mara gasped at the scene unfolding in her mind. "…They will stop the alp from birthing titans. The demons of the Second Sun wish to raise the monsters of the First!"

"And your son, what will he do?" Olessa asked.

Mara's eyes searched her son's pale features. He was so calm and placid in her arms. He was such a small bundle of flesh. Nothing so small and innocent could ever wage a war against forgotten gods.

"He will fight them. But he could fail. Oh, gods, he could fail, and if he does, they will make him suffer. I don't want that for him."

"No mother wants to see their child falter."

A mighty blast exploded behind Mara. She whirled around in time to see the temple doors collapse in a cloud of dust and smoke. The king's soldiers streamed inside, masked and hooded priests of the Serpent Sun among them. Ialane and Caspran stepped behind them, cloaked in white and clouded by rage.

The faithful did not scream. They did not panic. They clustered tighter and linked hands. Their voices rang out in a hymn of adoration that ordained a night born of violence.

"Mara!" Fear edged Gia's voice. "You know what your son will do. You know what he can accomplish."

"But he's dead, Gia. He never lived. He can never be a savior to them."

"He will!"

"It's true," Olessa added. "The fire will give him life. He will draw breath in the flames."

Mara turned from the slaughter and stepped closer to the fire. "But only if I give my own life. That is the bargain. That is the price. One soul wakes another."

Gia's hand clasped Mara's shoulder. "Such is the price of holy pilgrimage. Such is the lonely cost of saving souls."

"No, Gia." Mara clenched her teeth. She lifted her chin. Her fear flowed from her veins. Her trepidation vanished. A burning star ignited in her chest. "My life for my son's? This has been the easiest choice I ever made."

Mara spun around. Soldiers buried their sharpened blades in priest and acolyte. Serpent priests' blades whirled through flesh and robe. Ialane Donra and Brother Caspran screamed, vaulting toward her.

Mara wrapped her arms around her son. Her eyes met Ialane's. The demon alp scowled. Mara smiled. "The Serpent Sun will never rise, you hateful bitch."

She closed her eyes. She inhaled.

Mara backed into the flames. Their searing heat encased her, formed a pillar of crackling energy that swelled around her body. In the distance, beyond the light, Sister Ialane's poisonous scream split the air.

"Name him," Olessa whispered somewhere beyond the fire. "Dawn has arrived. Name him!"

"Hurry!" Gia said. "You must give him a name before the last star of Harvest Festival fades. Do it now, Mara. Name him now!"

Mara bit her lip. The fire engulfed her, and yet, it did not burn. She looked to her son. The flames had not touched his skin, either.

"I don't know what to name him," Mara said. She looked to the crowd beyond the flame. Ialane buried her swords in the flesh of the faithful. She hacked through them as easily as a gardener hacks through weeds. Those that fell before her were lucky to scream. Most just bled and died, their life staining the marble floor crimson.

"Who is he?" Gia asked. The panic in her voice had compounded tenfold.

"Name him, Mara," Olessa commanded, her voice also rife with terror. "Name him before she reaches you!"

"To survive the war he must be strong." Mara's voice tumbled into the barest whisper. "He must not falter. He must not bend or break."

Ialane sprang above the crowd. She brought her sword back. The alp flung the blade, its razor end aimed for Mara's heart.

Mara lowered her son and swelled her chest toward the demon's weapon. "And so, my son, my love, I name you Iron."

An infant's wail tore the air. Every soldier's sword stilled and serpent's blade faltered.

Mara raised her hand. A wrist once broken mended. She caught Ialane's sword, and with a flick of her wrist, she sheared the blade in half.

She tossed aside the remnants and looked at her son. Iron bawled. His tiny hands pushed from the burlap and clutched her hair. Tears wet his cheeks, their blue hue vanishing beneath a pinkish tone.

Mara stepped out of the Ever-Burning Flame. "I am the fire."

The pale inferno followed her. It formed wings sprouting from her back. It burned away the burlap and became the dress of a regal goddess. It circled her brow and crowned her with a fiery halo.

Sister Ialane landed before Mara. The priestess snarled and flung her second sword.

Mara caught the blade, and the steel cracked and turned to ash. "Demon of the Second Sun, have you learned nothing? Your sun has set. It will never rise again. The Six stand against you. You lost the war. You will not reignite it. Your dragons will not fill the skies. You will not raise the titans. You could not control them even if you did."

Ialane laughed and rotated to the crowd. "They all will die against us. No one will remember the Six. We will wipe you from eternity. You are forgotten."

You are dead. You are bygone."

The alp twisted around and flung a spell of dark clouds. Any normal person would have withered in the magical barrage. Any normal person would have shrieked and screamed and begged for forgiveness.

Mara stepped into the smoke, and it seized upon her entry and withered into pathetic wisps. Mara lifted her chin and gazed down at the demon she'd defeated in another form so long ago. "You listen to me, you murderous filth. Your brothers and sisters wage war upon this world. You have raised a monster for the wicked king to ride, and beneath his banner, your kind will work a horror unlike anything in the memory of man. I will witness it even as my power retreats within my son. But he will stop the alp. He will bury them, and then, he will bury the king, and our power will be reborn."

Ialane hissed, bearing the pale fangs hidden behind her scarlet lips. Her gold eyes glimmered with her hate. She raised a palm, and a swirling ring of fire the color of a scarab's shimmering wings surrounded her hand.

Wind billowed through the alp's hair. The wicked fire painted the scales of the serpent around her neck in shifting greens.

Ialane stepped forward. "Your son is mine."

Mara smiled. She held her son in the crook of his arm. She raised her hand, and a halo of white fire edged by crimson erupted around it. Hot wind washed in a torrent through her hair, and if an impurity remained on her, it faded with the heat.

A well of pride exploded from Mara's heart. She grinned, and it was a grin from deep within her soul. "He has a name, Ialane Donra. I will give you the gift of knowing it before I wipe you from this world, this Sun, and any others that may follow."

"No!" Ialane screamed. "He will not be the savior you seek!"

The priestess summoned all her power into her dark flames. The magic roared from her hand like an ancient dragon so enraged it would burn the entire world at once.

"Seek?" Mara laughed. "I never sought him. He came to me. He chose me, and I chose him. I was blessed to receive him, and we granted one another divinity by our sacrifice."

Ialane's flames met Mara's, and a clap of thunder rocketed the temple, flinging all but Mara and the serpent priestess to the floor. Mara stepped forward. Her flames flared and ate away at the demon alp's.

"His name..." Mara's voice no longer sounded like her own. It was deep as an ocean, vast as a cloudless sky, and mighty as the highest mountain. She looked to her son and smiled.

"...His name is Iron."

For the first time in his life, her son's eyes opened and met his mother's. He squirmed, and his cherry lips parted.

Iron giggled. Ialane shrieked.

The wicked priestess grabbed her serpent and flung it at Mara. "Do not let the boy live!"

Mara clenched her jaw. She reached through the fire and caught Ialane's snake. It writhed in her grasp. Its muscles flexed and bent in her grip. It bore its fangs. Mara tightened her grip. Red cracks spread along the creature's body. It twisted. It seized. And then, it burst into flame and ash.

Mara found Sister Ialane's panicked eyes through the wall of fire scorching the temple. "I know your king saw through that serpent's gaze," Mara said. "Now he has heard the name. Now he knows my child lives. I have shown King Sol all I wished him to see. There is no longer a need for you."

With a flick of her wrist, Mara flung her flames at Ialane. They tore apart the alp's fire and encased the demon's body. The alp fought the flames. She struggled against the heat.

But nothing, not even a demon, could stand against the Mother's flames. They forced Ialane to her knees. The alp raised her arms to shield herself and screamed.

The flames blackened her pale face. They blistered her porcelain features. They peeled the skin away and burned the bone to ash.

You will still die tonight, the alp's spirit whispered in Mara's ear. *And with you, so goes the magic of the Six. Good King Sol will bury you, and then, he will bury your son.*

Mara banished the alp's spirit to the endless void where her kind wailed into oblivion. Mara's white fire receded. The king's soldiers fled, and even the serpent priests fled with them. The last one to leave was Brother Caspran. He glared poison at Mara, his shadowed eyes swearing revenge. But like the others, he too fled into the safety of the wider world.

Those faithful to the Six who survived the massacre rose and cheered. They turned to Mara. She nodded to them and turned to the fire crackling before the statue of her likeness.

"And so it ends," she said, stepping toward the flames.

26

IRON

Death and carnage took a quiet turn as the last soldiers and serpents disappeared through the shattered temple's doors. The roiling, crackling flames encompassed Mara, but they did not burn. They were flames of her own heart, and so they only made her stronger. Yet, even as she became something of such great power, she felt herself slip from one world to a darker other.

Soon, the spark of life that she gave to resurrect her son would snuff out her own. The Burning Mother was meant to sit in the heavens and watch the world, not stand amongst its faithful.

With a mother's loving smile, she looked upon her son. "Iron, Iron, I will love you until the end of my days. When you cry, think of me to dry your tears. When you smile, know that I will smile with you. When you dream, know that I will dream of you."

Sander Hale and Cassandra approached Mara as one might approach a lioness napping in the summer sun. Their fear and wonder flowed from them on their deep breaths.

Mara grinned and looked to the two priests. "We have come far tonight, but there is still a step left for me to take before I leave you."

Cassandra stumbled forward. "Mother, I do not wish for you to leave."

"But I must, my darling daughter. I did not craft this flesh of mine to live beyond this sunrise. You know this."

"I do, do," Cassandra said, slowly closing her eyes.

Sander eyed Iron warily. "So…magic really will die then?"

Mara sighed and caressed her son's temple. "It will. It has already nearly faded from Sollan. Once I leave you, what spark of power lay within the faithful will diminish in the many lands of Urum. This haughty king of yours has begun a process that once started will not stop until it is finished. Like a mighty wave sweeping one end of the Sapphire Sea to the next, this will only stop once it crashes on the shore."

"And when the wave recedes?"

"Death and destruction and one child who holds all hope within him."

"We will lose our magic. What are we without your power to propel us?

I'm damn near nothing more than a common thief without the Sinner's smoke and shadows. I feel like my income is about to take a mighty hit."

Cassandra swatted the man's shoulder. "Do not curse before the Mother! The mightiest of the Six stands before you, and you speak like a sailor on his third shot of saltwater gin!"

Mara laughed at Sander's words. "Sander, Sander, it is not all fire and brimstone beneath the king's heel for those who still bend a knee to the Six. Magic will flourish for a small number. For those who follow my son, the spark of me within him will ignite their souls as long as they tread in his footsteps."

"Lucky them." Sander's lips puckered, and his shoulders slumped.

"Why so sad? Chin up, loyal priest and quick-witted thief, for you shall be counted among his number."

Sander's jaw went slack. His gaze shot up to meet Mara's, and he stumbled back. "What? M—M—Me?"

"You were right when you said you suspected you would have a companion on your journey to frozen Skaard. In a way, a piece of me will be with you, but it is not me who you will take. You will hold an infant boy, the savior born to battle a dark king and the nightmares he raises from the dead."

Sander swallowed. He rubbed the back of his head while it slowly shook side to side. "That's heavy stuff, Burning Mother. Are you sure I'm up for it? Hells, I'm no good at caregiving. My mom used to tell me I'd find a way to kill a cactus if I could."

"He's right," Cassandra chimed in. "Mother, should it not be one of your loyal acolytes who raises the boy, teaches him your ways?"

"No. He will never be safe with my faithful. Only one who knows the shadows and secret paths of the world can keep him from harm until he's ready." Her gaze shifted back to the thief. "Sander, take Iron to Skaard. Teach him the Sinner's magic. It will not die from you with him by your side. Teach him the ways of stealth and secrecy. Teach him to survive a brutal world. By flame I smelted Iron from the ashes. Should he die, so will what magic remains, and so will the door close for the Six on the world of Urum. The Third Sun will set, and the Serpent Sun will rise."

Sander's hands balled into determined fists. He clenched his jaw and bowed. "I will teach him to survive. I will keep him safe. I swear it, Burning Mother, on my very soul...even though it's not a particularly clean one. How will I know he is ready for this?"

Mara closed her eyes and let her spirit wash over the world she loved. She flew across the glittering Sapphire Sea. She breathed in the frigid air of Skaard. She sifted through the ancient forests of the Eastern Kingdoms. She sped over the rolling dunes of the Simmering Sands. There was so much beauty in Urum, so much she wished she could have seen through human eyes.

I will watch the world through my son's eyes, even as I am chased from it.

"I will always be with you," Mara said. She extended Iron, and the thief gently pulled him from her arms. Mara sucked in her breath. "You will know him ready by my sign."

A great weight lifted from her body, and with it, her flames faded. Her eyes closed, her spirit came upon the great city of Sollan. She saw the king's palace. In it, she saw Good King Sol. He reclined on a throne smelted from purest gold. He crowned himself with a golden serpent eating its own tail.

A beast slept before his throne. Two pale wings folded against its back, and it cradled its head in claws that could shred stone like butter. A trail of smoke drifted from its nostrils. It opened an eye rimmed by gold and hate, focusing on her.

So the alp have raised a dragon for you, Mara thought. *My son will cut it down, too, just like I cut down those demon steeds of theirs so long ago.*

Good King Sol lifted his head. She stared into his eyes, at the burning, writhing pit of hate that had replaced his heart. He grinned like a hungry wolf catching sight of wounded prey.

"I'm coming for him," Sol said.

Be careful what you hunt. A fox falls before a wolf. A wolf falls before a man. A man falls before a king. A king falls before Iron.

"Oh, I know my prey, Burning Mother, and you know by now I am much more than a man who wears a crown."

Mara turned away from Sol, leaving him and his dragon to their wickedness. *Indeed you are. But know that when you die, it will be as a man, fearing the endless void your heresy will bring you.*

Her eyes snapped open to the temple. Her flames cooled. Her body lightened. "I must leave now."

Cassandra sobbed, burying her face in her palms. "I do not wish to see you die."

"I must go, my child, but I will never die as long as some spark of my power remains."

Sander cradled Iron. Her son's tiny hand pressed against his dark garments. "He will be a great warrior, Burning Mother. Thank you for everything you have done for us."

"And thank you for all that you will do."

Mara's cooling flames flared like the heart of a sun around her, and a mighty light roared into the temple and shook the ground. Glowing lines appeared along her skin. A vision of the corrupted king flared within the fire. Every inch of his features emblazoned on her memory, his wolfish smile sending a shiver down her spine. His heart, his heart, she knew his heart. It was not the heart of a man, but something darker, something older, something that should have been dead and forgotten.

You, she thought as a horrible realization bloomed within her. *I remember you, my ancient enemy. I know your true name.*

And I know you, Mara, the most beautiful maiden in the House of Sin and Silk.

"I will speak of you often," Sander called, "and I'll teach the boy of his mother, who is the mother of us all."

"No!" Mara roared, her voice cracking the temple's foundation. "Sander Hale, I am the Burning Mother, and this is my last command. Do not speak of me to Iron. He cannot know the one who birthed him, for the knowledge will lead to a much darker path."

Sander shielded his eyes from her brilliant light. "But Mother, I don't—"

"*Enough!* Do not speak of me to him. Do not let him question this. Do not let him wonder. His past is his destruction. Let him look ever to the horizon and not to the long shadow behind him."

"Y—Yes, Burning Mother…"

Mara inhaled a breath of Urum's air. Slowly, she let it slip from her lips. She dipped her chin and clasped her hands beneath her belly, mirroring the statue behind her. The flames encased her like a coffin constructed from the sun. Her skin broke apart. A pillar of light exploded from the Ever-Burning Flame, tearing through the temple roof. As the sun rose on the darkest Harvest Festival in memory, for the briefest moment, a second sun blazed in the sky.

"Goodbye, my son!" Tears fell freely down her cheeks, but she smiled through them. She looked up, reaching to Iron, her child, her son, the boy who would save all mankind.

"I will come to you when the night grows dark. For you, I will be a light that shines the way. I love you, I love you, I love—"

The light vanished from the Mother's temple. No flames burned before the Mother's statue. Only a pit of ash once called Mara remained.

THE END

I hope you enjoyed Ashwalk Pilgrim, the first in the Unbreakable Iron series. You'd do me a great honor by rating this story online. If you want to know more about Mara and Iron and be the first to read the next in the series, check out my website at *www.abbradley.com.*

ABOUT THE AUTHOR

AB Bradley was born in Fort Worth, Texas and spent most of his time growing up there. He did everything most kids in suburbia do: school, sports, scouts, etc. and grew up slower than he liked but faster than he expected. He attended the University of North Texas, where he graduated with a Bachelor's Degree in English.

Currently, AB Bradley writes both professionally and personally, which means he's writing about eighteen hours a day and still loves it more every time he taps a letter on the keyboard. He's a resident of Dallas, Texas and loves Tex-Mex, days by the pool, and creating stories that will stay with you for a lifetime. You can find out more about him at www.abbradley.com.